I0657928

the Key to Time
Tempus Fugit

⊰ R.M. SEIDLER ⊱

This is a work of fiction. Names, characters, places, and incidents are either the product of the author's imagination or are used fictitiously. Any resemblance to actual persons living or dead, business establishments, events, or locales is entirely coincidental.

The Key to Time
Tempus Fugit

To the kid who reads in the corner of the gym during recess

CONTENTS

A Speedy Recap

Quincy Marie Katelyn Harris legally belongs to Miss Heatherwood's foster home in New York. It's supposed to be temporary until her mother wakes up from a coma caused by a terrible accident. Thankfully, during the school year, Quincy attends Oakley Academy, an institute where the most qualified and influential, Talented kids go.

Quincy's Talent is perfect memory which helps her recall any moment of her life in exact detail, or at least it will be when she's been fully trained. But it seems she might have a second Talent, something to do with knowing what time it is. Though she's not completely sure what that entails yet.

Not only must she learn how to use her Talents while finding a place at Oakley Academy, she also has a more pressing matter that requires her to open a mysterious door. One which requires four minor keys to open, including the master key passed down to her from her mother. With the help of her new friends, her garrulous raven guardian, and the Timepiece: a time-traveling clock, Quincy now has the first of the four Minor keys. She must master time travel to find the three missing keys if she is going to stop time from completely unraveling and ending the universe.

SCOTLAND: THIRTY SOME-ODD YEARS AGO

The older boy stood with his feet firmly planted on the ground, his head craning toward the sky. A cloud in the form of a rabbit soared across the horizon and he smiled delightfully. He looked down and watched his younger brother focusing on the earth. The younger boy sat down on the dry ground and delicately pulled a piece of heather from the terrain. He rubbed it between his fingers feeling the texture of the leaves. He inhaled the grassy scent, sighing contentedly.

The older brother felt a jolt of uneasiness in his stomach and looked behind at the house. "It's probably time to go inside," he admitted sadly.

His younger brother dropped the heather and looked up at him. "Wil, how do you suppose time began?"

Wil frowned and bit his bottom lip to keep from responding with annoyance to his younger brother. What kind of question was that anyway?

"How am I supposed to know? There's no beginning to time."

"Are you sure? How do you know?"

"Why do you have to know, Dwi?" Wil asked, frowning deeper at his brother's grin. He was saved from having to come up with a logical explanation by the dinner bell. Wil looked over and saw the kitchen door open and the small figure of a maid ringing the bell and waving a dish cloth rapidly toward them.

"And now we're late," Wil looked accusingly at Dwi who smiled sheepishly.

"Last one to the house is going to die an old maid!" Dwi called back as he raced toward the kitchen.

"I'm no maid, and that's cheating. Come back here!" Wil ran after his brother feeling the wonderful sensation of the wind rushing past his ears.

As they entered the house, they bumped into the cook who made a *tsking* sound with her tongue and wagged her spoon at the boys and their wind-tousled hair and clothes. They dodged the second maid and scooted past their aged aunt to be received by their father in the parlor. They stood side by side, both with perfect posture and eyes facing directly ahead.

Their father stared at both of them. Not a word passed between his lips, but his evident disappointment forced them both to cower and drop their gaze.

"Come now, Everett. Boys will be boys. Especially boys with exceptionally creative names."

Their uncle grinned at the boys as he walked into the parlor and stood next to their father. Their uncle was a good five inches taller than their father and instead of the family brown hair, his was black as night and it matched his mischievously twinkling eyes. Wil and Dwi both fought from smiling in response. It was a good day when he came to visit.

"I never should have allowed their mother to name them so soon after their birth." Their father said with a sigh, a sign of his deflating frustration. Wil stared at his father, and for the first time saw exhaustion and defeat carefully hidden in his expression.

Wil and Dwi looked over at their uncle.

"Yes, yes. By all means," their uncle encouraged gesturing them closer.

Each boy reached into their uncle's pocket and grasped a package. Wil from his right and Dwi from his left. It had become a favored custom, each wondering what odd gift their uncle had found for them. They placed the package in their pockets, knowing that they would not be allowed to open them until after supper and in their own beds.

The boys' mother, with the help of her lady's maid, joined them for dinner. Wil looked at her frail hand as she sipped her soup with disinterest. His great-aunt sniffed and blew her nose into her napkin. Dwi looked up at Wil and scrunched his nose. Their aunt must have a perpetual cold for she constantly complained about the dampness. After a polite inquiry about their uncle's health, which was always 'fine,' silence ruled the meal. Wil looked over at his brother and bit his lip and shook his head furiously. Wil knew all of his younger twin brother's expressions. He recognized this look all too well.

"Don't do it." He silently willed, wishing his brother could read his thoughts.

Dwi grinned at his brother. He had understood, but he would go on anyway.

"Da, how did time begin?" Dwi innocently asked.

Wil bit his lip until he tasted the blood in his mouth and slowly looked over to his father. He watched his father's lips tighten with irritation. Their uncle, however, laughed loudly and gulped in air after finishing.

"Why must you ask such odd questions?" Their father demanded.

Dwi looked down at his soup. "Because I want to know," he mumbled.

Their uncle reached over and patted his hand. "That is one of my favorite things about you. Always wanting to know everything. Let me tell you a story about it tonight."

Dwi looked up, happiness lighting his features, and even Wil felt his spirits rise. Their uncle told the best nighttime stories.

The rest of the meal dragged on and on until finally they were released for bed. They raced up to their room and had their teeth washed and night clothes on in moments. They dove into bed with their unopened packages on their lap. The twins shared a room despite having been offered to separate on multiple occasions. They

4

both felt secure being next to the other, though neither one would ever admit it. Their uncle took his customary spot on the window seat and motioned for them to open their packages.

Wil ripped open his present to find a book. He smiled with pleasure, but his face fell when he opened it. The blank white pages stared pathetically back at him.

"It's empty on purpose," his uncle smiled. "It's for you to place your notes in."

His uncle had noticed Wil writing in the dust four months before with some possible house schedules for the next month. Wil had even remembered which staff worked which days and had researched who had asked for which shifts off. He had never told anyone how much pleasure he took from putting everything into neat lines. It made him embarrassed, as if this wasn't normal behavior for a ten-year-old.

Wil smiled at his uncle and placed his book on his bedside table.

Dwi gently opened his package, being careful not to rip the paper. As usual, he was more interested in the construction of the packaging than the gift itself. Will fought from rolling his eyes at his brother. Finally, Dwi looked at the gift inside and giggled. He slowly opened the pocket watch and grinned at their uncle.

"It's broken," he said with glee.

"Think you can fix it?" their uncle asked.

Dwi opened the back of the watch and peered inside. "I think so."

Their uncle smiled. "Excellent. Now let's answer your question. How did time begin?"

The boys grasped the ends of their blankets and stared as their uncle transformed into a master storyteller.

"Before Time was called into existence, there was the One. One was profoundly alone and had no wish to remain so. Much like the rules of invention, a foundation or a set of rules must be made. Firstly, One created Time. The first guardian watched the present, past, and future. Poor Time would always have his hands full and would never remain in the moment seeing what is and what was and what is to come. All without directing any of it.

"That sounds annoying," Dwi whispered. Wil threw his pillow at his brother's face.

Their uncle grinned and continued. "The silent guardian governed existence. When One decided the invention worked, One then created Law. Law had the final say in the matters of earthly problems, and he was given great wisdom regarding humanity. Since Time had little desire to lead, Law would be in charge of all creation, including the three guardians.

Dwi yawned and Wil hated to admit that his own attention drifted.

Their uncle shook his head. "Let's move faster. Finally, One created Messenger. This guardian would be able to come and go as she pleased in Time, Earth and all the heavens, including One's very presence. She was the glue that kept all of creation together. None could match the beauty and grace of Messenger."

Their uncle paused and he closed his eyes and breathed deeply in and out. He slowly looked up and smiled sadly at the boys.

"As beautiful as our mum?" Dwi asked.

"Why must you keep interrupting him?" Wil hissed.

"Boys, boys. Yes, she was as beautiful as your mum. Let's continue?"

Both boys eagerly nodded and he started again.

"For a while, things prospered, the three guardians grew and took root in their designated areas. Humanity created governments and rules to grow and engineer a better world.

Their uncle shifted his weight on the seat and clenched his knuckles. "But all good things ultimately come to an end."

Wil snuck a peek at his twin who stared back at him, his expression of surprise mirrored his own feelings. They had never seen bitterness from their uncle.

"Humans by nature are curious. One man's curiosity became an unfortunate invention that ended Messenger's story. No mortal knows how Messenger sacrificed herself so that others would live. Both Law and Time loved her and each blamed the other for her death. Law, furiously released himself from his duties as high judge and left to plant seeds of deception in those who had ears to listen. Both guardians agreed that they never wanted to cross paths again, for if they did, one would cease to exist."

7

A harsh torrent of air threw itself against their window, breaking the boys from their dreamlike state with simultaneous gasps. Moments later, rain drops crashed against the glass.

"As Time began to fail his duties, all fell into chaos as the fabric of time began to unravel."

Dwi slipped deeper into his blankets after hearing a crack of thunder until only his head and fingers showed above the covers. "This isn't a terribly happy story tonight, uncle."

"No, it is not, but it is an important one."

Wil frowned at his brother, trying to discourage him from interrupting yet again. He wanted to know what happened next. Finally, his uncle continued.

"One, in great anguish called the remaining guardian, Time. Time was angry that One refused to step in to fix the mess and start over. One stripped Law of the powers of travel and his title of high judge. Law would now be a shadow of his true form, a phantom that could only hinder and create illusions. He could no longer lead all people, but would only play with only one weak-minded person at a time. He would always follow chaos for chaos is what he had created."

Wil's heart stopped in his chest when he felt something touch him. He quickly relaxed when he realized it was his twin brother sliding into the blankets next to him.

"Only Time remains, watching as moments dissipate into nothingness, gifted with powers of his own, and powers he never asked for."

"So, what happens next?" Wilbright whispered.

"Only time will tell."

CHAPTER ONE

BACK TO THE PRESENT

Quincy awoke with a start. Out of habit, she glanced toward the window and in the direction of the lamp outside. Her heart beat faster when she couldn't find the window or any other light in the room. She waved her hand in front of her face, but she couldn't see anything in the pitch-black surrounding her. She sat up and pulled the covers to her chin. After a long moment, she slowly pulled her leg from the bed to touch the floor, but her foot kept going. She tried again, this time with her hand. Still, she could not find the floor. Quincy held back the desire to scream for help. No one could help her here in her nightmare. She lay in the silence, waiting for the next act. As usual, she did not have to wait long. A voice cut the silence so sharply Quincy's heart skipped a beat. No matter how many times she heard it, she couldn't stop herself from shaking uncontrollably.

"Hello, Miss Quincy," it said in a silky, bass monotone voice.

Despite the darkness, Quincy squeezed her eyes shut.

"Your mother gave her life for that key. Are you willing to do the same? What's stopping you from following her fate?"

"Go away," she whispered in the blanket.

"You are nothing but a child. An insignificant child."

The voice coldly laughed, a dark contrast from the deceptively warm voice. Quincy shivered and involuntarily whimpered.

"Where are you hiding...?"

Quincy hid under the covers but someone grabbed the bed and capsized it, sending her screaming into the floorless void.

* * *

Quincy sat up on her bed in Miss Heatherwood's Home for Boys and Girls, screaming, "Talin!"

Quincy's eyes opened wide just in time to see Amanda's hands reach for her neck. Fearing she would touch the key, she jumped away from her. Without thinking, she fled from the girl's room outside to the stable. Barefoot, Quincy ran without stopping until she heard the familiar breathing of the horses. She closed her eyes and smelled the straw and the horse sweat, waiting until her heart calmed down.

A sudden realization hit her. She had broken one of the many rules of Miss Heatherwood's, and it forced her out of her moment of peace. No doubt Miss Heatherwood would use this mistake to her advantage. Because Quincy now attended Oakley, the government no longer paid Miss Heatherwood for Quincy's tuition throughout the school year. Quincy wondered how much money this had cost Miss

Heatherwood. The headmistress had been even worse towards Quincy than she could have imagined. It felt like she had been in and out of the detention closet every day while Miss Heatherwood turned a blind eye to the school bully. Quincy rubbed her bruised knee where Amanda had "accidentally" tripped her with the mop bucket.

The last few weeks had been hard, especially when Monty had written that he had already finished his school supply shopping while she had been stuck at Miss Heatherwood's. Quincy thought about the Latin book under her bed. On and off throughout the summer, she had attempted to study her Latin, but once again, even after reading the introduction to Latin twice, she still didn't understand the basics. Another student had swiped the tome but when they couldn't read it, they had grudgingly put it back in its place with some additional "artwork." Quincy was almost disappointed to see its return. She always imagined herself to be smart, but for some reason, Latin made little sense. She sighed again and kicked at the stable door. Annoyed, the horse snorted.

"Sorry," Quincy said as she fed the horse a handful of oats in apology. If it had been her horse at Oakley, he wouldn't have been so easily pacified. She rubbed the nose, surprised by how much she wished it was Consto, her horse at Oakley. She looked at the calendar on the peeling stable door, hoping Mrs. Adalin would arrive soon to take her away from Miss Heatherwood's.

The hardest thing to bear had been Talin's disappearance over the whole summer break. A couple of times she imagined seeing a raven or a crow that could have been Talin, but when she called after it, it never responded or even paused. Despite Talin's cantankerous behavior, she missed his companionship. Quincy had been the envy of the whole foster house during the weekly mail call. Eloise, Mikaela, and Colin all sent her letters on steady basis, including the weekly letter from Monty. The consistency in Quincy's summer helped her bear the daily drudgery. Eloise's letters had been sporadic, sometimes a package full of writing and other times a small note. It made Quincy smile, typical Eloise. Colin had sent a couple of sketches of birds and trees that Quincy kept on the wall by her bed, much to the jealousy of her roommates. She finally took down the pictures and put them in her trunk to protect them. That didn't stop someone from digging into her belongings to spirit the drawings away. Later that day, Quincy found them torn to pieces outside.

Quincy knew who had done the deed, but she had no proof to call out the bully. Not that it would have helped her or fixed her torn pictures, and it was doubtful Miss Heatherwood would have punished Amanda anyway. The rest of the foster kids left her alone for fear of drawing attention. Including Anna, who looked even paler than last year.

Quincy groaned and debated hiding in the stables until someone came looking for her. But then she would be guaranteed double the lashing. One for leaving her room earlier than allowed, and the second one for avoiding said punishment. Quincy kicked at the floorboard and gasped. She angrily reached out to pull a splinter from her bare foot. When she heard someone clear their throat, she immediately looked up at the rafters.

"Ah, much better, and faster than last year too," the raven said, chuckling.

Quincy smiled. "I was thinking about you."

"Fancy that."

Quincy's smile dropped and she crossed her arms. "You said I would see you this summer and you wouldn't leave me here alone."

"Hey, I did *exactly* what I said. You did see me this summer, and I never left you alone. You even waved to me. I never said we would talk or have a summer adventure together. One per year is quite plenty enough for me, thank you very much."

Quincy shut her mouth, momentarily pacified but she still felt the dull ache from her loneliness over the last few months. "So, I see you have your camouflage on again."

Talin preened his feathers as if showing off.

"Handsome, is it not?"

Quincy couldn't help but laugh at Talin's mock bow with his wing in front of him. Her laughter quickly turned back into a frown. "You know, you could have at least said hello or waved."

"And place you in the center of attention? Hardly." Talin looked around the stable as if expecting someone to walk in. "Can you imagine people's response to a talking bird? Or someone attempting to make conversation with one? Or even better, thinking you were having a little chat with yourself."

"Then why are you talking to me now?"

"Obviously because I need to." Talin rolled his eyes.

Quincy groaned. "What happened now?"

Talin looked puzzled. "What do you mean?"

"Well usually when you show up out of nowhere, you want something or there's a problem. Which one is it?"

Talin pretended to be offended. "I'm checking up on you to make sure you were ready for school, and other...things." Talin openly looked in the direction of her neck and to what Quincy imagined, her key.

"I thought once I took the key, I no longer had the chance to walk away?"

"You don't, I just hoped I wasn't going to have to use brute force to make you come back." Talin winked. "Miss Heatherwood's stick is further up her backside than last year. She's not going to be pleasant this next week," Talin warned.

"Tell me something I don't know. Speaking of which, what are we going to do in case she refuses to let me go?"

Talin chuckled throatily. "We'll remind her of the law of course. Mrs. Adalin has legal custody over your education. There's nothing Miss Heatherwood can do about it."

Quincy leaned against the pole, relieved.

"But unfortunately, Quinn, we don't control what happens to you now, and if you hurry up, you might make it before everyone gets ready for breakfast..."

"Not possible. When I left, I had fifteen minutes."

"Then I suggest you run."

Quincy waved goodbye to him as she ran across the field towards Miss Heatherwood's Home for Boys and Girls. Quincy dodged a couple of teachers who had begun to stir for the day and ran up the stairs towards the girl's room. She gasped as she ran past the clock, proving the whole conversation with Talin had taken five minutes. How was that possible? She checked her mental clock and frowned. How had time stopped?

She waited by the door until the grandfather clock rang the appropriate time to get dressed and ready for the new day. She managed to slip inside right before the Crone walked in, but too late for Amanda to corner her. The Crone openly stared at Quincy's unkept attire and her filthy feet, but said nothing. The Crone either respected or feared her. Quincy wondered if it was because of her Oakley student status. Few people attended the private schools, much less one of the big five.

At the beginning of the summer vacation, Quincy wore her Oakley sweater on a visitation day to her Mother's care home. She had never seen so many people stare at her. Not unlike their staring now. She pretended to ignore all their glances as she got dressed for breakfast.

***

Quincy knocked on the door and stuck her head inside.

"Hi, Mom," she whispered. After kissing her mother's cheek and dropping her bag by the bed, Quincy hoisted herself and curled up next to the comatose woman. Quincy pulled out paper and a pen to work on her correspondence with Monty. She looked over and resisted the urge to ask her mother what she thought of her new friends. She'd spent the entire summer updating her mother about her many experiences from the prior year. Of course, she wouldn't get a response from her unresponsive mother, but it made her feel better. She told her about Eloise and her umbrella, Rusty and his loud trumpet playing, and about Colin. She would love to get advice from her mother about Colin and boys in general.

She imagined her mom would giggle about Eloise's hair and comment on Rusty's obsession with his instrument, and Quincy knew her mother would tease her about the attention from Colin and Monty, despite the fact they were all just friends. Besides, Colin already had a somewhat girlfriend.

Quincy grimaced at the thought of Genevieve. She wasn't a bully like Amanda, but for some reason, Genevieve didn't like her. The feeling was mutual since she had taken Quincy's first choice horse.

"I wonder how you met Monty's mom though," Quincy wondered aloud for the hundredth time. The previous year Quincy had learned how to time travel and met Monty's mom who had been her mom's best friend. She wished her mother was awake to recount her adventures as a student and to explain everything.

Quincy laid her head on her mother's shoulder and breathed in her scent before she would have to leave her side. This would be the last time she would see her until the next summer holiday. Quincy once again felt torn between going to Oakley and leaving her mother behind. She sighed and rubbed her eyes to brush away a tear accumulating in the corner that threatened to fall down her cheek. Quincy kissed her mother goodbye and walked out of the home towards the court appointed official who would take her back. As they pulled up to the foster house, Quincy smiled as she viewed a smartly dressed woman wearing a peacock-feathered hat, leaning against the door checking her manicured nails. The carriage stopped and Quincy thanked the official before jumping out and walking toward the barrister.

"Hello, Mrs. Adalin."

Mrs. Adalin looked up and smiled at Quincy. "Ah, there you are, my dear." She looked behind her at the building and her smile tightened. "I'm guessing from your surprise you never received my letter."

"No, I didn't. What did it say?"

"Oh, the usual. That I would arrive fifteen minutes ago and I would expect you to be packed and waiting with your trunk so we could part..." Mrs. Adalin checked her pocket watch. "...exactly ten minutes ago."

Quincy gasped and ran past the barrister inside the foster home.

"Please hurry, the train leaves in less than an hour!" Mrs. Adalin yelled after her.

Quincy ran up the stairs to pack her few belongings for school. She sat on the edge of her bed, quickly folding her nightgown. Looking at her feet, she remembered her nightmare about the floorless void. She shuddered and quickly snapped her trunk shut. A waft of dinner reached her room and she grimaced at the unappetizing smell. The awful meal wasn't the cook's fault. She had to make do with what she had been given. Quincy sighed in relief that she would not have to be eating with everyone else, especially since she herself helped make the supper. The cook had taken Quincy under her wing for the summer making Quincy one of her summer helpers. She knew she had done it in kindness to keep her away from other students and adults, but Quincy constantly felt claustrophobic in the hot kitchen.

She dragged her suitcase down the stairs and stopped when she saw Thomas slowly walking up, rubbing his backside. Another victim of the Deathstrike. He stared at her luggage, depressed, and continued up the stairs. Quincy felt the elation in her heart diminish because she could leave, but he couldn't. Not until the day he turned eighteen.

From the corner of her eye, Quincy glimpsed Miss Heatherwood at the door of the dining room with arms crossed and a dark expression on her face. Quincy sucked in her breath and pulled her trunk out of the door. She breathed a sigh of relief as she viewed Mrs. Adalin and a carriage waiting for her.

"Are you ready?" Mrs. Adalin asked.

"I have been since you left me on the first day of the summer."

Quincy and the carriage driver hoisted her luggage in the back. When she jumped inside, she leaned over toward Mrs. Adalin. "By the way, are we taking the night train again?"

Mrs. Adalin nodded and Quincy bounced up and down in her seat, excited to be back on a train and soon especially on an eagle.

***

Quincy's excitement quickly dissipated after a couple of hours of jerky motions which kept her from falling asleep. There was little to see outside and the stars were hidden by the thick clouds. Quincy looked at her reflection in the window and stuck her tongue out at herself. She sighed and leaned her head on the glass, attempting to fall asleep.

The night train stopped suddenly and Quincy, who had been curled up on her chair, was thrown forward against the seat in front of her. She rubbed her temple and felt a headache creep into her forehead where she had bumped into the hard back. Embarrassed, Quincy looked next to her so she could share a laugh with Mrs. Adalin. To her surprise, Mrs. Adalin was not in her seat. Instead, a gentleman wearing curious clothing sat in the barrister's spot. He wore a plum-colored suit and matching top hat with a raven's feather sticking out of it. The plumage reminded her of the mysterious man in black that she continued to bump into at odd moments. On his left eye he sported a large monocle with a silver chain dangling from it. His crooked nose looked like it had been broken on more than one occasion. Terrified, Quincy gasped and clenched her hands on the arms of the train's seat until her knuckles turned white. She momentarily allowed her imagination to run rampart. *It's one of them,* she panicked as her throat tightened. Could this be the voice who haunted her nightmares?

As if reading her mind, he chuckled and shook his head. "No, my dear, you should have no fear. I do not desire, what I have already acquired. I simply require a moment to… inspire."

Quincy, not recognizing his voice from one of her nightmares, relaxed her grip from the seat, but remained poised for action if needed. She thought his odd penchant for rhyming, curious.

"Then who are you?" Quincy asked, defensively.

He smiled warmly. "You may ask, but my identity I must mask," he winked mischievously. "I do apologize, my dear, but to all the rules I must adhere. Time and space must not be erased. I trust you'll adjust."

Quincy looked with disbelief at the man and she pinched herself to make sure she wasn't asleep. She doubted her mind could dream up a rhyming man in purple.

"I have a small piece of time before the clock will chime. Please forgive the rhyme." The man grimaced and then looked down at her neck. "You have found the second key, to my complete glee."

Quincy tensed and stood up to run away from the man, but his height blocked her from leaving. Her heart pounded and she felt light-headed. She took a deep breath, forcing herself to breathe normally. He raised his arms with his palms open to Quincy as if in retreat. "Please, freeze."

He took one hand and slowly reached into his pocket. He pulled out a long chain and dangled it in front of her.

A key slowly swayed right to left like a pendulum. Around the keyhole were notches reminding Quincy of a clock.

"You have a key?" she asked breathlessly.

The man grinned much like the fox in Oakley's Dining Hall and he slowly placed the key in his pocket while gently shushing her with his index finger.

Quincy looked the gentleman in the eye, her face with a determined expression. The gentleman smiled down at her as he met her gaze. After a moment, the train lurched and Quincy broke the gaze to look over the seat in front of her.

"Quite a bumpy ride tonight. I think next time we won't take the late train."

Quincy looked over in surprise at Mrs. Adalin. "Where did he go? Didn't you see—how long were you—I thought..."

Mrs. Adalin gave Quincy a puzzled expression.

"Quincy, I told you not three minutes ago that I needed to visit the lady's room."

"Are you sure you were gone for three minutes?"

Mrs. Adalin put her hand to Quincy's forehead.

"Are you sure you're alright? Do you feel ill?"

"Yes, no, I'm all right, thank you."

Quincy settled back down in her seat, pondering her visit from the stranger with his key, curious clothing, and his rhyming speech until she heard the conductor welcoming them to New York City.

CHAPTER TWO

THE POWER OF THREE

L ord Wilbright laid in his bed with his eyes closed but fully awake. He shivered, cold despite the warm fire nearby. Even half asleep, he was still planning. Soon, it was time to face the girl. This morning, he would fly into New York and take the eagle with her to London. An inconvenience to be sure, but he needed a moment alone with her. If he stayed on top of his game, he should be able to speak to her during the flight while the barrister slept or at the very least, pass her a note. Her letters were carefully screened at school and he had yet to locate her summer home. Her guardians had made it difficult to find her, but at least he knew without a doubt where she would fly from. As his thought drifted to the items he should pack, an odd sensation pierced his heart. He slowly opened his eyes and saw who sat on the end of his bed. Her sleek blond hair hung loosely over her slender shoulders. Her deep blue eyes accentuated her pouty lips. She wore a flattering red nightdress and her hands were placed delicately in her lap.

"Eleanor," he gasped and quickly sat up.

She slowly slid toward him until she was inches away. It took every fiber of discipline in his body not to grasp her. Her lips slowly parted and she brought them to his ear and she longingly whispered a name.

But not *his* name.

He roared in anger and pushed her away. But instead of the love of his life, he touched a dark substance made of shadows. The silhouette slunk through the window towards his garden. He listened to the beat of his heart pulsating through his head. How could his greatest desire also be his greatest nightmare? He breathed deeply, in and out, trying to banish the pounding in his head. To his relief, it worked briefly, leaving him in eerie silence. The moment quickly ended by further pounding. He rubbed his head, attempting to banish it a second time. The pounding continued and he sheepishly realized it was someone knocking at his door.

"What is it?" Wilbright yelled.

"Is all well, my lord?" his valet asked, muffled behind the door.

"Yes. Leave me."

Wilbright waited until the footsteps abated before he grabbed his night robe and stalked down to the other wing of his estate.

Angrily, he pulled the lever shifting a bookshelf to reveal a secret room. He entered and stopped behind a man sitting in front of a window. The hawk perched nearby, cried at his entrance. Wilbright hissed in anger at the bird.

"Now, now, be nice, Wilbright," the man near the window emotionlessly answered. Wilbright crossed his arms, his anger fueled.

"I warned you about letting the Nocti loose in my home. I allow you to build what you want here, but they must not run rampant on my property. The death of an employee would be...inconvenient."

"Don't be so finicky, Wilbright. I've nearly fixed the problem. Soon they will stop disintegrating so quickly. It's a pity I can't find the Grand Master to ask him how he managed to make his Noctem Umbrem permanent. Dwi—,"

"Don't say his name," Wilbright angrily interrupted.

"So easily agitated in the early hours, aren't you?"

"Keep them away from me and my home," Wilbright snapped.

"You should be honored. They find those with the most hurt— with the most to lose."

The hawk squawked at him as if laughing. Wilbright resisted the urge to knock down his perch. The hawk hissed as if reading his thoughts.

"I need the sleep. I have an early trip to New York."

"Why bother? You will meet failure. Her guardian will make sure of that."

"I plan to catch them off guard. I only need a moment with her."

"Well, I won't argue with you." Prieler shrugged. "But if you must go, take that with you." Prieler pointed to a box. "I want to see how long they last."

Wilbright stared at the box and shivered. "Is it full of—,"

Prieler nodded. "But, not the finished copies, unfortunately, but they should help you to at least stop her for that moment you desperately seek." Prieler opened a drawer and handed him a ring. Wilbright rubbed his finger over the band. "Why wood?" he asked.

"It comes from a special tree. It keeps them in check and stops them from using your own emotions against you." He handed Wilbright a dried sprig. "If you place a piece of it over your door and window, they won't enter."

Wilbright stared at the box, the branch, and the ring. It was a dangerous game he played. But if he wanted to win, he would have to do whatever it took.

"Thank you," said Wilbright stiffly.

"As you will," Prieler dismissed him.

Wilbright retreated to his own room to try and catch a few hours of sleep. Prieler leaned closer to the window to peer outside. The hawk squawked again and it turned into human laughter. The dark and sickly-sweet laughter had long ceased to incite fear in Prieler's heart. He slowly turned around to face Iblis, the man in red who had transformed from the hawk.

"Wilbright's fear and his pride are his greatest weaknesses," he said simply to Iblis.

The hawkish man leaned in closer. "They are also our greatest strengths. The Scottish lord is a necessary annoyance. We need him, for now," Iblis whispered in his ear.

"If you say so."

"I do."

The sitting man nodded and gazed at the wall as if uninterested.

CHAPTER THREE

CLOSE ENCOUNTERS

Quincy barely managed to place the thought of the odd man and his key aside when they arrived at the NEFS New York Station. Mrs. Adalin and Quincy found a place near their gate and nibbled on pastries from the small refreshment cart nearby. Afterwards, the family lawyer reached into her purse and handed Quincy some money.

"This is for the trip. Feel free to spend it as you wish," she smiled. "We have half an hour if you would like to visit the shop."

Quincy grinned and thanked her. She meandered into the giftshop and passed by the snow globes and touristy keychains. She slowly walked past the magazines to look at the latest fashion and celebrity gossip until she found the book section. Quincy grinned as she ran her fingers against the books. She paused when she noted a constellation embossed on the spine. Smiling, she pulled out the book and traced one of the constellations on its cover. She

29

recognized a few of them. Her father had allowed her to gaze through his telescope as he recited all them, but it had been a long time ago. Could she find his voice again in the pages of this book? She continued down the aisle until she found the fantasy section. After reading the backs of few of the books, she chose one with a fascinating cover. The illustration depicted a woman clothed in white, in-between two men, one wearing a dark red, the other in black. The title, "The Rule of Three" sounded interesting enough. After the shop, she stopped by the coffee cart and decided to surprise Mrs. Adalin with an earl grey tea while Quincy chose her usual hot chocolate with raspberry.

"That's very sweet, Quincy" Mrs. Adalin said as Quincy handed her the tea. Quincy smiled and took her place beside her. She looked at her books before placing them in her school bag with a patch of Oakley's white eagle on the flap. Before she closed the bag, Mrs. Adalin peeked over at her books.

"Excellent choices."

"Have you read 'The Rule of Three?" Quincy asked.

Mrs. Adalin nodded. "I've read it to my niece a few times. It's a fantastical and slightly romantic take on the creation myth," Mrs. Adalin said as she took out her reading glasses.

"Oh," Quincy wrinkled her nose.

Mrs. Adalin laughed. "What was that for? Don't you enjoy a good romance novel?"

Quincy grinned. "It's not that. If this is based off the story my parents told me, I don't think it's going to be an interesting read. My parents told my sister and I the story when we were young. My sister drifted off toward the end and fell off the bed."

Mrs. Adalin sighed. "Well then you heard the boring version. This one will be much more interesting," promised Mrs. Adalin.

"Oh? How come?"

"The author claims there was some sort of relationship triangle between the three."

Quincy burst out laughing.

Mrs. Adalin smiled and shrugged. "You never know."

"I don't see three stoic figureheads in a love triangle. We are talking about the same story, right?"

"The legend, about the three created to govern, protect, and guide our world?"

Quincy felt herself falling asleep already. "Yeah, that's the one." They sat silently sipping their hot beverages. "Mrs. Adalin, do you believe the story is true?"

"Which one? The one about the three or the romantic triangle between them."

Quincy and Mrs. Adalin shared a smile.

"Some believe they were a story based off of people long ago, or an allegory." Mrs. Adalin paused and bit the end of her glasses before continuing. "I believe over time; truth can turn into stories.

I'm sure these fairy tales have been based on reality, but the original story no longer exists. At least to my knowledge."

Quincy took another sip and sighed. Bored, she pulled out the book from her bag to stare at the three. She wasn't sure why, but she felt a sense of familiarity at their illustrated gazes, especially the man wearing black. She dismissed the thought from her mind. After all, black was a popular choice for clothing.

***

Wilbright marched to the NEFS New York door, but a man a hair taller than him blocked his way, forcing him to look up. When their eyes met, Wilbright's gaze dropped first and he clenched his fists.

"Uncle, why are you here?" Wilbright whispered angrily.

"I already warned you I would not let you continue unchecked. I will not allow you access to her," he quietly growled.

"You're forcing her to hear one side?"

"Your people have tried to kill her and her best friend. What would you have me do?"

"Let fate take its course," Wilbright promptly answered.

"Do you speak for fate?" his uncle questioned.

Wilbright couldn't think of anything witty to answer and chose the first thing that came to mind. "Shouldn't you be someplace else?"

Wilbright's uncle sighed. "You haven't figured this out yet," he answered as a statement, not a question. His curt reply fueled Wilbright's anger. "Enough of your riddles." Wilbright frowned and tried to push past him.

"Absolutely not," his uncle growled.

Wilbright sneered. "Fine. But do you think I came alone?"

His uncle looked around the crowd. None of them bothered him until he saw three shadows loitering near the tree line. He sucked in a breath of air and glared at Wilbright. "You will regret this."

"Only if I lose," Wilbright purred.

An NEFS eagle called out and they both whirled around to see the magnificent bird land into the building. His uncle ran inside, freeing the door for Wilbright to follow. He held back a curse at how quickly his uncle managed to find the girl clutching a cup and a book. Nearby, a NEFS agent called out, "Paris, France," and a handful of people queued up to board the eagle. Wilbright lost track of the girl and the taller Scottish man in the crowd.

***

Quincy watched the eagle land and heard "Paris" from the NEFS official.

"Are we next flight after Paris?" Quincy asked Mrs. Adalin, who nodded without looking up from her paper. Quincy settled back down in her seat and sipped on her hot chocolate. She felt a push behind her and the rest of her hot chocolate spilled.

"Hey!" she said angrily.

Whoever had pushed her, now held her shoulders preventing her from turning around. She tried to squirm to face the owner of the shockingly tight grip, but she couldn't budge. She stopped fighting when Mrs. Adalin placed her hand over Quincy's, the lawyer's reaction wide from shock.

"What are you doing here?" Mrs. Adalin sputtered.

"Go. Now!" the voice from the tight grasp said from behind her. "NOW!"

With one hand, Mrs. Adalin grabbed two pieces of paper shoved to her while the other grasped Quincy's arm, dragging her toward the eagle.

"What's happening?" Quincy asked, barely grabbing her bag in time. "Why are we leaving now?"

"We'll talk later." Mrs. Adalin said as she cut through the line and handed the staff member the pieces of paper.

They weren't eagle tickets, but the passes allowed them to board the eagle without question. The staff member whistled and people hurriedly moved onto the eagle. A scream tore through the station and everyone in the compartment tried to look over the right side of the eagle. Even with the high view, no one could see anything with the sudden movement below. Within moments, the eagle took off and Quincy looked over at Mrs. Adalin. She tightly clutched her hands with her jaw clenched, not meeting Quincy's gaze.

Quincy noted the other occupants and wished they had privacy so she could find out what was happening and why they boarded the Paris eagle instead. Instead she gently squeezed Mrs. Adalin's shoulder and tried to smile encouragingly until the lawyer relaxed under her grasp.

***

Wilbright swore under his breath. How had she disappeared so quickly in the crowd? She must have jumped on the flight to Paris. He could follow her on his own eagle immediately, but all the chances pointed in the exact replica of what had recently transpired. He looked around in vain trying to find his uncle. He knew the man could easily disappear, as if he could materialize and dematerialize on command, so Wilbright quickly gave up. He stared back at the edge of the forest, angrily. Prieler's shadowy minions had already dissipated. *Useless!*

NEFS Officials looked around, confused. No one knew what the commotion was about. One woman sobbed into one of the official's arms. He gently patted her shoulder. "It's okay, miss. There ain't anything out there now."

"But I promise you I saw something wrong."

Wilbright shook his head. Time to regroup and re-plan.

***

Quincy and Mrs. Adalin arrived in Paris stifling yawns and rubbing swollen eyes. Neither had slept the entire trip and instead had remained silent, keeping their gazes on their hands and feet.

Now that she had arrived, Quincy momentarily stifled her exhaustion and looked around the ornately built Paris station. Gold paint covered the wooden door frames and accentuated the fine details. She wished she didn't feel ill from anxiety and lack of sleep so she could better appreciate the Parisian station. In line to buy tickets to London, Quincy eavesdropped on the multiple French conversations happening around her. She closed her eyes, listening to the wonderful cadence. As she snooped, she felt the hairs on her arms stand straight up. She recognized a handful of words similar to Latin. Almost enough that she could follow the conversation! It made her strangely happy and for one blissful moment, she lost herself in the language as she silently repeated the words. Maybe, after she finished Latin, she could take French? Or another language? Or multiple ones. She could speak any language she wanted to!

Her elation died as reality set in. What choice did she actually have? She needed to find the missing keys and save the universe. That didn't leave her much time to learn new hobbies or work towards a future *she* wanted. She had already agreed to this. *Too late now,* she thought bitterly.

Defeated, she tuned out the languages and stared unnecessarily at a clock, watching its moving hands. Finally, it was their turn in line and they quickly bought their tickets. She counted down the minutes until they could board for London. After the hour was up, the two boarded quickly. Mrs. Adalin breathed a deep sigh of relief. "Finally."

Quincy nodded her agreement. She opened her mouth to ask Mrs. Adalin what was going on when an older woman boarded with three children under the age of fifteen. Now, she would have to wait. Mrs. Adalin noted the family and patted Quincy's knee.

"Soon," she said.

Quincy nodded and mentally counted down when they would land. Thankfully, it was a fast trip, and in her desire to get off, she tripped on one of the rungs from the ladder and banged her knee against the metal. Fighting back tears, she stepped away from the eagle towards the door.

Her taunt shoulders released with the words, "Welcome to London" as the NEFS customs agent stamped her travel book. She silently followed Mrs. Adalin through the station and across the street.

When they arrived at Bailey's B&B's cheery door, Mrs. Adalin turned to her. "We'll talk about it in your room after we've settled down."

"Okay," Quincy answered, fighting not to collapse against the door.

Bailey opened the door, greeting them both with a smile.

"Hello, my dears! You both look done for. Come in, come in."

They followed Bailey into the warm home and Quincy sunk down into the comfy overstuffed chair while Mrs. Adalin signed papers.

"Where's your trunk, sweetie?" Bailey asked.

Quincy's eyes widened in horror. What had happened to her trunk? She whirled around to face Mrs. Adalin. Thankfully, most of her important things had been left at Oakley, but not her parents music box. Quincy felt her throat tighten.

"Don't worry; it has your name on it. I'm sure it will meet you at Oakley."

"I hope so," Quincy whispered.

Bailey gripped her shoulder. "Oh, you poor thing. I'll find you a nightgown in our lost and found. You wouldn't believe the things people leave behind. I once had a family leave a stuffed rabbit behind. They came back from the station for the crying child's animal. Mercy, that child wailed."

Quincy nodded and smiled, trying to follow the conversation up the stairs. She hid a yawn behind her elbow, and rubbed her gritty eyes from exhaustion.

"I thought you ladies would appreciate the same rooms as last year." Bailey winked at them as she handed them each a key. "Go ahead and enter. I'll hunt down some proper night clothes and soup."

"Thank you," Quincy called after Bailey, but she had already disappeared down the staircase.

Mrs. Adalin followed Quincy in the room and they both sat on the bed. True to her word, Bailey brought up some vegetable soup and bread rolls.

They silently and quickly inhaled the food, starving from the stressful day. Finally, Mrs. Adalin sighed and placed the empty bowls on the night table.

"Forgive me, Quincy, but I'm exhausted, so I will keep this brief. But I will try the best I can to answer your query as to what happened this morning."

Quincy gripped the blanket, the exhaustion suddenly gone.

"Someone tried to find you today. His name is Lord Wilbright. I'm not entirely sure what he wants from you. To be honest, I'm more of a middleman. Or rather woman," Mrs. Adalin smiled tightly. "My job is to make sure you make it safely to and from Oakley. Everything else is up to..."

Mrs. Adalin paused as if unsure what to say. "You have another guardian who knows and takes care of the details," she finally said.

"Talin?" Quincy asked.

"I don't know his name. He was at the station today and told us to get on the eagle to Paris."

Quincy frowned. So, it wasn't Talin. Then who? The mysterious man in black?

"I had been warned this could happen, but it was a precaution I wasn't expecting." Mrs. Adalin's shoulders sagged.

"Do you know Lord Wilbright?"

"By reputation. He's a Creative Engineer, but we move in different circles. He's not someone who I would like to know. Quincy, I believe he helped orchestrate the events leading to your family's carriage accident."

Quincy choked on her gasp. Her hands shook and her heart pounded from the onslaught of emotion. He had destroyed her family and ruined her life. She bit her lip in anger until she felt the skin break.

"I'm sorry, Quincy. I know you shouldn't have to deal with this, but you must be wary of him. He's cunning. And he's looking for you."

Someone knocked on the door and they both jumped. Quincy wasn't the only one with shot nerves.

Bailey opened the door and waved at them with a long night shirt. "Sorry, my dear, but this will have to do. At least it's clean. Washed it myself," she smiled and left it on the chair near the door. "Goodnight!"

Bailey closed the door and Mrs. Adalin stood up and stretched.

"Try to get some sleep," said Mrs. Adalin as she opened the door. She paused and turned around to face Quincy one more time. "Please lock it after me."

Quincy nodded and twisted the lock behind Mrs. Adalin. She changed into the nightshirt and curled up in the soft bed. Hot tears streaked down her face, landing on the sheets. She couldn't fall asleep, forced to replay the image of the cemetery with her father and sister's names inscribed in front of her, and the name of the supposed orchestrator of their deaths.

***

The next morning, Mrs. Adalin entered Quincy's room with a fresh croissant and an *I love London* tourist t-shirt for Quincy to change into. She also handed her a small bag filled with necessities to freshen up with before breakfast.

"Oh, I don't remember the last time I had a hot croissant," Quincy said dreamily. "Thank you."

"You're welcome. Please change quickly and meet me down for oatmeal."

Quincy nodded and walked into the bathroom. She had never been so thankful for a toothbrush. After cleaning up, she walked downstairs for breakfast and her mouth watered at the delicious smell of properly cooked oatmeal. She ate a spoonful and smiled. After a summer at Miss Heatherwood's, she had forgotten what true oatmeal tasted like.

"We have a busy day today. We need to get books and your clothes. Tomorrow we'll take a carriage outside city limits for you to catch up with your classmates."

Quincy nodded sipping her apple juice.

Mrs. Adalin allowed Quincy five more minutes to finish her breakfast before she ushered her away from the table towards the street.

"Would you prefer to visit Mr. Bauer's for books or Madame Joyeux for clothes?"

"Books first, please." Quincy pleaded.

Mrs. Adalin smiled. "Why am I not terribly surprised?"

***

Quincy looked around the door of the book shop, disappointed not to see anyone she knew. Mr. Bauer's Bookstore only allowed you to see the person you walked in with, as well as the store owner, a clever feat she still couldn't begin to understand the mechanics of. Quincy stared at the list of required books. They were similar to last year's list since the first two years at Oakley were designated to general education. On their way back to the register, she paused at the strange mirror. She wondered if she would see the strange woman from last year, but she saw her own reflection instead.

"Are you coming, Quincy?"

Quincy nodded and ran to catch up with the barrister. After they had purchased her books, she walked outside, trying to give Mrs. Adalin a moment of privacy to say goodbye to her brother, Mr. Bauer. Quincy kept an eye on the crowds of people, enjoying watching them, until she spied a family of five walk inside the shop, presumably for school books. She turned her envious glance away from the door and back onto the busy London street.

Quincy looked up when she heard the bell ring from the door and Mrs. Adalin briskly walked out. "Thank you for waiting. Lunch?"

Quincy's stomach audibly grumbled. "Lead on," giggled Quincy and Mrs. Adalin smiled, gesturing down the street towards one of the local cafés for lunch. They both enjoyed a cup of noodle soup and a sandwich while Quincy flipped through her history book. She stopped when she saw a chapter on the hierarchy of Creative Engineers and knew Eloise would be delighted. Eloise dreamed of one day joining the ranks of the Creative Engineers. The rest of the book was filled with government and politics and she groaned in disappointment.

"What's the problem?" Mrs. Adalin asked, looking up from her paper.

"It looks boring," Quincy admitted.

Mrs. Adalin laughed. "Yes, but it's crucial to know. Besides, you could end up running for parliament or take a position in government."

Quincy resisted the urge to roll her eyes. "I seriously doubt it."

Mrs. Adalin smiled. "That may be, but it's still necessary information to know."

Quincy grudgingly agreed with her and flipped through her other books until she hit the bottom of the bag. She pulled out a book she knew she had not bought. Quincy looked up perplexed at Mrs. Adalin and waved the book about watercolors.

"We can pick up the actual paints this evening if you like."

Quincy looked surprised. "This is for me?"

"You've mentioned in some of your letters how much you've enjoyed art. I hope this encourages you to continue with it. It may bring you joy in the future."

Quincy jumped up and hugged Mrs. Adalin while thanking her continuously. Mrs. Adalin stiffened from the hug and gently brushed her off.

"Yes, yes. You are most welcome. Let's go get your uniform. Those pants will clearly not work."

Quincy laughed as she looked down at the legs of the pants she borrowed from the lost and found and saw too much of her socks showing underneath.

Mrs. Adalin and Quincy finished lunch and slowly walked toward Madame Joyeux's for new clothing. Quincy excitedly called out, "Wait for me!" when she saw a small girl with a purple umbrella about to walk in the door. Eloise turned around, saw Quincy, and delightfully squealed loud enough for three people. Bystanders stopped to turn around and stare at Eloise who grinned and ignored them. The two of them linked arms and walked down the hallway to their own school uniform room. Quincy looked back at Mrs. Adalin who waved them off. Eloise had the list in her hand and they sorted through this year's necessary school uniforms.

"Come on, Quincy, I need a new purple dress. Let's see what's in fashion this year."

Before Quincy could say anything, or question how many purple dresses she already owned, Eloise whisked her away to another part of the busy clothing shop.

"So how was your summer, Quincy?" Eloise asked.

"Uneventful," Quincy shrugged. "Yours?"

Eloise jumped into her adventures from her summer, many of which Quincy had already read about. Quincy juggled her emotions of jealousy from hearing about her friend's summer and happiness to be with her again.

***

The next day, Quincy unsuccessfully suppressed yawns on the carriage ride to the eagle's field. She had not slept well for the second night in a row and she blamed it on the anxiety of being followed in New York and her trunk left behind. She fiddled with her new sweater while bouncing on the seat. They would soon be at the field and she would be released to find her friends and board an eagle. Quincy waited for the carriage to stop before beating the cabbie to open the carriage door. Mrs. Adalin smiled at Quincy and patted her shoulder.

"I know you want to leave as quickly as possible, so I'll be swift." Mrs. Adalin paused and stared into Quincy's eyes. "Please, please, please be careful. Watch who you trust, especially outside of Oakley."

Quincy nodded slowly. Her words sobered her excitement.

"But don't allow this to ruin your day. Please enjoy this year. Keep in touch!"

Quincy half-smiled and deposited her heavy canvas bag with the Oakley luggage piles. She glimpsed some now Year Twos of the Third Floor near other Oakley students. Rusty gave Quincy a bear hug and she joined the conversation. Colin offered to take Quincy's small side bag, to which Quincy politely declined. Eloise unsuccessfully stifled an Eloise-like giggle. Rusty looked side-to-side and back at Colin. "Where's Genevieve?" he finally asked.

"Family emergency. She won't arrive for a couple of days."

Quincy pretended to be sorry and then immediately felt guilty at her delight at not having to deal with her on the eagle ride. To Quincy there wasn't anything worse than a family emergency, but she had no desire to see Genevieve quite yet.

"Speaking of missing people, has anyone seen Monty?" Quincy asked, but everyone shrugged in reply.

Five lines formed in front of the five empty doorposts. The four of them got behind the Oakley line. Quincy kept looking anxiously back until she glimpsed a white blonde head of hair walking briskly toward her. Monty stopped next to her, clearly winded and disheveled.

"Have I missed anything of great consequence?"

Quincy smiled at her best friend. She wanted to hug him, but he didn't appreciate physical contact like she did. Instead she simply shook her head. "Not yet, but you cut it pretty close."

Monty grimaced. "Seizure on the ride here."

Before Quincy could respond, scattered gasps erupted throughout the field as the eagles approached. The magnificent creatures soared towards the students and stopped in front of the five lines. Cheers, and some groans from those not excited for school, erupted from everyone as students boarded the eagles.

The five friends boarded the eagle, and when no one volunteered to be a solo rider with the group, the attendant flagged the eagle to leave.

Rusty looked around and frowned. "Hey, Eloise, your sister could have ridden with us. Where is she?"

Eloise tightened her grasp on her umbrella. "Why should I know? It's not like she's in our year."

"She took an earlier flight with students her own Year," Monty smoothly interjected.

"Are you keeping notes on Mikaela?" Colin said with a forced smile. Rusty, who had grown over six inches, now towered above the rest of them, thought it was a joke and nudged Colin.

"Nice one!"

"So, did everyone have a fantastic summer?" Eloise interrupted the awkward laughter.

The conversation turned in a more pleasant direction comparing Rusty's height next to the much shorter Eloise. Eventually the conversation died down, and Monty pulled out a newspaper while Rusty and Colin switched to sports. Eloise started talking about her summer adventures and Quincy pasted a smile on her face, listening to everyone's exciting summer holidays until the small spec of Oakley appeared on the horizon.

✳✳✳

Quincy took a bite of her mashed potatoes and savored its buttery flavor. A loud *thump* interrupted her moment.

"Have you seen our history book? It's going to be a brilliant year!" Eloise squealed directly in her ear.

She suppressed a grimace, and quickly grabbed her water glass as Eloise dropped her umbrella next to her plate.

"Not on the table," Mikaela growled as she grabbed this year's new purple umbrella and thrust it back into Eloise's hands.

Eloise stuck out her tongue. She opened the book and pointed to the chapter about Creative Engineers.

"Eloise, could you please pass the bread rolls?" Colin begged. Eloise grabbed the basket in front of her and without looking, handed them to Monty. He raised an eyebrow and handed the bread to Colin.

"A whole section. That'll be like a month on Grand Master Creative Engineers!"

"Not a *whole* section," groaned Rusty as he slid off the bench and under the table.

"Eloise, I have found a fascinating book which I would appreciate your thoughts with," Monty smoothly interrupted.

Quincy stifled laughter as he successfully steered the conversation on a book about some invention or other. Colin muffled his with hot chocolate.

Quincy looked over and saw the headmaster Luther Marquam deep in discussion with the staff seated at his table. She smiled with anticipation for her Independent study class. Hopefully this year she could start to master her Talent. And master her horse, and Latin, and, and…Quincy groaned.

"Quincy?"

"Yes, sorry. What?" she blinked.

"Tomorrow? Art Corridor?" Colin gave her a hopeful look.

"Sounds good. Oh!" Her eyes brightened. "I have to show you my new book on watercolors."

Quincy and Colin talked about art projects and his new horse until they were released after dinner and walked toward the Third Floor with the rest of the Year Twos. Quincy waved to the painted fox who lived in the Oakley Dining Hall portrait. It winked at her before pouncing on a leaf. Quincy wanted to talk to Monty alone about what he had found from his research from over the summer, but Colin wouldn't leave her alone until they all separated for the night. She enjoyed seeing all of them but desperately wanted to be alone with Monty. As they all said goodnight, Monty nodded at her as if clearly understanding her frustration.

"Tomorrow night?" Quincy asked him. Monty nodded and said goodnight. She dejectedly walked up the stairs barely listening to the conversation about the new style of polka dots when she glimpsed the hallway with the detailed flowers. She took a deep breath, imagining she could practically smell the blooms. Quincy opened the door and felt the rush of laughter and the warmth of the cream and red colored room. She smiled when she noticed her trunk next to her bed and canvas bag. She opened her trunk and nearly cried aloud when she saw the music box carefully wrapped within.

She looked over and grinned. Alba and Mon-Aye were giggling over a picture. She walked up to Mon-Aye's bed and leaned against the post.

"Hello, lady." Alba purred.

"Gregory, again?" Quincy pointed to the picture.

"Oh no." Mon-Aye shook her head. "No thank you. Gregory was so *last* year. Keep up!" she grinned. "I have received special intelligence. The recently retired stage actor Rex Dafoe has taken a post here…"

"As an Oakley nurse." Alba finished. She handed Quincy a signed picture of a classically handsome man with a dimpled smile that made her melt. Just a little bit.

"But why *here*?" Quincy pondered.

"Who cares?" Mon-Aye answered. "But we're going to get all the details. You know, for *reasons*."

"Yes," Alba agreed. "The Rex Dafoe fan club requires it! I think I'm going to get sick often this year…"

"Oh, well that's why we have an Infirmary, isn't it?" Quincy giggled. She placed her palm over Alba's forehead. "You are feeling warm…"

"I knew it! I'm sick!" Alba declared.

The girls laughed until Mikaela demanded to know what she missed. After making a pact that they would dig up information on Oakley's new nurse, the girls said goodnight.

Quincy giggled as she closed the thick curtains around her bed. Having friends was the absolute best feeling in the entire world.

She laid down, but despite her exhaustion, she couldn't fall asleep. The lights above and underneath her curtains gradually darkened until only a glimmer of moonlight shone through. She kept tossing and turning until she finally fell fitfully asleep.

A *creak* woke her and she quickly jumped out of bed and slowly opened the curtain to peek outside.

Adrenaline coursed through her veins as she surveyed the dormitory. Everyone slept in their beds silently dreaming. She rolled her eyes at her jumpiness. What could happen to her at Oakley? Besides, weren't her curtains soundproofed? It must be all in her head.

Too bad her horse Consto was such a large creature. He would have known the difference between reality and her fear. Her steed had a sixth sense when unsavory people lurked about. Consto had arrived at Oakley, nameless, and for some reason he was enamored with the Latin word for "stop." Occasionally, he might even listen.

She could have asked for another mount this year, but Consto's keen sense gave her the perfect reason not to request another horse.

She thought about the current time, wishing it wasn't so late. Otherwise she could have justified a visit to the stables.

She rubbed her forehead and mentally calculated that she had been in bed for three and a half hours. She grudgingly went back inside her warm bed and continued to fall asleep and wake up every few hours afterwards.

CHAPTER FOUR

HARD PLACES

Quincy knocked her head on the table in a feeble attempt to wake up. She had slept so restlessly the night before; she might as well not have slept at all. Three nights of awful sleep. She stared at her ragged reflection on the window across from her and hoped she didn't have Latin on her first day back. Monty sat down next to her and grabbed a knife to butter some toast.

"Quinn," Monty gently nudged her with the back of his butter knife. "Did you know drinking water is often more desirable to aide in waking up the brain than attempting to knock sense into an exhausted and practically functionless mind?"

Quincy shook her head. "It's too early to do this. Besides, I..."

Monty interrupted her. "It is true, a night of no sleep is not helpful for Latin."

Before Quincy could relay her exasperation of his Talent, Monty grinned. "I know, annoying is it not? By the way, you might find sustenance helps."

"Helps what? Sleeping or waking up?"

Monty shrugged. "If I were you, I would stand on the grass."

Quincy frowned, too puzzled to respond quickly before Monty grabbed a second piece of cinnamon toast and walked away from her.

"Monty, we have to be in front of the Learner's Citadel in less than twenty minutes. Where are you going?"

"The librarian found a book on locks that I have been looking forward to reading all summer."

"Locks? You'd better grab it quickly before someone else does on the first day of school."

Quincy realized she had picked up a personality trait from Talin and needed to give up the sarcasm, so she smiled apologetically.

"Oh no, I already visited yesterday." He laughed. "I picked up an excellent book. The one in question is a limited printing and happens to be on loan." Monty gave Quincy a slight smile. "Not that you are truly interested."

"*Ddefnyddio'r amser yn ddoeth*," she laughed.

Everyone within earshot groaned and someone mumbled, "Stupid school motto."

He shook his head. "Eat," he said, pointing a finger at the table before walking out the door. He waved at Eloise who passed by him without seeing him. She sauntered towards the third table attempting to walk a straight line as if thinking the dinnertime illusion was currently in effect. Which it wasn't. The dinnertime illusion placed each table on a different plane of existence and if you were late to the evening meal, it became difficult to find your way to your table. The illusion never happened at breakfast. She sat down next to Quincy and Mikaela without saying a word.

"Well, Eloise you proved me wrong about being the most exhausted person in this room." Quincy tapped her spoon on Eloise's plate. "You know, it's odd though, because I didn't see a candle lit in your part of the room."

Eloise's head shot up and her bloodshot eyes widened.

"What? Who? Me? Of course, I was in my bed. Why would I have been awake last night?" she said while yawning. "I was happily asleep not creating or doing anything of any sort."

Realizing she had said too much, Eloise grabbed an apple and fled towards the main hall. Mikaela laughed after Eloise had left.

"What's her issue today?" Quincy pondered.

"Today? Who knows? I only live with her." Mikaela rolled her eyes.

Quincy's stomach heaved and she decided against eating the toast in front of her. She stood up and walked outside to wait with the other early students on the steps of the Learner's Citadel. After ten minutes, Colin and Rusty joined her to discuss classes. The school bells rang but she couldn't find Monty or Eloise. Bry had been chosen to say the arrival poem so he stepped up to knock on the doors. Everyone from the Third Floor cheered for their Floor Leader and he gave a slight bow. His powerful voice echoed around the courtyard. Before he finished the school poem, everything around her became fuzzy. The last thing she comprehended was how happy she was to be standing on grass. Everything became black as Quincy hit the lawn of the courtyard.

***

Quincy briefly awoke and wondered if she was in a strange dream when she heard Monty and Colin arguing.

"I was here first," argued dream Colin.

"A mature response," jabbed back dream Monty. "Do you not already have a girlfriend to attend to."

Finally, Nurse Watson came and shooed them away, leaving her in silence and to fall back to a deep sleep. After what felt like seconds, but in actuality had been exactly eight hours and seventeen minutes, she woke up from a deep sleep. Quincy poked her head out the door and saw the headmaster Luther Marquam talking to Nurse Watson. The nurse saw Quincy and motioned towards her. The headmaster turned around and smiled.

"Ah, Miss Quincy. I came because you missed my class this afternoon."

"I'm sorry sir." She paused as his words connected and sat up when she recognized the walls of the Infirmary. "Wait, what happened?"

"May I come in?"

Quincy nodded and the headmaster walked inside the small room and sat down on the visitor's seat.

"Probably nerves and not enough sleep," he gently chided her. He handed her an envelope with her name embossed in gold. "Here's your list of classes. You had two friends who came earlier and each wanted to be the one to give you your schedule." The headmaster smiled and shook his head fondly. "Boys."

Quincy remembered the visit between Monty and Colin earlier.

"Is it alright if I look at the schedule now?"

"By all means."

Quincy looked at her schedule, not surprised by any of the classes.

"I have a small assignment for you, I'm afraid."

Quincy couldn't contain her horror, and the headmaster chuckled and shook his head.

"Don't be alarmed. It's something for you to think about. A major part of your Talent is remembering your past. In order to make a concise and well-thought out decision, one must be familiar with the past so they don't make the same mistakes again. Our decisions affect not only ourselves. They are steps in time and you, my dear, must be willing to find all of the choices for every decision. From there, we learn if the decision was right or wrong. We study our pasts so that hopefully, we won't make the same choice, or mistake, again."

Quincy chewed on her lip. "That's a lot to think about," she finally said.

Headmaster Marquam nodded. "It is, but ponder it and be prepared to give me a clear explanation why studying choices and their consequences in history is important to understand. Any questions?"

She shook her head. "No, I think I can figure it out."

"Excellent. The fastest class I have ever taught." He chuckled as he stood up. "I'll see you in class the day after tomorrow." He paused at the door and turned to face her, his voice dropping to a whisper. "I was informed of what happened on your trip here." Marquam shook his head. "We have securities in place here. You have no need to fear for your safety at Oakley."

Quincy thanked him and watched him leave. For some reason, she doubted him. Could she be as safe here as he thought? As soon has he had left, Nurse Watson stepped inside. For some reason, Nurse Watson reminded her of her mom. She didn't look like her, but her capability of being both warm and terrifying, as needed, felt familiar.

"Alright then, Miss Harris. I encourage you to always eat breakfast. And," she threateningly wagged her finger, "You need to figure out what is stressing you out to this extent. I don't want to see you up here for a bit."

Quincy nodded. "I'll work on that. Thank you."

She grabbed her things and walked out. She grinned at Mon-Aye and Alba peeking out at the end of the hallway. They waved her over when they saw her.

"You're so confident!" Alba gasped. "You didn't even wait a full day! Tell us, did you see him?"

With everything happening, Quincy had forgotten about the actor turned nurse and shrugged. "I don't think so."

Mon-Aye shook her head. "Such a pity. I hear his Talent is his healing soft touch." She waved her hands at Quincy.

The two girls sighed dramatically. "We need to get more information for our fan-fiction… err… fan club newsletter. Do you want to feel faint again?"

Quincy grinned. "How about later? I have to go through my schedule."

"Boring." Alba said and dismissed her with her hand.

Quincy shook her head and walked down the main staircase toward the third floor. She already knew exactly what was constantly stressing her out. She looked down at her shirt and her hidden key before looking at her class schedule.

Quincy stopped walking when she saw which year of Latin she had been placed in.

First year Latin. Again.

The heaving sensation quickly came back and she wanted to be sick. All her friends had moved on to second year Latin, except her. She would be stuck with the Year Ones. And stuck having to use her book from last year that had misspelled foul language graffitied on the cover from Amanda. Quincy did not wish to speak to anyone and held her head down. She attempted to run past the family room and into her own room. Monty met her at the door. "Quinn, do you want to talk about it?"

She shook her head, "Thanks, but I'm fine." To her embarrassment, her lips trembled and her eyes watered. "I'll see you in a bit, okay?" Before he could respond, Quincy turned away from him and ran up to her room. She sat on the bed and held her pillow into her chest, feeling tears pooling into it. How could this have happened? How could she have failed and why was she behaving so ridiculously? It's not like it was the end of the world. A quiet knock at the door interrupted her pity party and she groaned at her mistake. She had forgotten to use her soundproof drapes.

In reply, Quincy gave a muffled "I'm fine. Please, go 'way."

The knocking stopped for a moment and she thought the knocker had left. She poked her head from out under her pillow and looked outside of the drapes to stare at the now silent door. After a minute, the door opened ajar and Monty poked his head in the door. Quincy wiped her face and jumped off her bed.

"Monty, you know you can't be in here. You'll get in a lot of trouble if you get caught."

Monty gave her a mischievous smile. "*If* I get caught. We have a few minutes. What is the problem?"

"Nothing."

Monty raised an eyebrow. "Well?"

"Well what?"

"Am I invited in?"

Quincy gave him a mock-sigh and shook her head. "I can't stop you."

Monty's lips curled and he sat down at the end of her bed while she plopped down on her pillow. He looked around the room, clearly interested.

"So, this is the ladies' room..." he grinned at her. "It is surprisingly messy."

She fought against smiling, and finally sighed. "I flunked Latin and have to retake Year One."

Monty nodded. "I am sorry for your distress."

"Me having to retake Latin with the Year Ones is... it's so embarrassing." Quincy crossed her arms over her knees. "I wanted to do better. I wanted to *be* better." How could someone who failed Year One Latin save the entire world? Shame turned her cheeks a bright pink from the ordeal she created for herself. This wasn't the end of the world, and there were more serious problems to face like the actual end of the world. What if she saved everyone but had to keep taking Year One Latin until she mastered it? Quincy imagined what she would look like as an old woman taking Year One Latin and for some strange reason, it made her giggle.

Monty unsuccessfully hid a smile on the corner of his lips.

"Monty, you can be so mean! Stop knowing what I'm going to tell you."

"I am terribly sorry for smiling. I truly am."

"Yeah, sure. Liar."

"Truly. I am sorry for your emotional…distress?"

Quincy tried to frown but started laughing again. Monty joined in but momentarily stopped to look at his watch.

"Monty, will you promise me you won't banish me from our part of the table?"

Monty nodded solemnly. "I can do that. Now, I would truly relish the idea of staying longer, but my handful of moments are up. I will see you later in the dining hall."

Quincy waved goodbye as Monty slipped out. She lay back down on her pillow, this time feeling better. Not even two minutes later the door opened and two of Quincy's roommates walked in.

Monty had just missed them. She laughed and wiped her face before anyone could inquire about the tears.

✳✳✳

Quincy walked down to the stables after dinner to greet Consto. The horse blew air out of his nose as if trying to intimidate her. He immediately stopped when he saw her peace offering. He happily grabbed the apple from her outstretched hand and chewed contentedly. Quincy heard someone walk up next to her and she turned around to face Colin. She smiled as he sat down on a stool nearby.

"Thanks for leaving me the drawing of your new filly in the Infirmary. She looks beautiful."

Colin glowed from the praise. "I should be able to ride her by next summer," he said, dreamily. "Maybe I can bring her with me next year."

"Did you finally decide on a name?"

Colin nodded. "I decided on Albion."

Quincy imagined Colin riding the white horse, Albion, on a windy day and had to admit he would have an elegant seat.

"Albion goes well with your last name," she teased.

"Albion and her Knight," Colin laughed at himself. "On a holiday, you should come home with me and I'll let you ride her."

Her cheeks grew hot and she hoped it wasn't obvious. "Thank you, but I don't think I'm allowed to leave school grounds during the holiday."

"You should ask. There are usually ways to get around it. I think you can fill out a request."

"Maybe," Quincy answered simply. How would Genevieve feel about the invitation and why make an offer to a girl who isn't your girlfriend?

The conversation changed to polo and Colin described his uncle's horse bred for the sport until the Timepiece rang for bed. The two slowly walked up to the third floor and he wished her goodnight. She sat in the family room, hoping to meet Monty, but he never showed up. After a yawn she gave up on seeing the Irish boy that evening.

***

Quincy had her Latin class planned perfectly. At the beginning, she nonchalantly stood by the door and then, at the last bell slipped in unnoticed at the back of the room. The professor looked down at her through his spectacles on the tip of his nose, effectively ruining her brilliant plan.

"Ah, Miss Harris. Delighted you have graced this classroom with your presence."

Quincy clenched her fists and her toes, but forced herself to look passive and stare at the chalkboard in front of her. The professor snapped his fingers, demanding the class' attention. As he droned through the introduction, Quincy hated to admit the perk of retaking Latin meant that at least the first part of the class would be easy if not incredibly boring.

As soon as the bell rang their release, she dashed out of the classroom. Monty waited for her at the end of the hallway and her humiliation instantly dissipated when he waved. Quincy gave him a quizzical expression. "I'm happy to see you, but what are you doing here?"

"I have a free period and thought I could meet you on my way to the library."

"Aren't you going to Physical Ed?"

Monty shook his head. "I have permission to take a personal study period instead. Doctors decided physical activity is the last thing I truly need."

"I'm sorry, Monty."

Monty responded with a wicked smile. "I am not."

Quincy laughed.

As they separated at the library, Monty paused awkwardly at the library door.

"I am sorry I was unavailable last evening. Would you please meet me in the family room tonight?"

Quincy nodded and she waved goodbye as she quickened her pace to the locker room. She paused before walking into the locker room. Even though she was almost late, she couldn't stop herself from reading the notice on the door.

Polo Tryouts for the Spring season. Coming soon!

She felt tingles down her spine to her toes. Polo. She was old enough for tryouts this year. If Consto would let her. Or an event for the Equospatium?

While debating with herself, she quickly opened the door and dashed inside. She looked over the empty room with dread until she saw a panicking Eloise desperately searching her bag.

"I can't find my left shoe," she moaned.

Quincy managed to throw clothes on and run after Eloise, who had found her left shoe still in her locker, to meet the other students outside.

Professor Pertinax gave the girls a death glare. Quincy wished her Talent turned her invisible.

"You would think that after a full year with me, you girls would know better. Two laps around the field. What are you both still doing here? Go!"

"Here we go again," Eloise rolled her eyes as they ran past Rusty who saluted them. Quincy failed to hide a grin. Even running laps and being stuck in Year One Latin at Oakley, Quincy couldn't imagine any other place she would rather be.

After the first lap the girls slowed down to a jog.

"It's too bad polo tryouts aren't for a few more months," said Quincy breathlessly, trying to make conversation. Eloise yawned and nodded slowly, clearly not having heard what Quincy had said.

"Eloise, what's the matter?"

"With me? What could be wrong?" Eloise frowned.

"Never mind, I guess." Quincy shrugged, dropping the subject.

"Football on the first day," Eloise whined and Quincy felt inclined to agree.

***

Quincy rubbed her sore legs and glimpsed her reflection on the library window. She could already feel the sunburn on her cheeks, the tips of her ears, and the part in her hair. Quincy hated Independent Study being scheduled right after Physical Education this year. She walked into the headmaster's office and plopped down on the chair in front of him.

"Football day?"

Quincy nodded grumpily.

The headmaster smiled. "My sincere apologies. How did your assignment go?"

"I tried. I'm not sure if I'm right though."

"Well, let's hear your thoughts."

Quincy pulled out a piece of paper from her pocket to read her notes. The headmaster politely coughed. "Your talent is memory, if I remember correctly. Less paper, more brain."

Quincy bit her lip, stifling a laugh, and continued without her notes.

"If history is the story of our past, in order to decide what to do with the future, we should know what we did in the past so we don't make the same mistake and know the consequences for all of our actions," she paused. "Basically."

"Exactly. Now in your own words please."

"Don't make the same mistake twice and expect different results?"

The headmaster chuckled. "True, give me an example?"

"When you don't do your homework and then you do fail a test. Then later don't do your homework again and... expect to do well on the test?"

The headmaster laughed loudly and cleared his throat. "It's more difficult than it seems. Learning from one's mistakes and then doing it differently is much easier said than done. Something I have personally found."

Quincy nodded and could not help but ask the question forming in her head. "Talking about choices, hypothetically, if you could time-travel to the future and you saw something you liked, would you ruin the chance of it happening by trying to make it happen? Or if you saw something you didn't like and you tried not to make it happen, would it end up happening because you saw it?" She paused, not quite sure how to continue.

"Is there a question in there?" the headmaster inquired.

Quincy chewed on her lip and leaned closer to the headmaster's desk. "I guess I'm wondering if you're not supposed to do anything or if you're supposed to try and make it happen... Or not. Does that make sense?"

The headmaster frowned and rubbed his chin. "I think I understand what you're asking, though I don't know how to answer that. What would you do, Quincy?"

Quincy shrugged. "I'm not sure. I guess it would depend on the situation."

"Excellent answer. But why the question?"

"Your question on learning from the past for the future made me think about time and the possibilities. Honestly, it makes my head hurt."

"It does tend to do that, doesn't it? Don't be too terribly frustrated. This is why I ask you these seemingly odd questions. It's good for you to think about them."

Quincy recalled one of her Language Arts class lectures and discussions from last year. Professor Archer asked them to write the definition of true love and then choose who wrote the best one. By the end of class, no one could decide. Her brain felt similar to how it felt now. She rubbed her forehead and found herself momentarily lost within the ticking of the countless clocks surrounding her.

The headmaster stood up and walked to a filing cabinet behind his desk and pulled out one of the drawers. He turned around to face Quincy and beckoned her toward the cabinet. Dutifully, Quincy joined him.

"See these files here?"

Quincy nodded.

"Last year I told you your mind was similar to a cabinet. That every memory stored in your mind is like this file of papers. Your Talent allows you to organize your memories and allow you access to a specific moment, like looking for a paper from this cabinet. You are now capable of recalling random objects in their particular order. We are going to move on to exercises to aid you in pulling specific memories hidden in your mind by searching for it instead of it being accidentally triggered." The Timepiece rang, and they both looked up.

"Sounds good to me." Quincy replied, standing up and grabbing her bag.

"Before you leave," the headmaster added. "Any news about the next key?"

The peculiar man on the train entered her mind, but she didn't want to admit her odd dream to the headmaster. Instead, she shook her head. "Nothing new from me. I'm waiting to talk to Monty about it." She sighed and wrinkled her nose. "It's frustrating, but there isn't anything I can do from Miss Heatherwoods."

Marquam nodded. "Don't be too hard on yourself. It's better for you to try to remain inconspicuous as possible there. We don't want unwanted attention."

Quincy nodded.

"Okay, thank you for keeping me updated," he finished, dismissing her.

Quincy nodded and left.

***

That evening, Quincy slipped into the family room and saw Monty staring vacantly out the window. His limp arms hung loosely against his blue night robe. Three students sat at one of the tables in the corner in deep conversation for the Year Four graduation project. Quincy stood next to Monty, but the Irish boy didn't welcome her and instead stared glassily into the cloudy night. She gently put a hand on his shoulder, but he didn't register her touch. She looked closely at his face and saw his empty eyes. She shivered and waited

71

for his seizure to finish. Finally, after two minutes, he sighed and leaned into the glass. He breathed deeply and slowly slid down the window until he landed on the floor. Quincy sat down next to him and he stared exhaustedly at Quincy.

"Sorry," he said simply.

"You seem to be having a lot of those recently. Are you okay?"

He nodded slowly. "I believe so," he answered, his shoulders slumping. "It seems this key business has been creating a bit of stress in my life." He closed his eyes and put his hand in his pocket.

"What did you see?" she whispered.

He rubbed the bridge of his nose. "You mentioned a man wearing purple, specifically plum. Or so you assume."

Quincy gaped at him. "But I'm sure it was a dream."

"Apparently it is more than that, if you will decide, or rather have decided, to tell me."

Quincy shrugged and told him about her accidental trip to Paris and meeting the man who rhymed on the train. Monty's eyes widened at the mention of the man's key.

"And you are sure you have never seen him before?"

"Completely sure," she nodded. "I would remember him."

Monty took off his glasses and automatically cleaned them. "Odd. I have not come across any mention of any odd men in plum in my research."

One of the other students in the room loudly laughed and Quincy and Monty both looked up. The group groaned and mentioned something about "coffee" and left the room, leaving them alone. Monty stood up stretching and motioned toward the empty seat near the fireplace. Quincy perched on the arm of the chair while Monty sunk into the cushion with a sigh.

"Did you learn anything new?" she asked.

"Many things, actually. But I am not quite sure what is relevant," Monty replied as he pulled out a notebook from his night robe pocket. "What I have found, has been difficult to sort between myth and the truth. To be quite honest, if you had asked me a year ago, I would have informed you anything dealing with the door and keys were tales of fancy," he admitted.

"Well, now you know," Quincy teased.

Monty smiled and checked the room one more time before pulling his hand out of his pocket. He opened his palm revealing his key and slowly traced the clover-like eye. "I am truly curious of what could be behind the door leading to the end of time."

"You didn't find anything at all about it?"

Monty shook his head. "Nothing definitive. All of it seems to be complete conjecture."

Quincy sighed. "So, what did you find?"

"I created a tedious chart of all the reports of minor keys being found. What it told me is no one knows where the stolen key is." Monty took off his glasses and rubbed his eyes. "The only thing that piqued my interest was a robbery in the vaults of one the famous banks in Switzerland. The first and only time in history."

"What does that have to do with the keys?"

"There is some conjecture that one of the keys is, or rather was, in that bank. Not that it helps us. We better hope the key hasn't been permanently lost, or this whole thing will be in vain. Speaking of lost keys, did the rhyming man want something from you for his key?"

She shook her head. "I don't think so?"

Monty frowned. "I will do some research and see if I can find anything on men who like to rhyme with some sort of connection to the minor keys. Though I doubt I will find anything of the sort." he admitted.

"Me too. Besides, what if he stole it? Minor keys can be given and taken away."

"True," Monty nodded. "Which makes it difficult to procure the genuine keys."

Quincy groaned, her shoulders slumping.

"I did however make further leeway on the door itself."

Quincy's shoulders perked up and she looked at Monty again.

"The engravings on the door entailed three birds. Are you familiar with our creation story?"

Quincy grimaced. "I haven't heard anything about the original three in years and suddenly it's all I'm hearing. I know there were three beings sent to protect humanity or something."

"A condensed version, but yes. Quite often, people in art depict the three as birds. I believe this may be of some importance."

Birds. Quincy stifled a laugh. Talin was a special bird, but she doubted he had anything to do with the story. Or did he? "Why birds?" Quincy asked. She remembered the cover of her book with the three of them represented as people. "Are they birds or people? Or something else?"

Monty shrugged. "No one truly knows."

"Do you know what the globe object is on the door?"

"My best guess is it is a representation of the world."

"So, what's next?" Quincy asked.

"I will do some more research on individuals who could be or have connections to the creator of the door and the keys. Maybe this will help us weed out candidates until we find the true Creative Engineer. Meanwhile, you should talk to Eloise. She might have knowledge that I do not possess regarding engineers."

"Okay. I guess I was hoping for more."

Monty nodded. "Likewise." He stood up and hid a yawn behind his hand. "Goodnight."

"Night," she answered as Monty left for his room. Quincy stayed by the fire and watched the flickering flames while grasping her key.

RIDDLES

Quincy woke up refreshed. After her fainting spell three days ago, she hadn't had a nightmare since then. The deep sleep had helped to lessen her anxiety. She sighed contentedly and snuggled in her cozy covers, closing her eyes. *Five more minutes,* she pleaded. As she slipped back into a doze, a pillow hit her directly in the face. She ripped it off her head to see Kalleigh grinning mischievously down at her. But before Kalleigh could revel in her victory, she growled after being hit with a painful-sounding smack to her backside by a smirking Mikaela. A smart tap on the door interrupted their glee and Quincy's sweet revenge.

"Ladies," Bry groaned. "I hate to remind you that it's our turn to help set up breakfast and we really don't want to be late. If you don't hurry, us gentleman will leave without you and we'll still get in trouble. Again."

"Good!" Alba added.

The girls responded with giggles.

"Aww, it's too soon to get reprimanded," a muffled male voice groaned in the hallway. "I don't want to do dishes all month again."

"Fine. Let no man say I didn't try."

Everyone waited until Bry's footsteps had disappeared and then commenced with the pillow fighting. Eventually, they grew tired and decided to come to the boy's rescue and help set up breakfast. After eating, Quincy had a moment of panic as she dug through her bag. "I left my book on my chair." She stuffed the last of her toast in her mouth and jumped up. Monty grabbed his own bag and followed her out.

"I am on my way to the Post Office. I believe you usually get a letter today from your solicitor?"

Quincy nodded. "Mind grabbing my mail?"

"It is no problem."

They separated and Quincy grabbed her book and dashed to her first class. Panting, she leaned against the wall next to the door. Monty briskly walked up to her waving a letter; his eyes unusually bright.

"Why so excited?"

Monty grinned and handed her the letter. "Look," he requested.

Quincy grasped the letter. It wasn't from Mrs. Adalin. Her throat tightened as she looked for a return address. There wasn't one, which meant this wasn't about her mother. She momentarily closed her eyes and sighed before looking at the spidery-like handwriting on the envelope.

"That's bizarre," Quincy said, peering closer at the ink. From the light, it appeared to be a dark purple. *Purple ink?*

"I thought so too."

"You could save me the time if you have already seen what it is," she replied, placing her hands on her hips.

"I have not. Though, that would have been nice information to have. Maybe one day I will get it to work when I wish." Monty shrugged and pointedly looked at the letter.

"Going to share?"

"Yes, but not now," Quincy replied, slipping the letter in her bag.

Monty frowned. "Why not now?"

"Later," Quincy replied grinning at his impatience. "We don't have enough time before class starts and I have to at least try to focus in Latin. Let's talk about it tonight?" He nodded and waved before walking away.

She turned the letter over and saw a strange melted seal. Curious, she held it next to the light coming from the window and saw an intricate design of a clock face. The clock hands looked odd. She tried to get a closer look, but the bell rang and Quincy slid the letter into her bag before slipping into class.

The thought of the unknown letter hounded her through the day making it difficult to focus on the Latin lecture. Her mind kept running back to the letter in her bag. Who would send her a letter?

She pondered the note's contents and the curious purple ink. Could it have been from...?

"Miss Quincy?"

Quincy looked up, suddenly realizing she was in Mathematics. She barely remembered leaving Latin. The Mathematics professor frowned at her and crossed his arms.

"And if you were paying attention you would know the answer is...?"

Colin, sitting in front of her, signaled four fingers and then three fingers behind his back without turning his head.

"Um, forty-three?" she smiled, innocently.

The professor frowned even deeper. "Very good, Miss Harris. I hope next time you will be able to answer me without the aid of Master Knight."

Quincy nodded sheepishly and counted down the minutes until class ended.

After fifteen minutes of painful waiting, Quincy launched out her chair and ran out the door. She decided to skip lunch and find somewhere private to read her letter. Nurse Watson entered her memory and so did her lecture about the importance of food.

Unfortunately, Quincy would not have time to do both. Grudgingly, she followed the rest of the student body towards lunch.

***

After class, Quincy managed to dodge her friend's request to visit the Templum in the forest. As much as she wanted to spend time with all of them, the letter felt more important today. The sense of mystery from the unknown authored letter lured her back to her room. Quincy took the stairs two at a time, leaving her breathless by the time she collapsed on her bed. She looked around the cream colored, and disorganized room, thankful most of her roommates were out practicing or studying. Lindy walked in after Quincy and closed her drapes to take a nap. Quincy closed her own drapes, laid down on her stomach, and pulled out the letter from her bag. Once again, she found herself drawn to the spidery handwriting. After looking under her bed, she finally found her letter opener. Slowly, Quincy opened the flap and took the letter from the envelope. She choked when she read the introduction.

Dear Miss Quincy Marie Katelyn Harris,

How did the writer know she had two middle names? She did not offer that piece of information easily. Not even Monty knew. Especially because she felt a mix of embarrassment and surprise that "Katelyn" was probably because of his mother. Puzzled, Quincy continued to translate the difficult handwriting.

I have a proposition. It's something like a mission.
Of sorts.
In order to learn, you must earn,
My praise.

Riddles

Three is the lucky number to plunder,
My treasure.
Number one will be done at a quarter past one
to watch them shun the one who will run for the
deed he has done.
You will find the man who they will ban from a
position of power from the great tower
that he has built.
To win my favor, you must savor the flavor of failure,
of yesterday's past.
Find the dial and filled with guile,
travel behind and rewind the time.
With a thought, three clicks will do the trick.
Search for a feather that you find tethered
to one whose tracks are black.

~C

How strange. Quincy looked over the letter again even more confused before she had read it the first time. Who was "C?" What kind of treasure? Travel behind? Was she supposed to read something or go back in time via the Timepiece? Quincy wondered if Talin would know, but unfortunately, she had not heard from the bird since Miss Heatherwood's. Further thoughts were interrupted when the football team barged in, laughing loudly from an incident on the field involving a missing shoe and a lost jersey. Quincy put the letter in her pocket and got ready for dinner.

At dinner, Quincy twisted her spoon in her lentil soup. She looked up to ask Monty if he had chosen the topic for his English paper, but he had a frozen expression on his eyes and stared unblinking through Quincy. She turned around to see what had captured his attention, but only saw the feet of the fourth-floor table. Quincy sighed and continued to stir her soup. She wanted to get hot chocolate with him so she could get his advice on the bizarre letter.

"Is everything fine, Quincy?" Colin inquired hesitantly.

Genevieve looked over Colin's shoulder and frowned icily at Quincy for presumably taking Colin's attention away. Such a pity Genevieve had arrived. Quincy had hoped for a few more days before the ice queen's arrival.

"Me? Yeah, sorry. Just tired." She smiled at Colin and looked over at Monty blinking rapidly like a nocturnal animal exposed to light.

Quincy open her mouth to inquire if Monty felt alright, but before she could say anything, he looked at her, smiled, and grimaced.

"All is well." He waited until the conversation switched to other topics and then he again looked at Quincy. "Hot chocolate would be wonderful."

Quincy frowned and before she could tell him how much she hated when he did that, Monty grinned at her. "I know."

An hour later and armed with hot chocolate, they sat down on a table in the café and looked over the letter. Monty wore a focused expression while he pondered over the letter multiple times and then at the seal on the envelope. While she waited for him to speak, she stared at the seal in better detail. The wax had been engraved with not one, but three feathers as the hour, minute, and second's hand of a normal clock. Quincy listened to the clock tick in the café and wondered when he would finish so she could speak. Finally, after ten minutes, Monty stretched and sighed. "Riddles. I simultaneously adore and loathe them."

"Exactly!" Quincy threw her hands in the air. "Why can't people say what they mean?"

Monty reached into his bag and pulled out a pad of paper with a fountain pen and eloquently wrote notes. "My preliminary thought is that you have been invited to participate in a treasure hunt. This letter could be clue number one. Have you received any other seemingly odd letters or anything out of the ordinary?"

"Just the man on the train. But he was a..."

"Dream?" Monty finished, and grinned at her irritation. "Maybe he is as alive as you or I. And who is to say he is not the same man who has sent you this riddle?"

"C?" she questioned.

Monty shrugged and sipped his hot chocolate, smiling wickedly as he licked the whipped cream from the corner of his lips instead of using his spoon. "Going back to the riddle, it makes use of the number three. I have never heard of three being a particularly lucky number. However, it is considered to be a whole number. Perhaps it is a code and you will have to remember it for some reason?"

"Possibly?" Quincy shrugged. "I don't know if I want to see someone banned 'from a position of power from the great tower that he has built.'" Quincy paused. "Do we assume it's an actual man?"

"That would narrow it down. However, it truly is not of much help. And reading the next few lines, it seems this has already happened. How are we to view this? Are we supposed to read about it in a book?"

"Maybe? But how do we win his favor? And what is it?"

Monty shook his head. "Have not the foggiest. Hopefully something to do with the 'treasure. Or the key that "C" taunted you with?"

"A treasure hunt for the key?" Quincy wondered.

"Find the dial and filled with guile, travel behind and rewind the time. Three clicks will do the trick. Search for a feather that you find tethered to one whose tracks are black."

"It would seem this is an instruction manual on time traveling." Monty looked up at Quincy as if expecting her to fill in the blanks. Even though Monty was Quincy's best friend, Talin had made it clear the Timepiece was to remain their secret. She had never told Monty how she managed to fix the last years' time disruption that had threatened to ruin his own existence. Monty had never asked, though she recognized his curiosity. Monty looked disappointed with her reluctance to share. He quickly rallied and stretched his arms. "Well, from the location it seems you would have to find a feather of some sort. Though I am not sure what it has to do with treasure or a key, but it seems the clue requires it. If this is in fact what it is? It may all be a hoax for someone's entertainment at your expense."

"I hope not," she answered before finishing her hot chocolate. "Well, thanks for your help. I wonder if I should forget about this," she said, waving the letter before putting back in her pocket.

But she knew she wouldn't easily forget the letter and the rhyming man in plum. As she walked back to her dormitory, she decided she would hunt for Talin this weekend to show him the letter and to talk him into letting her tell Monty everything. And should she ask Professor Marquam?

Now to search for the annoying raven. If she could find him. She had a feeling she would need all the help she could get for this treasure hunt.

***

Quincy kept finding excuses during the weekend to walk around Oakley hoping to find Talin in a dark corner or stalking the kitchens for snacks. Finally, one of the cooks threatened Quincy with a spoon and warned her not to come back for the rest of the day. She even went to visit Talin's quarters. She knocked on the door multiple times and silence answered. Talin would not be found unless he wished to be. Unhappily, she trudged back to her room to work on homework.

***

Quincy walked into her Latin class and sat down in her now customary spot at the back of the classroom. The professor lectured in Latin while she fought to stay awake. She stifled yawn after yawn and felt her eyelids begin to grow heavier and heavier. A book slammed shut and Quincy jumped in her seat. Embarrassed from having fallen asleep, she looked up at the professor, ready to apologize. Instead of looking at her, he pulled out a stack of books from inside the podium.

"Close your books. You have forty-five minutes to complete your exam."

The professor passed the unusually thick test books to the different rows of students. Quincy felt her heart pound in panic. This test wasn't supposed to happen for another week. Sweat gathered on her forehead. Before she could yell out the professor's mistake, movement in her peripheral vision caught her attention. The window behind the professor darkened and shadows formed a menacing hand with crooked fingers. It slipped through the open window. Quincy ran past the professor and attempted to shut the window before the hand could enter the room. Another hand slipped in and held the window open while the first hand reached for Quincy's face. She tried to swat it away, but like the other hand, it had taken physical form. It blocked her vision until the whole room became black. Quincy screamed and her shoulder landed on hard ground.

She opened her eyes and waited for her vision to adjust to the darkness. She rolled over and felt the warm floor by her bed. She had fallen from her nightmare and still shook from the adrenaline. After waiting a minute for the effects of the nightmare to wear off, she gingerly stood up and rubbed her sore shoulder. She looked at her tousled bed, and frowned. She had little desire to fall asleep so soon, so she grabbed her robe and a rose-colored flamed candle and walked out of the dormitories. Thankfully, the weather still allowed her to visit the Timepiece without a coat. Sadly, she had already missed the morning song, but the dial's movements helped calm her. It was too late to meet the headmaster so she didn't expect company until she felt a blast of wind and heard feathers fly past her. The raven swooped around her in warning before landing on her shoulder.

"I heard you were looking for me?" Talin said.

"Hi, Talin. Where did you hear that?"

"A little bird told me. So, what did you want?"

"Permission."

"For what? Should I be worried?" The feathers over his left eye raised.

"No? Probably not. I got a letter in the mail and I would like to do some traveling."

"A letter? Who else has seen it?" Talin groaned. "No wait, let me guess. You showed the Irish kid. The one who lives in the library?"

"You don't seem to have much to do if you know where everyone spends their time."

"Impudent ingrate," snorted Talin. Quincy grinned.

"Do you have the letter with you?" he asked.

She groaned. "Yes, let me pull it out of my nightgown..."

"Hilarious. Okay, before I grant you anything, I need to see that letter. Meet me in your family room tomorrow night at eleven. Oh, bring your friend."

"You're going to meet Monty?"

"I swear I just said that. Yes, I'll meet him. Let me do the talking. Just bring him. Oh," he paused and grinned at her wickedly. "Don't tell him anything."

Quincy's eyes widened. "You're so mean!"

"Eh. It depends on your definition of mean. I'll see you tomorrow. And get some sleep. You look exhausted."

Quincy rolled her eyes. "Thanks. I'll see you tomorrow, Talin."

Talin saluted and flew toward his tower.

***

The next evening, Quincy kept her robe on as she slipped into bed. She blew out her green flamed candle, and curled up in-between the covers. Slowly, conversations started to dwindle as girls drifted to their own beds. Finally, only the four communal candles remained lit by the door. She fought to keep her eyes open for more than a second as the fatigue settled in. She wondered if Monty was having the same trouble staying awake as she was having at this moment. The

Timepiece rang eleven times reminding Quincy to get out of bed and put on her slippers. She picked up a blue candle by the door and walked away from her dormitory hallway toward the family room. Monty, poised and completely alert, waited for her by the fire. When he saw her, he smiled and wiped his glasses on his blue robe. Quincy stared enviously at his calm and aware expression. She looked around the room, relieved she had arrived before Talin.

Monty failed to completely hide a yawn behind his hand. Quincy joined him near the fire and chose an overstuffed chair nearby.

"May I inquire who we are meeting at this hour in our family room?"

"You're meeting me." Talin flew in from seemingly nowhere and landed on the arm of Monty's chair. Monty jumped up; his blue eyes widening from surprise. He stuttered a sentence in a language Quincy could not decipher.

"Yes, you heard me in Gaelic, and yes I understand you. However, Quincy, does not."

Monty closed his gaping mouth but continued to look at the raven quizzically. Quincy frowned, confused. "But Talin, you never spoke another language? I only heard English."

Talin rolled his eyes and sighed as if bored. "People hear what they want to. Let's move on to something actually important."

Talin's statement reminded her of another conversation from last year about the raven having a flawless Scottish accent that only a true Scot could hear. Quincy looked over at Monty who frowned with his lips pursed; his external signal of his mind trying to connect information. From time to time, Monty would shift slightly, as if uncomfortable next to the talking bird. Talin flew off the arm of Monty's chair and landed on Quincy's head.

"Ouch, Talin!" she growled swatting him off.

Talin snickered and flew off, finally settling down on the arm of her chair.

"Showoff," hissed Quincy.

Monty once again opened his mouth about to speak but closed it when it seemed he thought better of it.

"What *is* it with your generation? Never being happy with what you know and always having to ask questions. At least he knows when to keep his mouth shut." Talin looked over at Monty and winked. "I think we'll get along fine."

Quincy grinned at Talin; glad she no longer took his comments personally. She had learned to recognize Talin's idea of humor. Quincy looked over and to her surprise saw Monty silently shocked. Quincy grinned, remembering her first meeting with Talin and with it the realization that ravens, or at least this one in particular, could speak its mind. Monty seemed to be taking things surprisingly well.

Monty coughed politely and then his eyes narrowed suspiciously at Talin.

"I have read quite a handful of stories about talking ravens."

"Oh, I'm sure you have. Hasn't anyone ever told you not to believe everything you hear? Or read."

"I have, as a matter of fact. So then tell me what I should believe."

"I don't tell you what to do. Make up your own mind."

Monty and Talin tested each other and Quincy felt uncomfortable as if eavesdropping on a conversation. It made her feel like a trespasser. Monty did not reply and slowly nodded his head in agreement, but his eyes never left the bird next to Quincy.

"If you're both done, gentlemen?" Quincy shook her head at them.

Talin whistled and then poked her with his talon. "Fine. Let me see it."

Quincy pulled out the envelope from her robe and took out the letter. Talin glimpsed the seal and she saw a flash of recognition on his face.

"You know who it's from?" she questioned.

"I know this seal. Do you?"

"No. Should I? Will you tell me?" Quincy asked, sitting up straight in her chair.

"That would be cheating, so no," Talin laughed.

"Seriously? So, then why did you agree to look at it if you won't help us?"

"I didn't say I wouldn't help you. I said I wouldn't *tell* you. Helping is not cheating like telling is."

Quincy looked over and saw a small smile on Monty's face. Talin played a game which Monty, but not her, knew the rules. A game played with words and wit; Monty's weapons of choice.

"So, then sir, how are you able to help us?" Monty asked.

Talin looked approvingly at the Irish boy. "Finally, some respect," he rolled his eyes at Quincy. "Unfold the letter."

Once she had opened it, Talin hopped closer and scanned the letter. After a few seconds he cleared his feathery throat.

"How far have you two gotten with this?"

Quincy let Monty explain what they had figured out over hot chocolate until he paused. "It would seem it is directing us towards a time in history. However, it does not say when or what book in which to find the answers," he finished.

Talin returned Monty's unblinking stare. "One day, Master McCalister, you will find that not all the answers are found in books tucked away in the library." Monty frowned, but said nothing as he took off his already immaculately cleaned glasses and rubbed them against his robe again. Talin turned his stare in her direction. "Now I understand why you wanted permission. It's given. But you both need a chaperone." Monty's eyebrows rose and his cheeks reddened. Quincy laughed triumphally. She would get to use the Timepiece. They would time travel to the time mentioned in the clue. "So, are you volunteering as our 'chaperone?'"

Talin rolled his eyes, again. "Who else would go with you? I take it both of you are coming?"

"We can both go?" Quincy asked.

Monty blinked. "Where are we going?"

"Yes. Meet me at dinnertime on Friday at the usual spot."

"Where?" Monty asked again, this time, clipped with irritation.

Before Quincy could reply to Monty or thank Talin, the raven flew out the door.

"I hate it when he does that." Quincy informed Monty.

"I believe I need to go to sleep," said Monty weakly. He slowly walked out of the room without saying goodnight. Quincy felt a little guilty when she laughed at his shock.

CHAPTER SIX

A TREEHOUSE HERMITUDE

Quincy hated the fact that she was presently stuck in Wednesday instead of Friday. She set her head on her desk in her room, sighing. Two and a half hours of studying and her head felt full of unimportant knowledge. Could information literally spill out of her ears if she tried to read anything more? She looked at her history book, knowing she should at least get a start on her report, but instead, she poked her head around the corner to see if Eloise wanted to go in search of fun. But her umbrella toting friend wasn't in the room.

Quincy looked back at the empty page on her desk. She struggled with the best way to begin this paper. Giving up, she placed the paper underneath the pile. Now on the top of her assignments, Latin glared up at her. And this one had to be done before class tomorrow. Despite the habitual horror of being stuck with Year Ones, Quincy secretly admitted it had become easier learning Latin the second time around. She looked at her most recent paper and felt the desire to crumple it. The grade had been better than last year's, but she wanted to do better. She found Latin sentence structure difficult because everything seemed to be placed opposite to the English language.

A *tap tap* interrupted her thoughts and she looked up from her desk at the window in front of her. Talin perched on the stone edge of the frame and tapped on the glass with his beak again. Quincy quickly jumped up and pulled the curtain around her area for privacy. She opened the window to let Talin inside. He hopped in and landed on the un-lit candle holder on her desk.

"I can hear your mind complaining miles away."

"Hello, Talin. I'm doing well, thank you. How about yourself?"

Talin rolled his eyes. "What are you finding so difficult?"

"Oh, the usual. Latin and History."

"Want a break?"

"Well of course I do, but some of this stuff is due tomorrow."

"Trust me; this break will be worth it. Well, at least it will be in the long run."

"But homework…"

"Fine, ignore the call to adventure."

Quincy rolled her eyes. Why must he be so cryptic and melodramatic? "Okay, fine. "But not for long, okay? I have to finish this today."

"Excellent. I'll get you back at a decent time. Cross my heart." Talin saluted her with one of his wings. "Now meet me by the stables."

"Stables? You mean we have to ride to get there?" she moaned. "Can we walk? I still have bruises from my "pleasure" ride yesterday."

Consto enjoyed reminding Quincy who was in charge. Her horse took pleasure in making rides difficult, but his sixth sense was invaluable to her. Quincy involuntarily shivered. The headmaster couldn't protect her from everyone. Or at least from *him*. It reminded her of the moment when she caught sight of the man in burgundy in a mirror hidden in a memory of the Oakley stables.

"Aw, poor baby. Stop whining." Talin mocked. She frowned at the raven.

"It's too far to walk and it will be worth it, I promise." Talin rolled his eyes. "Besides, if I'm with you, your horse won't dare buck me off. You're safe in my careful talons."

Quincy thought about it and finally nodded. She hated that her horse behaved perfectly with Talin. "Okay, I'll meet you at the stables. Give me ten minutes to change and walk down."

Talin acknowledged her with a nod, launched off the candlestick, and flew out the window.

Less than ten minutes later, Quincy met Talin in the stables. He landed on the horse's head and Consto froze like a statue.

Quincy groaned. "That's not fair."

Talin snickered. "Life isn't fair."

With Talin perched on Consto, Quincy had no issues putting the tack on the horse and leading him outside. He didn't even move when Quincy mounted him.

"Let's go, we're losing daylight and I could have sworn *someone* was complaining about getting homework done."

She rolled her eyes behind his back.

"I saw that," Talin growled and she stifled a laugh.

"So where are we going? I need to be able to guide Consto."

"Not a problem. As usual, I'll do all the work." Talin turned around and winked. "Hang on tight, kiddo."

Right after the warning, Consto started to gallop, giving Quincy barely enough time to grab the reins. Talin remained unfazed by the speed of the horse.

"I forgot how fast he runs," she gasped.

"Who, this guy? Yeah, he was bred for speed."

Quincy's hands turned white from holding the reins so tightly. She wondered if blisters were forming. Looking behind her, she watched Oakley fly past and disappear into the distance. She had a brief daydream of her accepting a ribbon for the Equospatium for the fastest time. The path ended and Consto jumped over the barrier. Once again, she barely had time to prepare herself from flying off the horse.

"Talin?" she yelled. "I'm not allowed to go past this boundary and I know I'm not supposed to go into this side of the forest."

"Stop worrying. You're with me, remember? It's like a free pass from getting in trouble...Usually."

"Why doesn't that make me feel better?" she questioned, narrowing her eyes.

After five minutes of galloping, they slowed down to a trot on a small and unkempt dirt path. They stopped in front of a large sign with a hand-written notice.

DO NOT ENTER LEST YOU BE TRANSMORGAFIED!

Quincy caught her breath and stared at the sign. "Talin, what does 'transmorgafied' mean?"

"Honestly, I haven't the slightest idea."

"It doesn't sound good or...safe?"

They slowly plodded around the sign and continued on the path until they were stopped from another sign.

STUDENTS, POLITICIANS, AND 99.9% OF CREATIVE ENGINEERS WHO PASS THIS POINT WILL BE ROASTED... ALIVE!

"Hmm, I understand this sign all too well," Talin laughed.

"Yeah, of course you do. But should *I* be worried about where we're going?"

"Nah, like I said, you're with me. He doesn't roast horses or birds. At least not since the last time I saw him."

"Why are you taking me to see this person? I seriously don't have a good feeling about this."

Talin turned around and pointedly rolled his eyes at her and then focused again on the path. The forest grew darker the further they went in and the trees became substantially larger and thicker with age. They stayed on the overgrown path until they were stopped by yet another warm and welcoming sign.

THIS IS YOUR FINAL WARNING BEFORE YOU INVARIABLY FACE INSANITY AND A RAVING LUNATIC!

"Oh! This is a new one. I like it," said Talin, impressed.

"Talin, how well do you know this...individual?"

Talin snickered. "We have history. Excellent, we're here. Wait here a moment." He had stopped them between a large circle in the humongous trees.

"We are? I don't see anything."

Talin ignored her and flew up towards one of the trees. Quincy watched him fly up and stared at the view over her head. In the middle of the circle of trees, high in the canopy, someone had constructed a large platform with a bridge connecting to other trees.

Quincy looked around, hoping to find a ladder or something that would connect to the platform above, but she couldn't see anything besides the forest around her. She crossed her arms, waiting for further instructions from Talin. But after five minutes alone, she felt uneasy. Finally, she pulled on the reigns to leave, but as Consto took his first step, a piercing laugh with a thick Scottish accent broke the eerie silence.

"I'm delighted you like it. I'm rather fond of that sign myself. I admit it makes me smile every time I think about it."

Quincy heard Talin join in and then suddenly, both became silent. The Scottish voice continued without the laughter. It had become surprisingly cold.

"No. You promised me...Absolutely not! NO."

After another minute of awkward silence, one of the massive trees shook. She slowly encouraged her horse closer to the quivering tree and paused when she glimpsed a small candle on its base. On the top of the light, a small bell with a string led her inside the tree. Suddenly a part of the base opened up like a door and she jumped at the shadow of a tall, lanky man. After a pause the Scottish shadow spoke. "So, you must be Quinn. If you would be so kind, please follow me." He took two steps away and quickly turned around again. "And don't touch anything."

Quincy didn't know if she should follow him until Talin's voice echoed from inside the tree. "Quinn, follow the nice man."

She uncomfortably laughed as she hitched Consto to a lower branch and followed the man through the passageway into the tree. She anxiously rubbed her fingers together and attempted to break the silence.

"So, I'm not going to be roasted?" Quincy asked in a small voice.

"No, not at the moment at least. I've recently finished my tea and I'm rather full," he answered back, not bothering to turn around.

She gulped. Why did Talin bring her here?

Tiny twinkle lights lit up the small staircase inside the tree. It opened up to a large room of a mixed creation of glass and wood. Quincy momentarily forgot her fear from the elation. She was standing in an actual tree house! She walked around and looked at the oddly created and mismatched furniture and the unknown knick-knacks around the room. Engrossed by the details of the domicile, Quincy's uneasiness faded away.

"How does the fire breathe in the round containers in the staircase?" she wondered aloud.

"By magic, obviously," he replied. She heard the humor in his voice and relaxed. He walked into the light and faced her as she entered the room.

She could not help herself from staring at his strange attire. He wore a dark magenta bath robe with long and wide arms. His hair stuck out in countless directions. Quincy looked down at his feet half expecting to see slippers. Instead he wore slick black loafers that shone as if recently cleaned. He laughed forcibly at her expression.

"I'm an eccentric hermit. I'm allowed to wear whatever I wish."

Quincy said nothing and instead nodded. He sounded friendly enough now but she felt something dark lurking underneath.

Talin gave a false laugh to break the silence that had been created yet again.

"See, didn't I tell you? Anxious in a place she's never been to and still curious. You both will get along excellently."

The man's eyes widened and then he sighed as if torn as to what to say to his guests.

"Indeed. Talin, may I have a word?" The man looked at Quincy and added, "Please, make yourself at home on the chair in the corner. You may look, but don't touch anything."

Quincy sat down on the patched-chair and warmed her hands by the small fireplace while Talin flew out of the room after the odd hermit. She continued to look around, awe-struck by the ingenuity used to create the house. She peeked over and saw a small kitchen with a sink in it. She wondered how he managed to get water. She looked outside the window of the tree house and saw a well-kept garden on the surrounding branches. She heard their voices from yet another room. She listened to snippets of the conversation until she overheard, "I thought the whole purpose of being a hermit was to be left alone? You're invading my hermitude."

Quincy briefly wondered if hermitude was an actual word.

Talin had not given Quincy the reason why he had brought her here to a man who obviously didn't want visitors. She started to squirm in her seat counting the seconds. She didn't want to be in a place where she wasn't welcome, so finally she stood up to leave. After she took the first step, Talin flew in and landed on her shoulder before she could continue.

"I don't think this is such a good idea," she whispered to her shoulder.

Talin disagreed. "I promise it is. He's just…"

"Just bitter."

The hermit walked in and leaned against the door frame on the opposite side of the room.

"My rudeness is not excusable, but I still beg your forgiveness. I'm used to being alone and other than Talin, it's been quite a while since I've had visitors. And truthfully, you remind me of someone." The hermit rubbed his forehead. "Please, let's try this again?"

Quincy looked over at Talin who motioned towards the fire place with a wing while the hermit disappeared again. She sat back down and Talin perched on one of the arms while they waited for the hermit to come back from his kitchen. He came back, balancing a tray with two cups and holding a chair. He smiled at Quincy. "One can never have enough tea. Please, call me Dwilight."

"Dwi-light?" Quincy repeated the name out loud to make sure she had heard it correctly. This time Dwilight laughed easily.

"My mother was an artist and purposely chose a ...unique name. My father doted on her and accepted her choice. Ironic since my brother and I are not remotely artistic. And so, you have two Creative Engineers stuck with bizarre names and the surname of Fairnight."

"Wait, so your full name is..."

"Yes, Dwilight Fairnight. I won't even tell you my middle name."

Talin snickered next to Quincy. She tried to recall where she had heard his name before. An odd name like that is not easily forgotten. Before she could look backward, Dwilight interrupted her thoughts.

"Talin tells me you need a study partner for Latin and he thinks I need company."

Quincy turned in Talin's direction and frowned. She did manage to contain herself from sticking out her tongue at him.

"Hey, don't look at me like that. It's the truth!" Talin shot back, defensively.

Quincy looked back at Dwilight and unhappily nodded.

"Excellent. A smart person knows not to fight an obnoxious raven, especially one who brings me cinnamon for my cookies. I suppose you're always welcome to visit because I never leave. Ring the bell by the door and if I don't answer, feel free to come in. If I'm not in the garden, I'm in my lab back there." He motioned to a separate staircase near the kitchen. Quincy had completely missed the other area and wondered how many rooms were in the treehouse.

"Would you like to begin today?" he asked.

Before she could reply, Talin answered, "Not today, I need a ride back to Oakley."

"Lazy raven, you have wings, don't you?" Dwilight teased the bird.

Talin sniffed at the Scotsman and looked at Quincy. "Ready?"

She nodded and smiled at the hermit. "Thank you for the tea."

"Thank you for coming, Quinn. Until next time." He smiled tightly as they left. Quincy looked up and glimpsed the hermit peeking out from the window above them. She swung into the saddle and slowly left the forest.

"Why did we leave before talking about homework?"

"Dwilight has been mostly alone for over a decade. He is a wonderful person and one of the best I have ever known," Talin paused for a moment and sighed. "Even the short visit wasn't easy for him."

"Why does he live alone?"

"He's had some terrible things happen to him and he wishes he could forget." Talin's voice dropped, sadly. "Since he can't, he chooses to hide from it. Oh, by the way, the next couple of times you visit, don't stay longer than half an hour. Okay?"

Quincy nodded. "It's alright to come back here without you?"

"You may as long as you *only* go to see Dwilight. If a professor or monitor catches you, tell them the headmaster gave you permission. Yes, before you ask, you have my permission to say you have the headmaster's permission."

"You introduced me as 'Quinn.'"

"And so?"

She shook her head. "Just curious about your choice."

Talin shrugged.

"So then why did you introduce me as Quinn?"

Talin harrumphed. "Everyone should have a nickname. It's important to me that you two get along."

"Am I just Quinn to you?"

"To your face. I could have any number of nicknames for you that you'll never know."

Quincy stuck out her tongue at him.

"How mature," Talin sniffed.

"You would know," she laughed. She breathed in the forest air and felt the anxiety from the visit fade away. "Besides, isn't maturity over-rated?"

"Oooo, touché," Talin replied. "Let's test the speed on Consto, shall we? I vaguely remember someone complaining about homework..."

Quincy grinned and released her tight hold on Consto's reins. Now free, Consto shivered with anticipation and took off, galloping to Oakley. Quincy found herself laughing, delighted with the speed without the fear of getting kicked off. When the stables came into clear view, Talin and Quincy slowed Consto down to cool off before taking him back to his stall. Once Quincy finished unsaddling and brushing Consto down, Talin flew back to her shoulder. "For Friday, wear comfortable but nice-looking clothes, please. Pass the message to McCalister, okay?"

"What, no nickname for Monty?" Quincy prodded. He snorted and launched off her shoulder. She smiled and waved at the retreating raven.

CHAPTER SEVEN

PARLIAMENT

Quincy looked at her reflection in the third-floor mirror. Hopefully, she had chosen a proper outfit to meet Talin's expectations. Thank goodness if was finally Friday. She checked her mental clock. She had five minutes before meeting Monty in the family room. Quincy brushed her hair one more time until it shone. She gave herself one more look over before putting on her wool forest green coat over a long-sleeved blouse and her dark brown skirt. She wore knee-high socks and a comfortable, but clean, pair of brown shoes. Mikaela stopped Quincy with a whistle before she left the room.

"Where are you off to?"

"Going on a walk," Quincy attempted to nonchalantly shrug.

Mikaela's eyebrows rose. "Looking like that?"

Quincy smiled. "What are you implying?"

"Fine. Have your secrets." Mikaela smiled and waved her off.

Quincy quickly escaped before anyone else could question her. She paused when she glimpsed Monty waiting patiently by the family room door. Monty had slicked his hair and had combed to one side. He wore black slacks under his navy-blue coat. After clearing her throat, Monty looked over at her. Wordlessly she beckoned him to follow her out the door.

"You look...nice." Quincy said, turning away to hide a blush.

Monty cleared his throat. "Thank you. As do you."

Quincy and Monty walked outside and into the courtyard towards the Timepiece.

"Why are we here, exactly?" Monty whispered.

She shushed Monty and waited for Talin to fly in. They didn't have to wait long. The raven flew from the forest and landed on her shoulder. Monty, instead of Quincy, jumped with surprise.

"Are we ready?" the raven asked.

Quincy nodded and walked over the boundary toward the Timepiece. "Are you coming?" she turned back to Monty.

Monty raised one eyebrow and pursed his lips, but reluctantly followed.

She drew out her key from under her coat to open the side door. Talin cleared his throat.

"Hang on a moment, Quinn. Monty, do you have your key?"

Monty frowned at Quincy.

"He knows everything already," she admitted.

Monty looked betrayed and Quincy bit her lip. She had forgotten to tell Monty that Talin had known about his mother's key even before she had. Before she could explain, Monty pulled out the key from his breast pocket which had a braided string tied to the shirt.

"What would you like me to do with this?" He asked, coldly.

Talin rolled his eyes. "It's a key. What do you think you should do with it?"

Monty looked peeved but placed the key in the lock. He didn't look surprised when it opened. He stared at Quincy and stiffly gestured into the darkness. "After you."

Quincy awkwardly walked inside the Timepiece and reached for the rail.

"Not to be weird, but it's easier if we go down together." She gestured towards Monty with her hand open. He nodded and took it. Together, they slowly walked down the stairs. Finally, she reached the bottom and lit the room. Monty stared, awestruck, at the room surrounding him.

Talin yawned loudly, ruining the moment. "Welcome to the Heart of the Timepiece. Soon you will know exactly what power you wield with your key. Blah, blah, blah. I will tell you the same thing I have already told Quinn. Time has enough problems on its own without key holders changing time and creating loops, among other complications. I would hate for you to not have been born, again. So, don't use the Timepiece without everyone's favorite raven present. Understand?"

Slowly, Monty nodded. "Understood."

"Good. There's another rule for you, blondie, but we'll talk about it later. Now when are we going?"

Quincy pulled a specific line of the clue from memory. *"With a thought, three clicks will do the trick."* She pushed the dial in the center of the room counterclockwise until she heard three clicks.

Monty leaned in, closer to the sundial. "May I inquire what we are doing? What do the clicks mean?"

Talin tightened the feathers over his eyes. "Oh, please. You know exactly what we're doing. I know you recall the alternate timeline. You're going to see how we fixed yours. One click is ten years. I'll let you do the rest of the calculations."

"Thirty years? But didn't we already go back thirty years last year?" Quincy asked, looking at Talin on her shoulder.

"Thirty years from this year. We're traveling one year past our last adventure."

Quincy looked over at Monty who held his arms tightly against his chest and looked ill. "Is it of utmost importance that I come?"

"Courage, Irish. Not even you can spend eternity behind a book."

Monty narrowed his eyes at the insult and looked at the stairs as if wondering if he could run out of the clock before being stopped. Finally, he sighed dejectedly and leaned against the wall.

"Talin, what does it mean 'with a thought?'" she questioned.

"It's not easy to explain. A thought is not unlike an anchor. You need an anchor to make sure you get to the day mentioned. It takes practice or incredible luck. Otherwise you could end up in any random day of the particular year."

"So how do we know if we made it to the right day?" Quincy asked.

Talin groaned. "We're going to have to trust the illustrious "C" knows we will travel to the right day."

"So, we're trusting the riddler will happen to appear on the exact day he wanted us to? Seems risky."

"It is." Talin rolled his eyes. "Come on, let's move."

Quincy nodded and looked at Monty before continuing. "Are you ready?"

Monty nodded nervously.

"Should we go up to watch the seasons?" she asked, hopefully. She wanted to watch the time relapse, again.

Talin looked at Monty and whispered in Quincy's ear. "Eh, I wouldn't. Your friend is already anxious enough."

She reluctantly agreed and pushed down on the dial. At first, nothing happened. Quincy crossed her fingers, hoping she hadn't messed up the dial. The last time she had done this, she went outside so she could enjoy the scenery rewinding in time, so she had no idea what happened inside of the Timepiece. Quincy felt an odd sensation as the ticking of the Timepiece ceased and the room became deathly silent. Suddenly the ticking began again, but faster and faster until the ticking became one unending sound. She wondered if she had stepped into one of her nightmares because she could no longer tell the difference between reality and dreams. Right before she screamed, the noise ended and Quincy relaxed to the soothing ticking and mechanical whirring of the Heart.

Quincy looked at Monty who had curled up on the floor with his head tucked in between the knees. She walked over next to him and sat down. He sheepishly looked up at her. "I apologize," he mumbled.

She squeezed Monty's arm. "You don't have anything to be sorry about, I felt the same way when I first traveled."

Talin hopped down closer to Monty. He gently poked his shoulder. "How are you feeling?"

Monty slowly sat up and groaned. "I am not sure how to qualify that with an answer."

"Let's try this again. Do you feel like you're being torn apart from the inside out?" Talin asked, this time louder.

Monty shook his head. "I do not think so. And I do not believe I am in any danger of a seizure, if that was your line of questioning."

"Fair enough. Time to go."

"Are you ready to see Oakley thirty years ago?" she asked.

"Oakley thirty years ago?" Monty had a thoughtful expression. "Could we see certain...individuals...accidentally?"

Quincy felt like she had been slapped. Of course. Monty's mother who he had never met was an Oakley student thirty some odd years ago.

Talin sniffed. "I know you both would enjoy seeing your respective parents, but they all graduated last year. So, no chance of accidentally bumping into family."

Disappointed, they walked up the stairs and opened the door. The sudden natural light made them blink rapidly before their eyes could acclimate to the day-time.

"What next?" Quincy asked.

"We walk to Oakdale."

Monty's face paled and he sucked in a breath.

***

Half an hour later, Quincy, Monty, and Talin made it to the outskirts of the town of Oakdale. Monty's breathing came out in raspy breaths, but he did not complain.

"We won't go inside the town, the station is on the outskirts," Talin gestured with a wing.

Quincy sighed. She wished she could see the town, even from thirty years from her present. Only Year Threes and Fours were allowed to visit the town unsupervised. The three walked toward Oakdale's large glass building and opened a thick glass door. Directly inside, they found an ornate desk engraved with an eagle flying with a coach tied to its back. The woman behind the desk wore an outfit with the NEFS insignia on top of an eagle's wing. Quincy scanned the board behind the staff member and sorted through the list of flight locations, times, and dates. Without looking up from her desk, she welcomed them with a bored tone.

"Welcome to National Eagle Flight Services where we take you where you want to go in a timely fashion. Where is your destination today?"

Quincy looked over at Talin.

"London," he answered.

The woman with the name tag "Louisa" pointed behind her. "Which one do you want?"

Talin growled at the annoying attendant. "How about the one on the board behind you?"

Louisa gave an exaggerated sigh and without looking up, began to file her nails. "How many traveling today?" She didn't seem to comprehend that the voice came from a talking bird.

"Three." Quincy answered before Talin could be snarky to Louisa.

"That'll be twenty-five quid," Louisa said, popping her gum. Talin whispered to Quincy, "hand," and he pulled out a few pound notes from under his wings. Quincy wondered if he had a pocket somewhere hidden in his feathers.

The woman gave them their change and pulled out nail polish from her desk.

"Youths." Talin quietly growled.

Quincy held back a laugh as they walked over to the currently empty platform and sat down.

By the platform, a small cart sold delicious smelling pasties and Quincy's stomach rumbled at the smell. Even Monty perked up.

Talin chuckled. "Take the change and buy some lunch. Your stomach's rumbling is getting on my nerves."

"Um, thanks?" She laughed as Talin flew to the back of a bench.

"Hey, Monty. Go ahead and sit down. I'll get you food."

"Remember, I do not...."

"I remember. No meat." She grinned. "Weirdo."

He shook his head with a small smile and she walked away to buy two pasties. For herself she bought a beef pasty with carrots and potatoes and for Monty she chose cheese and broccoli. She made sure to offer Talin some of the crust which he greedily inhaled making contented smacking sounds.

"So, London is not a popular destination on a Friday?" Monty pondered aloud.

"It's Tuesday." Talin and Quincy answered in tangent. Talin snorted and cleaned the crumbs from her shoulder.

Monty raised one eyebrow at Quincy. "But we left on a Friday? How can it be Tuesday?" He rubbed his forehead as if fighting off a headache.

"Time traveling is weird. It doesn't make any sense. It's a time thing. I've learned not to bother asking. He'll give you an answer no one but him could ever understand." Quincy pointed accusingly at Talin.

Monty, who had regained some color to his face, smiled tightly at them and shook his head. The three sat in silence until a bell rang, and outside, an eagle cried in return. The ceiling creaked above as it opened. A large eagle landed on the platform and a man ran out from the office and opened the doors of the coach. An older woman walked out, leaning heavily on her cane.

The three of them gave the man their tickets and travel books and jumped in the empty coach. Within ten minutes, the eagle took to the air towards London. Monty quickly fell asleep and Talin stared blankly out the window. Quincy sighed, bored. Too bad she hadn't brought her homework along.

Finally, after half an hour, she dozed off, curled up against Monty's shoulder.

***

Quincy awoke as they landed in London. She yawned and stretched as Monty fixed his glasses. They walked out of the coach and into the London underground station.

Monty motioned toward the stairwell exit. Quincy and Monty had to fight against the crowd, dodging elbows and handbags. She stared at the onslaught of commuters, surprised at how many people traveled on a Tuesday. Before they could leave the station, Talin grasped a piece of Quincy's hair.

"We're not going to London. We need to get back to the ticket station to the right."

Quincy nodded and grabbed Monty's shoulder, motioning for him to follow. He nodded and dutifully walked behind her toward the NEFS ticket master. This time they were met by a young man with a big grin on his face. Before he could use the usual welcome, Talin interrupted. "Three for Oxford in twenty minutes."

The man looked at them and smiled tightly. "Of course."

After they had received their tickets, the three retraced their steps to find their platform. Quincy followed the sign for *Oxford* and found seats in the large underground chamber. They were surrounded by people of all backgrounds, ethnicities, and ages. Some were professionally dressed with briefcases, others in more casual clothing. They stood around waiting, some checking their watches, others sipping hot beverages and scanning the newspaper. Quincy easily counted thirty people.

"Are we all taking the same eagle?" She whispered to Monty.

He shrugged. "Possibly. Depends on the eagle. If it is a brown, then no. With the number of individuals in this room, I assume we are riding a white." He pointed to the eagle on his sweater.

Quincy nodded, remembering her meeting with a large white eagle the year before.

Talin interjected, "There are few of those in existence today." His voice dropped and he sighed.

For some reason, she felt his sadness and turned away. She craned her neck, curious to see what eagle could carry thirty odd people. The tunnel near the platform opened with a large whoosh and people had to hold on to their hats from being swept away. An enormous white eagle soared in and landed eerily silent. It was at least double the size of the eagles Quincy had previously traveled on.

It turned its head and for a second, she imagined it looked directly at her with its massive blue eyes speckled with gray. She quietly gasped. She had met this eagle before. Last year for her, but in the future of this bird. She wanted to say something, but what do you say to a creature who hasn't met you yet?

The eagle called out and the sound reverberated throughout the entire underground station. This must have been the signal because three staff members ran out pushing three large ladders with wheels and attached them to each row of the boxes. There were more coaches on the eagle than Quincy had expected; three boxes on the bottom, three in the middle, and three on the top. All together Quincy mentally counted around fifty available seats on this eagle. A staff member in his NEFS vest waved his hands to the crowd.

"The bottom row is for our elderly passengers and women with small children, afterwards, the rest of you may sit where you wish. Safety belts are required at all times on board. Failure to comply will result in harsh repercussions."

Since Monty looked tired, Quincy chose seats on the bottom coach. He looked relieved to be spared the climb to the top. Quincy hoped one day she could ride on the top coach. As she mounted the eagle, she could have sworn it winked at her. But it said nothing.

After everyone boarded, one of the NEFS staff members poked their head through the window to check that everyone had their belts on. After he had done so with each coach, he gave a sharp whistle and the eagle ran down the massive passageway.

Quincy anxiously tapped her fingers on her knee as the eagle picked up speed. With a violent jolt the eagle took off and flew out of the wide-open ceiling. Quincy looked down from her place in the box and watched the closing ceiling. Had there been a monstrously large eagle there at all?

They shared the box with a young boy who played hand games with his mother and occasionally looked outside with wide eyes. Quincy grinned at his look of awe every time he glanced out. Rain splattered against the windows, and Quincy wished she had brought a raincoat.

Her heat sunk as the eagle slowly descended toward a platform outside of Oxford. The trip had been too short. As they landed, Quincy stared at the rooftops of Oxford, instantly in love with the city. When the doors opened, she left the eagle quickly to stare at cobblestone streets flanked by magnificent buildings covered in spires and creatures with silly faces. Talin gestured to the street with his wing. They walked briskly away from the station. Quincy silently berated herself for forgetting to thank the Oakley mascot.

"What should we search for?" Monty asked.

"The man who they will ban from a position of power from the great tower that he has built so that we will savor the flavor of failure." Quincy replied automatically. "All so we can search for a feather that you find tethered to one whose tracks are black. Hey Talin, couldn't we have one of your feathers and be done?" Quincy tried to be amusing but the humor was lost on Talin who rolled his eyes at her.

"Quinn, be a dear and hail a carriage? I hate being wet."

Quincy shook her head in disbelief at the bird and waved at a passing carriage. After three refused to stop for them, Quincy frowned at the street, disgusted by their rejection. A sharp whistle sounded near her ear and she turned to glare at Talin. She stopped when she saw Monty's lips curl with a satisfied grin. When he saw her watching, he placed his two fingers in his mouth and whistled again. To her relief, a passing carriage stopped in front of them. She entered first, relieved to get away from the rain.

"Where to?" asked the cab driver.

"High Street, please," Talin answered.

"Where on High Street?"

"Anywhere will be fine."

The cab driver nodded and they were on their way.

"Erm, excuse me, sir." Monty mumbled to Talin.

"Sir?" Talin snickered. "At least someone has manners. What's your question?"

"The cabbie, and the ticket masters, do they see you like we can?"

Talin shook their head. "Not like you. I'm allowing you to perceive me. They see me, but they can't understand what they're seeing. This way, I don't seem out of place to them," he winked.

Monty's eyes widened. "Indeed? Then you have essentially created an illusion?"

"Isn't all life an illusion?" Talin growled.

Monty cleared his throat and stared at the opposite window away from Talin and Quincy.

"Not nice," Quincy hissed at the bird.

"No, I'm not."

She frowned and stared out at her own window, watching buildings go past.

After swerving around traffic and watching pedestrians giving rude gestures, they were dropped off on High Street. Talin gave instructions as they walked. They took another smaller side street and finally stopped in the center of town. All of the other buildings encircled a piece of architecture which was unlike anything she had ever seen. It looked like someone had stacked three circular building blocks on top of one another largest to smallest on top. It created an odd circular tower.

"What is this building?" Quincy asked, her awe leaving her with the feeling that her voice was detached from her body.

"Parliament." Monty answered.

Quincy tried to see her surroundings as she followed the large crowd pushing their way inside. The closer they came to the doors, the louder the noise became.

"Should we follow the crowd inside?" Quincy asked Talin.

"Sorry, Quinn, I cannot hear you." Monty called.

No one could hear much of anything over the uproar of the Parliament building so Talin responded directly into Quincy's ear, "I don't think we'll have any trouble walking in."

Quincy stared at the crowd and nodded at Talin's assessment. The Parliament outer chambers were filled with people listening to the echoes of the argument from the Secondary and Primary Chambers.

"Can we get closer?" she asked.

Monty simultaneously attempted to clean his glasses and dodge the throngs of people. "We cannot. There are three chambers to parliament. The Outer chamber is where we are allowed in. The secondary chamber is opened to invited guests and the primary chamber is reserved for the elected government, scribes, and delegates."

Talin whispered in her ear, again. "I think I know what this is. Take me to the guards at the secondary chamber. Only you and I can get in."

Quincy explained the situation to Monty who nodded. "I will happily wait for you both by the door," he answered.

She watched him walk away and then turned back to push her way through the crowd. On the door to the secondary chamber were three birds intertwined; a black and a white bird gracefully flanked the centered red bird who stared forward. Her eyes widened at the bird on the left.

"Talin, you're on the Parliament door?"

"Later. Now is not the time for questions."

Quincy frowned, and wondered if he would ever answer her. At the gate the guard recognized Talin and allowed both Quincy and Talin to enter. Quincy looked at Talin skeptically. "Why can he see you?"

"Remember, I have—had—friends in high places and at this time knew a number of people."

Quincy narrowed her eyes but followed his winged gesture toward a flight of stairs to reach the Secondary Chambers. The staircase took her to the balcony above the Primary Chamber. Quincy felt out of place with all the adults in the balcony.

"Move closer to the far door. We'll be less conspicuous over there," whispered Talin in her ear.

As soon as she found her spot, Quincy peeked over the side to watch the commotion. Pandemonium reigned as people yelled, trying to be heard over their neighbors. Even the Secondary Chamber teamed with people trying to get their say in. In the center of the Primary Chamber, three magnificent chairs were filled. She didn't recognize any of them. The first sat a man who hid his face in his hands and leaned heavily against the arm of his chair. The second held a quiet but focused lady in her early fifties who grasped the arms of the chair tightly. The occupant of the third chair stood up and pushed his long black braids over his powerfully built shoulders. He waved one hand over everyone as he tried to quiet down the uproar. Finally, as if she had had enough, the smaller lady stood next to her comrade and whistled, shrilly. Immediately, everyone quieted down. After getting a nod from the man with the black braided hair, she spoke in a loud and clear voice. "We have come together to discuss the imminent problem of one of our Thirds. He is in violation of Section 313, which we voted unanimously that no one may experiment in any form or fashion with the powers of nightmares. We saw the results with The Grand Master who, unfortunately, is not here today. This is the second reprimand for Frederick who was caught *in flagrante* in the experimental stage. No one, not even a Third, is above reproach."

Gasps were heard throughout the entire Primary and Secondary Chambers. Even the Outer chambers were silent, desperately attempting to hear the sequence of events.

"Master Frederick knows the consequences since he himself helped to create them."

At this, the lady sat down dejectedly and the other Third continued.

"From this moment, I hereby revoke his power as a Third, and strip him of his title and lawful abilities as a Master Creative Engineer."

Everyone averted their eyes as Frederick slowly walked out of the room from the Third's entrance. Quincy could not help but watch his retreat. As he left the room, her eyes met another man who seemed to be the only person not watching the withdrawal. Instead, his dark eyes were focused on her. Quincy had an eerie feeling she had met him before. The man from London. Her present-day

London. But how could he be here in the past? He wore a black velvet coat and clutched a device chained to his pocket. A dark hat with a matching colored feather covered most of his dark hair. He crossed his arms and stood with perfect posture. Quincy felt herself being examined from within until he broke the connection to turn his piercing gaze to the door where the demoted Third had departed. Could this be the feather mentioned in the clue?

"Quinn, it's time to go. If we don't leave now, it's going to be difficult to get out."

Quincy stood up and moved to leave. As soon as she walked out the door, panic ensued behind her. Monty looked up at them at the entrance.

"What transpired inside?" he asked.

"Keep moving," hissed Talin. "We have to leave right now."

Quincy looked behind one more time and saw the man wearing black looking at her from the entrance of the secondary chamber. He tipped his hat and Quincy noticed the absence of a feather before he melted into the crowd. She wanted to go back and see where the feather had fallen, but Monty pulled her outside and away from the building.

"Did you get the feather you were supposed to find?" Monty questioned.

"Go, Quinn!" Talin encouraged.

Quincy finally allowed herself to be ushered from the Parliament building and into the busy street.

A scream pierced the air, sending shivers down Quincy's spine.

"Keep moving," growled Talin.

Quincy and Monty hurried away from the building and finally stopped once Parliament had disappeared from sight.

"What happened?" Monty asked, rubbing his shoulders. He shivered as he leaned against the stone building.

Talin shook his head, sadly. "Frederick didn't want to leave easily. He set off a Noctem."

Quincy frowned. "A Noctem?"

Monty sneered. "The Noctem Umbrem do not exist. Fairy tales to force children to eat their dinner and go to sleep."

Talin snorted derisively at Monty. "You're too young to know everything. The woman who came across the monster will lie about it, not capable of trusting her own judgment, and this whole thing will be forgotten," he shook his head disdainfully. "I promise you; they do exist."

Monty shivered again and grasped his jacket tighter against his body.

"What's a Noctem?" Quincy asked Talin.

"A creature created from one's worst nightmare." He cocked his head to face her. "It takes the form of a dark silhouette unless it solidifies into the form of your greatest fear."

Quincy shook and felt moisture gather on her forehead. Though she wasn't sure if from the rain or cold sweat.

"Time to go back. Monty, grab another carriage, will you?" Talin coldly commanded. Monty nodded and walked toward the street.

"Is that—was that?" she asked, her voice sounding weak in her own ears.

Talin cleared his throat, interrupting her. "Yes, you've seen one before," he paused and shifted his weight on her shoulder and pressed his beak in her ear. "At Miss Heatherwoods. They seem to be drawn to you."

Her heart plummeted and she felt like she needed to vomit.

She did not remember any details of the trip back to the Oxford station. The one thing she recalled was the vivid smell of bleach that first night when she had met the man's silhouette at Miss Heatherwoods. The Noctem Umbrem. Night's shadow.

As they stepped into the station, she gasped. "But we didn't bring back the feather. What will happen now?"

Monty shrugged. "I assume you watched 'the mighty man fall from his place of power?'"

Quincy nodded. "Yes, but I have no idea what I was supposed to learn?"

Talin shushed them both as they were called up to buy their tickets.

Quincy chewed on her lip, quickly replaying the whole scene. It felt like a warning, but was it meant for her? Not that it mattered anyway. She had already failed. No feather no key?

She let Monty do the talking as he paid for the tickets. Luckily, they were in time to catch a smaller flight that would take them directly to Oakdale. After waiting for half an hour, she followed Monty onto the eagle and sat down next to him near the far window. Talin remained completely silent.

When the eagle landed at Oakdale, they slowly made their way back to the school grounds. Quincy placed her key into the Timepiece and looked back at Monty. He stared longingly at the school.

"I'm sorry," she whispered and reached down and clasped his hand. He smiled sadly and followed her down into the Heart of the Timepiece. When they reached the basement, Quincy waited for Monty to sit down and Talin to be perched on the sundial before she pushed down the gnomon. Once again, the clock stopped and then the ticking started again much like it had that morning.

Once the sounds of the clock dissipated and the nausea abated, Talin cleared his throat. "It's nearly midnight on the same day we left. I suggest we slip you two back onto your floor?"

Quincy nodded and looked over at Monty. His head stared blankly at the floor and his hands were visibly shaking as he unsuccessfully tried to hide them in his coat.

"Are you alright?" she cried.

He nodded. "Yes, I believe I need a moment."

Talin flew over next to Monty and whispered unintelligibly into his ear. Monty shook his head slowly.

"Are you sure?" Talin asked. This time loud enough for Quincy to catch.

Monty nodded. "Of course. I would know."

"That's strange." Talin finished. He flew on to Quincy's shoulder. "Quinn, you're going to need to help him up the stairs and into the Infirmary."

"She will do nothing of the sort," growled Monty. "I will be safe to continue in a moment."

"Fine. Your decision," snapped Talin.

Monty frowned and slowly stood up. He walked purposefully up the stairs, but halfway, slumped against the banister. Quincy quickly caught up with him.

"It's okay. Lean on me."

Monty nodded and slowly walked up the rest of the flight of stairs, his shoulders against Quincy. The three exited the Timepiece into the nippy evening air. They slowly made their way into the Main Hall and toward the dormitories when they heard a slight cough. Quincy and Monty whirled around and Talin dug his talons in Quincy's shoulder to keep from falling off. The three found themselves face to face with the headmaster.

"Good evening, sir." Quincy smiled. Monty tried to smile, but it came out as more of a grimace.

"You three are up late." the headmaster said, amused.

Quincy looked at the headmaster who stared at her shoulder. Quincy wondered if Talin allowed the headmaster to see him or if Marquam wasn't so easily fooled.

"I think you two should go to bed. I look forward to seeing you both on Monday."

They nodded as he walked away, sipping a steaming beverage.

"Well, this has been fun, but I have other things to worry about. Catch up on sleep, will you?" Talin launched off Quincy's shoulder and paused on the banister. "Oh, and Quincy, you should find time to study." He added before flying away.

Her cheeks burned. She recognized the code to visit Dwilight, but did he have to say it that way in front of Monty?

Monty yawned and motioned toward the dormitories. "I would like to go to sleep now."

Quincy nodded her head in agreement. The exhaustion finally overcame her feelings of failure.

She could be frustrated tomorrow.

CHAPTER EIGHT

LESSONS

Eloise yawned and Quincy teasingly smacked her book on Eloise's arm yawning herself.

"I wonder why yawns are contagious?" Eloise murmured. "Monty would know."

"Probably," Quincy answered flipping through the chapter to see how many pages she needed to read for History. She groaned and rolled over on her back and sprawled on her bed. Next to her, Eloise rubbed her blood-shot eyes and yawned again. Quincy poked the purple-haired girl.

"Why are you so tired?"

Eloise shrugged and sat up on Quincy's bed. "I'm not tired," she frowned.

"Oookay then." Quincy muttered. She knew Eloise was up to something, but the smaller girl didn't want to share. Quincy felt an overwhelming sense of curiosity, but she understood the need for privacy all too well.

Quincy turned to the first page of the chapter and pushed the book over to Eloise. "Which one of these is your favorite?" Quincy asked, trying to change the subject and interest her friend.

Chapter two gave a brief summary of each Grand Master Creative Engineer, with pictures, and Quincy swung it around to face Eloise.

Quincy's ploy worked and Eloise's face lit up.

"Well, let's see..." she turned each page with a focused expression on her face. "That's a hard choice... Ah! It would have to be Xavier Reed because he created all the rules in which all creative engineers are bound to, or Helen Thomas the first lady Grand Master."

Eloise scrunched her nose and paused. After a second of silence her eyes opened wide. "But my absolute favorite is Fairnight. His first name is Dwilight. Isn't that a brilliant name? He is the youngest GMC Engineer ever! Until I break the record of course." Eloise rolled on her back and giggled.

Quincy stopped mid-laugh. "Dwilight?" She looked at the picture. She felt like she had been slapped on the face. The picture below matched the portrait of D. Fairnight in the Grand Master Creative Engineer Hallway. In her memory, Quincy compared the portrait in the book to the face of the hermit living in the forest behind Oakley. She couldn't believe that she hadn't tied them together before. After all, who else had the surname Fairnight?

Why was the current Grand Master living in the Oakley forest?

"So, Eloise, where do Grand Master Creative Engineers live?" Quincy innocently asked.

"Oxford, England of course. By Parliament. Creative Engineers have their own meeting place in the city but they also have a special seat in the Parliament building."

"Please remind me exactly what Grand Masters do?" Quincy asked, hoping to continue to brighten her mood.

"The Grand Master is in charge of new inventions and enforces rules laid down by the Three. Remember last week's lesson?"

Quincy nodded. "Vaguely," she grinned.

"So much for your memory Talent," Eloise giggled. Quincy laughed along. Eloise looked down at her book and continued to talk about her many favorite Grand Masters while Quincy's mind drifted to the hermit. She interrupted Eloise with an inquisitive thought.

"So Fairnight lives in Oxford?"

Eloise looked up in surprise. "I'm...I'm not sure. He hasn't been seen in over twenty years."

"How can a Grand Master not be seen in over twenty years?"

"There was an accident, I think. No one except for the Thirds of the time know what actually happened. Only one of the original Thirds is still currently in office. They had to take over the enforcement of the Creative Engineers and won't allow elections for a new Grand Master. No one new has been elevated to Master Creative Engineer since." Eloise sighed sadly and placed her head flat on the bed. "Many Creative Engineers think this is the reason so few inventions have been made in the last two decades because they are afraid to take a risk."

"What risk?"

"Well, there's usually some risk involved in inventing. That's why there's supposed to be a separation between the Thirds and the Creative Engineers."

"So why won't they allow elections for a new Grand Master?" Eloise shrugged. "There's multiple theories but my favorite is the one where no one is qualified enough to be in charge. Dwilight's inventions were extraordinary. He created the elevating box and the ship that's run from both steam and turning wheels. My father told me everyone dearly loves and respects Dwilight and when he speaks, he enthralls audiences. But my favorite thing I've heard about him is his excitement is contagious. Or at least it was before he disappeared.

"I wonder what happened?" Quincy pondered.

"You and every Creative Engineer alive."

✳✳✳

After finishing her study session with Eloise, Quincy grabbed her riding boots and walked down to the stables. As she saddled Consto, her train of thought kept wandering to Dwilight Fairnight. Quincy bribed Consto with a carrot as they trotted around the Oakley fields. She laughed, surprised she had unintentionally ridden to the edge of the forest, the way to Dwilight's. She felt tempted to go in and visit the hermit, but quickly decided against going today. She tried to turn the bridle toward the stables, but Consto refused to move.

"Oh, come on," she pleaded. But Consto huffed and stayed still.

"Fine, do what you want." Quincy released the reigns and spoke without thinking. Immediately after, Consto galloped into the forest passing the warning signs until they were at the doorstep of Dwilight's treehouse. Quincy hated to admit she was impressed that her mount had known where she had been reluctant to go. She dismounted Consto and tentatively knocked on the door. After hearing no response, Quincy attempted to climb on the horse but he snorted and kicked at the ground loudly.

"What is going on with you today?" she murmured to the horse.

A creaky window opened above Quincy. She looked up and saw the hermit poking his head out.

"Excellent timing. The cookies have dinged. Let yourself in."

Quincy narrowed her eyes, skeptical about dinging cookies but walked up the stairs despite her misgivings.

"What do you mean 'ding?'" Quincy asked as she walked into his living room.

For the first time, Quincy saw delight in the man's eyes as he motioned toward his kitchen. "Allow me to show you."

Quincy smelled a mix of smoke from the fire heating the oven, and cinnamon. She looked at the wall behind where he pointed.

There were rows of different hourglasses attached to the wall with one large cord with a bell attached to the bottom.

"This is my kitchen watch. Let's say I'm cooking my dinner and it's going to take one hour and ten minutes. This is what I would do."

Dwilight strung the cord through a metal rung in the second hourglass and looped it back to the first one on the second row. He turned the first one and Quincy watched the sand begin to fall.

"The first one is ten minutes and the second one is one hour. When both are finished, the cord will be released and the bell will fall. Like this."

Dwilight unstrung the second hourglass and the cord fell, ringing the bell on the floor. His eyes danced with delight.

There was no doubt that this was the same Dwilight Fairnight from her history book.

"I kept losing track of time and burning the cookies, so I needed a device to call my attention. Wonderful as it may be, I know you didn't come to see my latest creation. You probably should eat a cookie while they're hot." Dwilight gestured toward his living room. Quincy left the kitchen and chose a seat next to the dying fire. Dwilight brought over a plate of cookies and a cup of tea.

"I wondered if I had scared you away the first time we met. Since you're here, I have answered my own question. However, another one arises since you do not have homework with you. Unless things have drastically changed since my student days." Dwilight narrowed his eyes above his teacup. "So why did you come to visit me?"

Quincy squirmed in her seat unsure if she wanted him to know her reasons. So she stalled and had a sip of tea. She forced herself not to grimace from the taste. She had never had tea sweeter than this in her whole life.

"Too much sugar?" he asked innocently. "I tend to forget that others don't care for tea as sweet as I do." He laughed.

Quincy grinned. "It is sweet."

Dwilight smiled and took another sip of tea. "Ask your question. I haven't finished my transmorgifying invention yet, so you're safe for a while."

Quincy laughed, her shoulders slumping with relief. "Are you willing to help with subjects other than Latin?"

Dwilight sipped his tea and *hmmed*. "That would depend upon the subject," He finally answered.

"History?"

"A broad and long conversation. Could you possibly be more specific?"

"Government elections."

"Still too broad. What would you like to know?"

"Is it possible for someone to be elected for life?"

Dwilight added another massive spoonful of sugar to his tea and stirred it thoughtfully.

"Thirds cannot. Once elected, they serve their term until it is over or they are voted off due to a vote of no confidence."

"A term is six years? It's possible to be re-elected, right?"

"Yes, it is, and yes they can be as many times as wished by the general public."

"Oh, but how come Grand Master Creative Engineers don't have a six-year term?" She blushed at her audacity and wondered if he would realize where she was going. By his smile, he knew exactly what she wanted to know.

"Grand Master Creative Engineers when titled are always Grand Masters, they keep the title for life. They take charge for as long as they wish or until they are voted out unanimously by the three Thirds."

"Why aren't they elected by the people like the Thirds?"

"Oh, people still have a say with their Grand Master. They can choose to support or make their leader as miserable as possible. Why do you think William Humperdink lasted seven months?" he winked.

Quincy quickly scanned her history book from memory and recalled a smug man. Eloise had rolled her eyes when she saw it.

"But wasn't he sick?"

"Oh, by his fifth month he was." Dwilight smiled wickedly. "My uncle told me he had never met a better plonker. Living proof that money and connections does not a person, or a leader, make." He wagged his finger.

"So how is a Grand Master chosen?"

"Do you mean how was *I* chosen?"

Quincy's cheeks reddened again. "Sorry, if I shouldn't ask."

Dwilight shook his head, smiled, and reached over to pat her arm.

"Don't be too embarrassed. I've always admired pluck. They asked me to step up because my predecessor died from an... awkward...situation and I tend to be well-liked," he grinned.

Quincy looked at him closely. When he smiled, his face lit up, and she instantly warmed up to him.

"My friend Eloise told me Grand Master Creative Engineers live in Oxford. Why do you live in the Oakley Forest?"

"You do ask quite a few questions."

"Sorry," Quincy bit her lip failing to hide a grin.

"So not truly sorry then. Good. That wasn't an insult. It was a compliment. How else are we expected to learn if not by questioning?"

Quincy smiled and curled up comfortably on the chair.

"In answer to your question, I am Grand Master in title which allows me to live where I wish."

"Why wouldn't you want to live in Oxford?" Quincy felt if she could live in a city with magnificent buildings, she would never leave.

The Grand Master in self-imposed hermitude paused and looked out the window. "The opposite gift to asking questions is the freedom not to answer them," he replied, wincing. "Please forgive me, but I'm feeling...a bit tired." He smiled tightly and stood up. Dwilight opened a panel in a wall and walked in. After he had closed the door Quincy heard a muffled, "Don't be alarmed, I'm a smidge tired. Stay by the fire as long as you wish, but when you're done, please let yourself out."

Quincy looked at the closed door and left, slowly walking down the tree. She would not inquire about why he left again.

***

Even after three weeks since her time-traveling adventure, the nagging feeling of having failed continued to plague her. Without any new messages from her mysterious writer, Quincy consistently fought to hide it in the back of her mind. Hide it, not forget it. The headmaster had been right when he had warned her that eventually she wouldn't be able to forget anything and all of her memories would be easily accessed. Instead, she focused on her breakfast, grabbing the butter and violently applying it to her toast.

"You need to let it go." Monty murmured as he handed her the cinnamon before she could ask.

"I'm trying. Thanks for the cinnamon."

He nodded and suddenly frowned, pursing his lips tightly. He quickly reached over to push her hand away from her mouth but wasn't fast enough. Quincy had already taken a bite of the toast, instantaneously triggering another memory. The memory of the taste transported her away from Oakley and into her past. Blinking to adjust to the light, she found herself back in her childhood kitchen. She stood behind a small girl who she instinctively knew was her younger sister, Emily.

"What are you trying to do?" she heard herself judgmentally say.

"I want more cinnamon on my toast." Emily turned around glaring.

"Don't you know a little bit of cinnamon goes a long way," Quincy answered. In her memory, she caught the strong whiff of cinnamon and melted butter. Or was she smelling her toast from Oakley?

Oakley?

She frowned. How could she be in two places at once?

She turned around to face the laugher from her mother. Emily giggled and jumped off her chair, accidentally knocking the cinnamon shaker from the counter.

Eight-year-old Quincy reached for the falling cinnamon, but when she blinked, she instantly transported back to her seat on the Third Floor Table in the Dining Hall at Oakley. The rapid change left Quincy numb. For a moment she had been eight years old again and for that second there were no such things as lost keys and failed scavenger hunts. She felt a gentle touch on her elbow. "Are you okay, Quincy?" Colin asked, leaning over toward her, concerned.

Genevieve, Colin's still unofficial girlfriend, sat down next to him, but he still watched Quincy, waiting for her answer. Quincy nodded, but stayed silent. If she spoke, she didn't think she could hold back the tears already pooling in the corners of her eyes.

"Do you want to talk about it?" he pushed.

"She is fine," Monty hissed.

Quincy forced a smile and shook her head. "I'm ready for the holiday," she forced out.

"Two more weeks!" Rusty howled loud enough that students from the surrounding tables looked over. Rusty flailed his hands over his head and made another whooping sound. Eloise rolled her eyes and picked up a bread roll to throw it at the red-head. She unfortunately missed the look of horror on Monty's face right before she launched it at Rusty's unsuspecting head.

Eloise had many good qualities. Intelligence, quirk, fun, and many more wonderful attributes.

Aim did not make that list.

The roll completely missed Rusty's head and sailed past the Third Floor table and landed with a thump on the back of a head belonging to a Year Four from the Second Floor. Seth was notoriously known for trying to create an after-school league for baseball. A sport Quincy was more familiar with than her European friends so when the would-be baseball captain stood up with a bread roll of his own, she instantaneously ducked under the table. The bread roll whooshed past where her head had been seconds before and into the back of a girl who subsequently screamed. Someone from the far end of the hall excitedly hollered, "Food fight!" and afterwards an avalanche of breakfast items dispersed over heads, in hoods, on shirts, and on seats. Quincy looked over at the painted wall and saw Oakley's resident fox dive into his hole inside the painted cherry tree to avoid an apple.

Quincy dodged a buttery pancake and saw an orange explode next to her. She slid under the table and saw Monty already there. At least she thought it was Monty. It was difficult to tell with all the maple syrup and cinnamon in his light blond hair. His glasses were smudged from the sugary substance and he shook from anger.

"I hate getting dirty," he growled as he unsuccessfully attempted to wipe his sticky hands on an already dirty napkin. Quincy looked at her hand and grimaced from someone's baked beans. Beans on toast was definitely not her first choice for breakfast.

"Enough!"

From her spot under the table, Quincy watched the final pieces of food land on the floor. The entire hall had become eerily silent save the lone sound of juice dripping from the table to the ground. Quincy and the others who were taking refuge under tables stood up to face their headmaster.

The headmaster pursed his lips and his cold eyes dared another student to defy him. He spoke in an even and surprisingly steady voice.

"I am incredibly disappointed in all of you. This is a school, not a zoo."

The headmaster stopped talking and watched the entire student body squirm under his icy glare.

"I would be a poor teacher if I allowed a mass evasion of class cleaning up this disaster. At the same time, I will not allow others to clean the mess you have all created."

The headmaster tapped his fingers over his table setting.

"Here's what we'll do. You all have fifteen minutes to clean yourselves as best as you can and make it to class. No tardiness will be excused today. For lunch you will be served sandwiches in the Main Hall. After your final class of the day, you will *all* meet here to clean up. All after-school activities are cancelled for the day."

There were some isolated gasps and groans, but for the most part everyone remained eerily silent.

"I'm not sure why you are all still here?" The headmaster pointed in the general direction of the Timepiece. "Time is passing."

After his pronouncement, all the students stood up and bolted toward the dormitories in order to clean breakfast from their hair and clothes in the short time allotted. Fifteen minutes was not nearly enough for her whole floor to shower. She quickly washed her hands and changed her clothes before running downstairs to class.

***

Quincy pulled *Spei Altus* from the bookshelf and jumped out of the way as the shelf fell down and opened the passageway to the headmaster's office. She had been dreading his class all day, even more than she had for Latin. Of all days to have class with the headmaster, why did she have to have it on the same day they were all in trouble?

She sighed and resolutely walked down the dark passageway toward the headmaster.

She paused at the open door and poked her head into the room. Marquam's attention kept him focused on the papers at his desk. Her entrance had been disguised from the hundred off-timed clocks and the numbed roar of the waterfall above. He paused from his work and sniffed. He sniffed again and without looking up, smiled. He finished his paper and noted Quincy apprehensively waiting at the door.

"Pancakes for breakfast?"

"No, but I'm pretty sure it was Mika—I'm not sure whose breakfast this was." Quincy pointed at her buttery and blackberry syrupy hair.

147

"Indeed. Would you like to come in, or hover by the door making me hungry?"

Quincy smiled awkwardly and quickly sat down. He looked up at her with a slight smile and she released the tension in her shoulders.

"Are you ready to begin?" he asked.

Quincy nodded and twirled her finger in her hair. She grimaced as she touched a sticky wad of syrup.

The headmaster opened his desk drawer and pulled out a detailed map of Oakley, a miniature version of the one hanging in the Main Hall, and handed it to her.

"For your assignment, I want you to memorize this map. Next class I will test you by making you fill in the blank parts of the map and answering questions. Does that make sense?"

Quincy stared at the lines making up Oakley academy and its surrounding grounds. She looked up at the headmaster and nodded. "Is that it?"

"Yes, that will do for today."

Quincy nodded and stood up. She paused before leaving, noticing how early her class had ended. "Are you unhappy with me...about today?"

The headmaster smiled and shook his head. "No. Not at all. Your hair is making me hungry."

Quincy grinned.

"Besides, the sooner I let you go the sooner you can finish cleaning the Dining Hall with the rest of your classmates."

Quincy groaned and walked away from his desk. She paused at the doorway and turned around again.

"Sir? May I ask you a question."

He looked up at her and clasped his hands. "Of course."

Quincy gulped and licked her lips. "Why do certain scents make me remember things?"

"Smelling and memory are located near each other in your brain. Why do you ask? Did something trigger a memory?"

"Yes, this morning with cinnamon. Is it okay to accidentally go back in my memory?"

"It's a natural progression of your Talent. It's possible your memory Talent is allowing your subconscious to pull you back to those memories on purpose. Perhaps to learn something?"

"The question is what, though?"

"Indeed," the headmaster nodded. "It might be of some worth to you to try to replay all of your flashbacks and see what they have in common."

"But definitely after a shower."

The headmaster laughed. "It would be difficult to think about cinnamon when you smell maple syrup. Oh, and Quincy?"

She paused and turned.

"You're most welcome to discuss your adventures with Talin and Monty here if it helps you. This is a safe place."

She sighed. "Thank you, but I don't think it's necessary. I'm pretty sure we failed."

Marquam frowned and clasped his hands. "Perhaps. Perhaps not. Please keep me posted?"

Quincy nodded and fled the room towards the Dining Hall.

***

It took Quincy three attempts with the shampoo before she finally got rid of the sticky substance from breakfast. As she walked out of the shower, Mikaela dashed in without a word. Five other girls waited unhappily in line, each grimacing when their disgusting clothes touched their skin. She shuddered when she still saw grime under her nails. While cleaning the hall, the syrup had stained her knees, hands, and made her shoes stick to the floor. The sickly-sweet odor insinuated itself to the hairs in her nose.

It would be awhile before she could put syrup on anything.

Quincy sat on her bed and frowned as she combed through her hair hoping to rid herself of any leftover bits of food. She looked at her uniform on the floor by her bed and saw the knees of her pants. How would she get the stain out? She looked over at Eloise's bed hoping to see how she had fared in the Great Oakley Breakfast Debacle, but the bed was empty.

***

Quincy sat on her bed screaming into her blanket. When she ran out of breath, reality forced her awake. She slowly caught her breath and felt completely wide awake. She poked her head out of the curtain and saw Eloise's curtains open and no Eloise. What was going on with her?

CHAPTER NINE

THE COROCULARUM

P lease pass me a bread roll?" Colin asked. Rusty made a show of handing him the bread instead of tossing it. Everyone nearby groaned. Quincy grinned and took a bite out of her salad. She looked at the empty spot next to her.

"Where's Eloise?" Quincy pondered aloud.

Monty and Colin shook their heads and Rusty shrugged. No one had seen her.

"Hey, Mikaela!" Quincy waved her arms, trying to get Mikaela's attention. When it failed, she hollered, "Oi, Trindle!"

Mikaela looked over at her and rolled her eyes. Quincy beckoned her over and Mikaela carefully walked over, obviously trying not to get confused by the dinnertime illusion, and slid over next to Monty. As soon as she had sat down, the headmaster stood up ending the illusion of the floating tables. Students slowly dispersed for their evenings. Mikaela leaned in. "What's up, nutter?" she grinned.

"Nutter? I hope that's a compliment," laughed Quincy.

"Sure," Mikaela innocently replied, taking a bite from Monty's slice of pie.

"Certainly, Mikaela. Please taste my dessert," he muttered.

"Seriously? Don't mind if I do," she replied, having another bite.

"Unbelievable." Monty turned his attention toward Quincy. "Were you not going to ask her about Eloise's present location?" he hissed before standing up and grabbing his book bag. "I'll be in the library."

"Of course, you will be," Mikaela said sweetly.

Monty frowned, pretending to be angry, but his lips curled with a smile. He walked away, waving without looking back.

Quincy grinned and turned her gaze to Mikaela, her mood quickly sobering. "I haven't seen your sister since the whole food fight fiasco. Do you have any idea where she is?"

"Huh." Mikaela scrunched her nose. "Come to think of it, I'm not sure."

"She didn't go to bed last night." Quincy added.

Mikaela bit her lip. "Okay, follow me." Mikaela grabbed the rest of the pie in a napkin and walked out of the Dining Hall and then out of the Main Hall until they were outside.

"Where are we going?" Quincy asked.

"Learner's Citadel," replied Mikaela.

"Why would she be here?" Quincy wondered. Eloise was a decent student but not an exceptional one by choice. There were too many other important things to do than to sit at one's desk and study.

"Her Independent Study professor is the Creative Engineers Studies prof and his students are given small workshops on the very sturdy, and mostly soundproof, fourth floor."

Quincy followed Mikaela up the stairs towards the fourth floor. After passing the second floor, they found Eloise slowly making her way down the stairs while leaning heavily on the rails. She looked like she had not slept in days and yawned as she half-heartedly waved. While waving, she tripped on her un-tied purple shoelace and her brown shoulder bag dropped on the stairs as she flew toward them. Mikaela and Quincy fell on their backsides but managed to stop Eloise's fall.

"Eloise!" Mikaela yelped as she shook her incoherent sister.

"Help!" Quincy hollered. A door opened nearby and the burly Professor Thurlsworth ran over and picked up Eloise as if she weighed nothing. Sawdust fell to the floor as the woodworking professor walked down the stairs carrying the unusually silent Eloise.

Mikaela continued to try to wake her sister in the professor's arms until Professor Thurlsworth stopped and gently chided her. "Let me take her to the Infirmary? How about you girls pick up her bag and her...things?" Quincy looked over at Eloise's bag and saw most of its contents strewn all over the staircase. Mikaela looked helplessly at the mess of papers with unintelligible writing, pens, small gears, a screwdriver, a half-eaten sandwich, her umbrella, and a pair of spectacles with odd lenses attached.

Quincy saw Mikaela torn between following her sister and cleaning her possessions.

"Go, Mikaela. I can take care of it."

Mikaela did not need to be told twice as she followed the professor down the stairs.

Quincy tried not to invade Eloise's privacy by reading her papers as she put them back in her bag, but she could not help looking at the intricate calculations. Eloise had never bragged about her proficiency with mathematics. The equations were clearly above Year Two or even Year Three work. She continued to stuff things in the brown bag when something metallic caught her attention. *A pocket watch*, Quincy grinned. Obviously, it hadn't been helping Eloise be on time. She grasped the pocket watch in her palm and grabbed Eloise's bag and umbrella. Walking down the stairs, she studied the plainly curious pocket watch. She placed it to her ear and frowned at the silence. *Must be broken* she decided. She pushed the button on the top to release the front of the watch. When she saw inside, she nearly dropped it on the floor. In the place of a clock-face, a large brown eye stared back at her. But it didn't remain brown for long. It continued to change colors to green to grey then blue to hazel and then back to brown again. It creepily followed her face whenever she moved side to side as if watching her every move. The movement captivated her and Eloise came to mind. She wanted her friend to tell her what this device did. Suddenly the eye blinked and she saw her reflection on the eye-lid, exactly like a mirror. Suddenly, she felt an odd sensation of being lifted towards the sky as if she weighed nothing.

Two gasps interrupted her gaze and she looked up to see herself face to face with Mikaela and a groggy Eloise. Quincy looked at the wallpapered walls of the Infirmary.

"But—but I was in the Learner's Citadel a second ago," Quincy gasped.

Eloise's eyes grew wide and she fainted again. Nurse Watson walked in and shooed Quincy and Mikaela out of the room.

"You can visit her after she has been examined and slept."

Mikaela waited until they had left the Infirmary before grasping Quincy's elbow and stopping her from walking away.

"How did you do that? It takes a good five minutes to get here using the lift, another three to use the stairs. Professor Thurlsworth just placed her in bed and barely left before you showed up."

Quincy thought about trying to pretend she had no idea how she had been abruptly transported from the Learner's Citadel directly to the Infirmary. But, looking at Mikaela's fixated glare told her she couldn't stretch the truth.

She passed the device in her pocket to Mikaela who scrutinized it with a frown.

"Why is this warm?"

Quincy shrugged. "It felt cool when I found it with Eloise's junk," Quincy blushed. "Sorry, her stuff."

Mikaela smiled and opened the device. "What the..." her smiled dropped. "Blimey, what is this?"

"Creepy, isn't it?"

"Yes," she shuddered. "How did it get you here?"

"I'm not sure," Quincy shrugged.

"Why did it transport you to my sister? Why not somewhere more exciting?"

"Maybe because she built whatever this is, it wanted to go back to her?" Quincy pondered.

Mikaela shook her head fiercely. "I know my sister is brilliant and all, but there is no way she created this alone. If she in fact built this, it's from someone else's blueprints."

"How can you be sure?"

"Because this device has nothing to do with levitation, flying, or floating." Mikaela rolled her eyes.

"What do you mean?"

"The only inventions she creates have to do with air."

"Why?" asked Quincy.

Mikaela leaned over the railing and looked down the staircase. "You didn't hear this from me but when she was like ten, she played in the garden after we'd had weeks of rain. The ground shifted and a piece of earth collapsed, creating a decent sized sink hole. She fell in and got stuck there for over a day."

Quincy widened her eyes. "Is that why she keeps inventing new umbrellas?"

Mikaela nodded. "She thinks if she falls again, she'll be able to float away on her umbrella. Weird, I know, but it works for her. Anyway, what were you doing when you opened this?"

"I was walking out of the Learner's Citadel." Quincy shrugged.

"Okay, so open it again," demanded Mikaela. She passed the device to Quincy who opened it and looked at the eye. She waited to see her reflection but it never blinked.

"Last time the eye stopped blinking. Now it's not."

"Hmm. Did you say anything?"

"I don't think so."

"What were you thinking about?"

"I was wondering what this was and wanted Eloise to explain it."

"So, you were thinking about my sister. What if it transports you to what you're thinking about?" Mikaela took back the object, opened it, and closed her eyes. After a minute she opened one eye and then the other.

"Too bad. That would have been fun." Mikaela wistfully sighed and gave back the metallic device. "Please try it again." Quincy touched the warm object and remembered a diner where she used to eat with her family in Portland. She opened the device and saw the eye blink and suddenly she felt an odd sensation in her stomach. She yelped when she felt hot liquid on her shoe. She looked up at a disturbed waitress dropping her coffee from the shock of

Quincy appearing out of nowhere. People around the room gasped and stood up to look at her. Quincy noted the diner had changed the paint from cream to a rusty red before realizing she needed to leave the diner. Right. Now.

She quickly opened the now scalding device and panicked. She tried to recall Oakley and her comfortable bed and saw the eye blink again and for a third time felt the weightless sensation.

Instead of her own bed, she found herself outside and in the rain. The device had become so hot it burned her hand and sizzled from the rain. She quickly dropped it in her pocket and looked around. The twilight and the dark rain clouds made it difficult to find her bearings. Within seconds, she had become completely soaked, so she searched for a dryer location. She ran for an awning and pulled out the sweltering device. She gingerly opened it to reveal an unblinking eye, the iris completely opaque. She closed it and imagined her toasty, dry bed, and opened it again. Nothing happened. She groaned when the rain fell heavier. A door across the street had an embellished sign *The Home Away from Home Café* over the red door and a small *open* sign in the window. She ran across the street and smiled when a small bell rang out her arrival. She stopped by the door unsure if she should go in.

"*Liebchen*, are you going to come in or are you going to drip on my doorstep?"

Quincy walked in and sat at the empty counter by the register. The café owner finished putting away mugs and turned to make a beverage. Embroidered calla lilies embellished her apron and another had been fashioned into a hair pin keeping her hair in a bun on the top of her head. Quincy wondered if the proprietress was truly German.

"It's a bit late for students. Come have a seat, you look like you're in need of this." The woman gave Quincy a cup of hot chocolate and she gratefully took a sip."

"Thank you."

"Certainly."

Quincy looked around trying to get a grasp on her location. She could be anywhere. Luckily the woman spoke English because if she had happened to land in Germany, it would be difficult to find her way around.

Quincy turned the cup slowly in a circle. "I'm embarrassed to ask, but, where am I?"

The woman burst into laughter. "School prank gone horribly wrong?"

Quincy pretended to laugh along. "Something like that."

"Living in a school town, I've seen it all," the owner sighed. "Well, wait for the rain to slow down, finish your hot chocolate, and please borrow one of my umbrellas. You can walk back to school. You are a Year Three, correct?"

"Wait, am I in Oakdale?"

The owner knitted her brow. "How long were you outside?"

Quincy forcibly laughed. She dug around her pockets, horrified she didn't have enough money for the drink.

"It's okay, *Liebchen*. It's on me tonight. Make sure you get back before they shut the gate."

Quincy smiled with relief. "Thank you." The owner waved and walked over toward a gesturing customer.

Quincy grabbed an umbrella and walked outside into the drizzle. She desperately wanted her bed. She followed the signs toward Oakley, and within five minutes of walking, her socks and shoes were soaked. The only thing warm came from the metal device in her right coat pocket. She continued to trudge up the pathway towards school. She jumped when something heavy landed on her shoulder. She groaned. "I'm tired, Talin."

"So, I see," he replied. His humor lost on Quincy. She wondered if she ignored him long enough if he would leave.

"It looks like you've had a long evening." He tried again.

Quincy gave a short laugh and grimaced when the metal device rubbed against her leg.

"Why the scowl?" Talin questioned.

"It's what I get for playing with Eloise's toys."

"Oh, do tell."

Quincy grabbed a leaf from the ground and used it to pick up the metal object from her pocket and showed it to her shoulder.

Talin burst out in laughter. "That's not Eloise's."

"You know what this is?"

161

"I haven't seen one of these in a long time. Not too many were made because it's a feisty device and it won't work for everyone. It's called a Corocularum."

"Coro-cu-larum," she said, drawing it out. "Isn't that 'eye of the heart' in Latin?" she asked hopefully.

"Close enough. You should be surer of yourself. Have you figured out what it does yet?"

"From what I've seen, it takes you where you want to go or find someone you're looking for."

"Two high marks for you today."

"So if Eloise didn't create it, who did? And why does it work for me and not Mikaela?"

"I'm muzzled by the rule of friendship on both accounts."

"Okay, could you please at least tell me why it stopped working?"

"It gets hotter every time you use it right?"

"Yeah?"

"You have three charges before it needs to be...recharged. You might be able to get five if you're not traveling far."

"Recharged? How does it "recharge" then?"

"Think of it like recuperating."

"How long will it take?"

"Only time will tell."

She had a suspicion Talin had no idea.

They remained silent until she reached the Oakley gates and she sneezed violently into her sleeve. Talin flew off her shoulder towards his tower without a goodbye.

"Bye to you too," Quincy yelled as she walked into the large doors and up the stairs toward her bed. She sneezed again and grimaced, hoping she had not caught a cold.

When she opened the door, Mikaela accosted her.

"Are you alright?" she asked grasping Quincy's shoulders.

"I'm fine, but I'm…" Quincy sneezed yet again and rubbed her nose on her sleeve.

"Where did you go?"

"Can we please do this in dry clothes?"

Mikaela nodded but followed Quincy around as if making sure she wouldn't disappear again. Quincy dropped the hot Corocularum on the bed and peeled off her wet clothes. Mikaela reached for the device, but Quincy quickly grabbed her wrists. "It's hot."

"But, how?" Mikaela sat down on the bed and peeked over at the Corocularum.

"I think I used it all up."

"You broke it?" Mikaela looked judgingly at Quincy.

"I don't think so. I think it needs to recuperate."

"Recuperate? What did you do?"

Quincy sat down on the opposite side of the Corocularum and faced Mikaela. "Well you were right. It takes you where you want to go. Three times to be exact. Afterwards it gets insanely hot and stops working."

Mikaela's eyes widened. "Oh yeah?" Her eyebrows lowered into a frown. "But why didn't it work for me?"

Quincy shrugged. "Let's ask Eloise?" She glanced over at Eloise's bed, still empty. "Is she still in the Infirmary?"

"Yeah, apparently she hasn't slept for a full night in over a month. They've given her medication which should help her sleep for a while."

"Then she'll be all right?"

"As all right as she can be." Mikaela put a finger to her ear and made a circular motion. "'Cause my sister is nutters!" Mikaela informed Quincy with a singsong voice and jumped off the bed. "Just like you!" she winked.

"You're so mean!" Quincy smacked Mikaela's arm with her pillow. Mikaela dodged the pillow and Quincy sneezed again. Mikaela grimaced. "Ew. You should probably get some sleep too."

"Good idea." Quincy mumbled as she fell asleep.

Mikaela giggled and left Quincy alone but failed to close the drapes behind her.

***

Quincy turned over in her sleep and managed to wake up right before she fell to the floor. She looked over and felt the comfortable sensation of being cloistered in her room with the darkness and her personal piece of space. She stretched and peeked under her bed at the Corocularum. Quincy gently touched it and felt the cool exterior. She could not help but wonder at the speed in which it had cooled down. Quincy grabbed it and sat up in her bed. She knew she should keep it closed and wait for further instructions from Eloise, but curiosity won again and she opened the device to see the eye watching her while simultaneously changing colors. Quincy thought about a flower garden back home and decided to visit. As usual the eye blinked and she saw her reflection. After a moment, her portrait became blurry and instead of herself, she faced a man staring back at her with lifeless eyes. His lips parted as if trying to smile but instead it turned into a demented leer due to the inability to use the facial muscles properly. Quincy yelled at the man to "Go away and leave me alone!" but he became bigger until he stepped out of the Corocularum and into her room. Quincy screamed.

***

Quincy felt something tugging at her shoulder and she jumped up. Multiple pairs of eyes stared at her with mixed terror and shock. Mikaela released her hands from Quincy's arms.

"What happened?" Mikaela demanded. "Are you okay?"

Quincy blinked her eyes, and to her horror, saw the drapes completely open. What should have only woken her up, had awakened the whole room. Footsteps came from the hallway, telling her the whole 3rd floor must have heard her scream. Quincy groaned and rubbed her sore head. She desperately wanted to be alone with her embarrassment.

"It was a nightmare. I'm fine."

Before anyone could question her further, Quincy grabbed her coat and ran out the door. She did not stop until she stood in front of the Timepiece. She felt hot tears run down her cheeks and fall on the ground. She looked down at her cold, wet feet and realized she had forgotten to put on her slippers. She shivered and wondered how long it would take for people to go back to bed so she could slip in back to her bed un-announced. She rubbed her toes together in the attempt to warm them up. She heard the wind change behind her and braced herself for the extra weight on her shoulder. The raven landed unusually gracefully, but as always, uninvited on her shoulder.

"It's too cold to be out here without shoes." Talin said, surprisingly gentle.

Quincy nodded. "Yeah, it is," she whispered. She shivered and crossed her arms.

"Next time it would be better not to run out of the room and instead laugh it off and go straight back to bed."

"I'll try to remember next time I wake up my entire floor."

Talin sighed.

"I'm sorry. I don't mean to be mean, but I don't feel like talking," she muttered.

"Fair enough."

The two remained silent in front of the Timepiece until five minutes later when Talin cleared his throat. "It's safe for you to go back up."

Quincy nodded and slowly made her way back inside toward her bed. Thankfully, Talin stayed on her shoulder to keep her company as she walked up the stairs towards her dormitory. He did not move until she reached the door to her room.

"Everyone is asleep except for Mikaela waiting for you on your bed."

"Okay. I'll wait for her to go to sleep." She backed up a step towards the family room when Talin dug his talon into her shoulder.

"Ouch!" she hissed. "That hurts you know."

"Oh, I'm sure. Go talk to her. She's not going to bed until you get back anyway."

Quincy grumbled and walked back to the door. When her hand grasped the handle, Talin flew away. She tiptoed towards her bed, and sure enough she spied Mikaela on it, leaning against her bedpost. She yawned and smiled when she saw Quincy. Mikaela stood up and gently patted her head. Without saying a word, the older girl walked toward her own bed and curled on her side. Quincy gratefully took off her coat and put on warm socks before closing her drapes and going back to bed.

***

Quincy expected to wake up and be the chosen topic of conversation, but to her relief, no one mentioned her nightmare and her fleeing the night prior; until breakfast.

Mikaela sat in Eloise's usual seat and helped herself to toast while adding a ridiculously filled spoonful of honey. The exuberance of sweetness reminded Quincy of Dwilight. She should go and visit him today. Mikaela narrowed her eyes at her and Quincy braced herself for the impending questioning.

"I think last night might have been my fault."

Quincy frowned. "What do you mean?"

"I think you had the nightmare from Eloise's creepy eye object."

Quincy nearly laughed. "That's weird." She hated the idea of admitting she had nightmares frequently.

"I think we should get rid of it."

"Get rid of what?" Rusty inquired as he sat down next to Mikaela.

"Nothing." Mikaela and Quincy answered simultaneously.

"Fine, don't tell me," he winked. "Has anyone checked on Eloise?"

"She's alive. Apparently, she needed more sleep from working on class work before the holidays and inventing who knows what." Mikaela informed Rusty while rolling her eyes. "She's the only person I know who forgets to sleep."

Rusty grinned and reached for the plate of eggs. A fellow band member walked up with sheet music, grabbing Rusty's full attention.

"I'm serious, Quincy. I think it's dangerous. We should, I don't know… bury it?"

Monty sat down next to Quincy and shook his head.

She had not had a chance to talk to Monty about the Corocularum, but once again he knew exactly what was going on.

"I don't know. I still think we should talk to Eloise about it," Quincy answered.

Monty inched his head in a nod for Quincy alone.

"Okay, fine. I don't think you'll get a chance to before the break. But I don't think you should use it again though."

"I won't. I don't think it's ready anyway. It's still too hot to touch."

Mikaela nodded and patted her back. "Fair enough. Let's continue this later?"

Quincy waved as Mikaela left for debate.

Quincy looked over at Monty who gave her a sheepish look and rubbed his glasses on his shirt.

"Now would not be the finest timing to discuss this." he mumbled.

"Okay." Quincy grudgingly agreed. She finished her cereal and walked out of the Dining Hall toward the Post Office. It had become a daily habit to visit out of curiosity since her first odd letter. Even though she had failed to find the feather, she could not help but wonder if she would be given a second chance to receive a mysterious note.

Today her persistence paid off when the aide handed her a long and thin package. She ran back victoriously into the Dining Hall and sat down next to Monty with her package.

"I have an unscrupulous feeling we are going to be absent from our first class," he sighed.

"It's the same handwriting. This could be more important than class."

"Oh, I am sure, but I truly dislike missing Language Arts. Especially right before the winter holidays." He grinned. "Despite this, I am pleased to open this with you. Star Room?"

"After you," she grinned.

✳✳✳

Ten minutes later, Quincy and Monty walked up to the Star Room and sat down on the plushy floor, the package in-between them.

"Okay, Monty. First things first. I doubt you could have foreseen everything about yesterday. How did you know about the Corocularum?"

Monty sheepishly cleaned his glasses. "I am afraid this whole debacle with Eloise is my fault. Do you remember the first day of classes?"

Quincy shrugged remembering fainting in front of the school. She hoped he couldn't see her red cheeks in the dark room. "Vaguely," she answered.

"Do you recall the book I had to find on our first day back?"

"Sure, if I looked back in my memories," she laughed.

He grinned. "Fine. The purpose of my enthusiasm in this case was due to the schematics I found in said book. The night after my..." Monty lowered his voice despite the fact they were alone. "...seizure, I saw it would be important for one of these devices to be made for some unknown reason. Then, I asked Eloise if she knew

170

what this was and how it worked. Apparently, she knew and became obsessed with figuring out how to build it correctly. She nearly broke down when she could not get it to work for her last week."

"But how did you know it worked? Did you have a premonition?" she questioned.

"Not this time. I overheard it overheated and assumed it worked for you," he shrugged.

"Why do you think it's important?"

"Well, we both comprehend the Corocularum is not the reason for your nightmares so it is not harmful in that regard. Think about it. How much time would we have saved in England if we had not needed to take eagles to get to every location? You could have simply transported there."

"You think this will work in the past and even the future?"

Monty shrugged. "We have no way of knowing without a test."

Quincy shook her head. "Nope, Talin would kill me. No, I'm serious. He would end me if I used the Timepiece without him."

Monty nodded. "To end you seems a bit severe. However, you know him better than I do. Besides, we truly do not know how it works. For all we know, it does not work unless you have been to a specific place before."

"I don't know. I plan to ask Eloise and see what she knows."

"I have no doubt this will be of interest to her since it worked for you and not her. Please forgive me, but I am missing one class and do not wish to miss another. The box?"

171

Quincy bent over to slowly open the package. She ripped open the paper and saw the box underneath with a purple ribbon around it. She looked over at Monty who had the vacant expression on his face. "Monty?" Quincy waited a minute before trying again and this time tapping his shoulder. "Monty, are you alright?"

"I am fine. I apologize. And to answer your question, yes I do know what is in the box."

"You couldn't wait for me to ask it?" she teased. "Do you want to tell me?"

"No, please go ahead. I do not wish to ruin your surprise." Monty yawned and leaned against the wall.

Quincy untied the ribbon and opened the box. She gasped when she saw its contents. A long, black feather nestled on purple velvet next to a letter with now familiar spidery handwriting.

CHAPTER TEN

THE SECOND RIDDLE

Quincy found it completely impossible to focus on classes after opening the package. Unfortunately, they had a group project meeting during lunch so the letter had to wait until after classes. Grudgingly, she made her way towards the Back Library for her Independent Study with the headmaster. She respectfully knocked on the open door and walked in. The headmaster looked up and recognized Quincy with a wave of his hand.

"Are you ready for your map exam?"

Quincy sat down and nodded. Her gaze drifted from his face to the window behind him and the letter in her school bag.

"Something on your mind?" he prodded.

Quincy forced her attention back to the headmaster and nodded. "I received a letter today and I haven't had time to read it yet. I think it might be for the key quest."

Professor Marquam's eyes widened. "I hope it's good news." He silently rubbed his salt and pepper stubble. "Well, as it happens, I have two rather pressing things I need to take care of. Let's postpone your exam until next week and you can update me if you wish?"

She nodded, relieved. "Thank you."

She left his office and walked toward the Star Room to read her letter. She wondered if she should wait for Monty, but in the end, she carefully broke the wax seal to read the letter. The same spidery handwriting filled the page.

Time is like an animal untamable.
Of a fable.
It is not drawn like a line straight,
Much like fate.
It mines and defines,
Times designs.
Every day and for every nay, there is a yea
that disarrays every day which leads it astray
from your line you might say.
You need to travel to unravel
the concise price of sacrifice
for what is gained and what is lost.
To win my favor, you must savor the flavors,
of your alternate, alternate self.
Grasp the dial and filled with guile,

Click the tip, and then you must flip.
Do NOT twist to assist, or it you will miss,
51.5194° N, 0.1270° W, which is where you will go,
to find a circle of stars to see how they glow.

Quincy instinctively knew she would have as many problems, if not more, with this second clue. She folded the letter and placed it safely into her pocket. Now what was "C" trying to send her? She casually walked down the stairs and toward the Main Library in search of Monty. In the hall, students worked to place a long green banner with painted words, "Welcome, Parents."

Quincy grimaced. Tomorrow afternoon parents would be arriving from all over the world to look at their children's grades, artwork, and assignments. Once again, no one would come to claim any of her pictures and show her off with pride. There would be no one to tell her she had been missed.

She picked up her pace as she passed the crafts being shown off by the door. Quincy paused and looked at the art work. She saw one piece of hers had been chosen. She had turned in three of her best watercolors but only her night sky had been placed in the Hall. Not that it mattered anyway, since no one but her would be looking at the painting tomorrow.

She looked at the clock and decided she wanted cinnamon cookies. She walked over towards the barn and shivered in the crisp air. She approached Consto, who for the first time, welcomed her with a nicker without bribes.

"You want to eat out of Dwilight's garden, again, don't you?"

Consto bobbed his head in agreement.

"Yeah, I thought so," she grumbled.

Even though Consto enjoyed going towards the forest, he occasionally liked to speed up or suddenly stop as if to make sure Quincy never forgot he was in charge.

After a smooth ride, at least smooth in Consto terms where Quincy stayed in the saddle, she jumped off the horse and knocked on the door. When he didn't answer, Quincy pulled the bell and waited for Dwilight to let her in. After another minute of no response she hollered at the tree.

"Dwilight?"

Quincy frowned. He never left the radius of his tree house so she guessed he must be in his lab working on a project. She tried the door and found it unlocked. She kept calling his name as she walked up the staircase and towards his lab. When in the lab she saw why Dwilight had not heard her ring. Violin music played loudly from the corner of the room and Dwilight's head was hidden under a table. Quinn walked over and knocked on the table and waited for him to see her. He pulled his head out and gave her a friendly smile. As usual his brown hair stuck out in all directions and today it smelled lightly burned.

"Quinn! Delighted to see you!"

"Hey, what are you looking for?"

Dwilight looked sheepish and pulled out a small nail from his bathrobe pocket.

"What's that?"

"A nail."

"You were desperately searching for a nail?"

"Not just any nail. This nail is made from a special metal not easily bent. This beauty is never where you want it but somehow manages to show up when you need it."

Dwilight delightedly showed off the nail and Quincy tried to be impressed. Dwilight grinned and patted her head.

"It's understandable. You would have to have Creative Engineer tendencies to appreciate this."

Quincy dropped her book bag on the ground, jumped up and sat on the counter near a window. Dwilight took his extra special nail and walked over towards one of his projects. He paused and seemed to think better of it and dropped it back in his pocket.

"Dwilight, could I ask you a question?"

"Always."

Quincy shifted uncomfortably and was unsure how to continue. Dwilight stopped tinkering and turned around from his project to face Quincy. "I have a philosophy about asking questions. Would you like to hear it?"

Quincy nodded eagerly.

"My personal philosophy is not to be embarrassed to ask questions. Because those who stop asking questions, stop thinking, and those who stop thinking could stop living, and those who stop living are most certainly dead. So please, by all means, ask away."

Quincy grinned and tucked it away to use on Talin later.

"Besides, what's the worst thing that could happen? Either I don't want to answer it." Dwilight shrugged. "Or I don't know. Either way, you have new information."

"That's fair. I feel that everyone has something they're good at. Like art, or music, even studying, or engineering." Quincy motioned to Dwilight's work desk. She twiddled a pencil with annoyance.

"And?"

"And, I don't think I'm like that. I enjoy a lot of things, but I'm not particularly good with any of it."

Dwilight sighed and sat next to Quincy on the counter.

"You enjoy, what is it... oh right, water coloring. Yes?"

"Water colors, yeah? But I'm not good. I'm just okay."

"Good by whose standards?" he winked. "But you enjoy reading, do you not?"

"Uh-huh. But not as much as my friend Monty."

"You like horseback riding, exploring?"

"Yes...but not well."

"Jack of all trades, master of none."

"A what?"

"It's a person who is good at many things but not the best at any one thing. Not a bad thing, it means you have many interests instead of one." Dwilight grinned. "It means you will be much more interesting at parties whereas me," Dwilight pointed at himself. "Well, I'm a generally friendly chap but I know more about gears than art history. Not terribly interesting party conversation. Besides, if it brings you joy, you shouldn't care what anyone else thinks of it but you." He stood up and stretched. "Well, I'm hungry for something sweet. One should never do work on an empty stomach."

"Sounds good, but do we have to start with Latin?"

Dwilight laughed. "We do not." He opened his cupboards and sighed dejectedly. "I should attempt to go to town and restock before it snows." Unhappily, he offered some stale cookies with the tea.

"Sadly, I have four cubes of sugar left."

He divvied up the sugar cubes as if they were priceless gems and plopped two into his tea. Quincy added one cube to her own cup.

"Are you going to use the other one?" he asked, innocently.

Quincy grinned and shook her head.

Dwilight smiled, and added the third cube to his own cup.

Quincy shook her head and Dwilight laughed. He took one sip and sighed in content. "Now, I have a feeling you aren't depressed about your hobbies or being the life of the party. Would you like to tell me what's going on?"

"Tomorrow is Parent's Day."

"Ah." Dwilight replied, not needing to say another word. He already understood.

Quincy took a large sip of tea to hide a sob and instead choked on the hot water. Dwilight tapped her back until she stopped coughing.

"Do you have any pressing homework due tomorrow?"

Quincy shook her head. "Just my presentation in History, but I'm ready for it."

"Let's start a project. Is there anything you want to invent?" he winked.

Quincy smiled at his attempt to make her feel better and then an idea crossed her mind.

"Dwilight, do you know what a Corocularum is?"

Dwilight's eyebrows rose, surprised. "Of course, I know, but the question is, how do you know?"

Quincy explained how Monty found blueprints in a book and how Eloise built one.

"She built it?" Dwilight nearly dropped his tea cup on his lap but managed to catch it before it spilt on his bathrobe. "*Crivvens*! How old is this lassie?"

"Sixteen."

Dwilight howled with laughter. "A sixteen-year-old tried to build it from the blueprints? That's brilliant! It would have been a miracle if she had managed to get the blasted thing to work."

"But it did. It worked when I looked into it."

This time Dwilight did drop his cup and it spilled all over the floor. Surprisingly, the cup did not shatter.

"Sorry, but did you say it worked when you looked into it?"

Quincy nodded.

"As in you managed simultaneous inner-planetary travel?"

Quincy nodded again. This time unsure. Is that what she had done?

Dwilight sat back with a look of shock. "A sixteen-year-old, what is this world coming to? The device itself is so intricately put together, one incorrectly crossed wire and the whole thing doesn't function. And finally, it works for seemingly random people."

"Random?"

"Yes, no one could figure out why it worked with one person and not the other."

"Is it dangerous?"

"No! Well, a bit. Once someone had a difficult time focusing on one place and thought about something else while trying to travel and ended up...well let's not talk about that. If you choose to use it again, make sure you know where you're going."

"Is it possible to travel from a photo?"

Dwilight pondered for a moment and shrugged. "I don't see why not as long as you don't think about some other object that reminds you of a place that isn't that place. Make sense?"

"I think so. But you're not going to tell me not to use it?"

Dwilight pulled the nail from his pocket and played with it. "I should, but I would be the wrong person to say it. My own failing is to play with unknown powers and then pay the price later." Dwilight frowned and got up to go towards the kitchen with the now two empty cups. From the kitchen he yelled back, "As long as you're safe about it. Or at least as safe as you can possibly be. You should be fine and dandy!"

Quincy did not feel reassured.

Dwilight laughed at her facial expression. "There's always a gamble with adventure. If you knew everything about it ahead of time, then it would cease to be adventurous."

"Yeah, that makes sense."

"Of course, it does. Be prepared to pay the repercussions," Dwilight wagged his finger.

CHAPTER ELEVEN

HERMITS AND THIRDS

Parent's Day left a bad taste in Quincy's mouth and her face hurt from pretending to be happy. She wished she knew why she was required to show up to Parent's Day even if she did not have any here. Thankfully, she wasn't forced to stay for the entire duration. She remained cordial with Monty's cold aunt and uncle as well as the Trindle family and Mrs. Knight before ambling toward the exit to her room. Quincy yawned and imagined a nap on the overstuffed chair nearest to the fire. It would be quiet since once again, she would be the lone soul on her floor. Before she could walk up the stairs, Rusty stopped her.

"You're back," Quincy said. "Did you forget Savannah?"

Rusty looked horrified. "No way I could forget my lovely lady!"

Quincy bit her tongue to keep from laughing. His lovely lady, Savannah, being his trumpet.

"I almost forgot this," he showed her his mathematics book with a frown. He waved goodbye but then stopped and turned around. "Oh, by the way, I didn't know you had an uncle."

Quincy frowned, completely confused. "A what?"

"Your uncle. He's here you know?"

"My uncle?" Quincy narrowed her eyes. "And he's here?"

Rusty ran his hand through his hair and shrugged. "Yeah, he's over in the Main Hall."

"How do you know he's my uncle?"

"He told me he was. I noticed him looking at student art and he pointed yours out."

Quincy turned around, and without saying anything to Rusty, ran towards the Main Hall. A tall man with a large gray cap stood in front of her mediocre painting. She walked over to him and looked up at her artwork. He turned around and gave her a cheery smile.

"Hello, Quinn."

The Oakley hermit had left his hermitude. For her. She grinned back and looked up at her picture.

"According to your stars here you painted this in September?"

Quincy nodded.

"It's quite good, however you did paint Altair a smidge too far from Tarazed to my taste. Otherwise I quite like it."

"Even despite the mistakes?"

"Of course. It's what makes it unique. And a good excuse to study astronomy." He chuckled.

Quincy beamed. "Thank you." She peered over to note his wardrobe.

"No bathrobe? You've left on the loafers though."

Dwilight grinned. "Nope, no bathrobe."

Dwilight wore his customary loafers with grey corduroy pants and a striped grey and dark green sweater instead of the burgundy robe. Even though inside, he wore a large grey cap and kept it down low on his brow to hide most of his face.

"Thanks for being my uncle today. I know you haven't been around this many people in a while."

"True, but I don't mind it for a few moments." Dwilight winked at her. "I think I would make a good uncle."

Quincy nodded, whole-heartedly agreeing.

"Now if you would be a dear, please point out the sixteen-year-old."

"Eloise?"

Dwilight nodded.

"There she is." Quincy pointed towards the Trindle family and the smallest one with the purple in her hair. Eloise failed to stifle a yawn but otherwise looked happy.

Dwilight shook his head in disbelief. "Sixteen years old. I was twenty before I could get the damn thing to work."

"Did you invent it?"

"Unfortunately, I can't take the credit," Dwilight grinned. "I found the schematics in a book." He handed her a small box. "Here's a treat for later. It was delightful to play your uncle today but now I need to get to Oakdale to get sugar. It smells like snow outside."

"You'd better hurry." Quincy laughed. "And thank you again."

"As it so happens, I find myself alone for the next couple of weeks so if you want company, you know where to find it." Dwilight tipped his hat and walked outside.

Monty walked up next to Quincy and frowned.

"Why the frown?" Quincy asked.

"I don't know who he is." Monty motioned toward Dwilight's retreating figure.

"He's a friend Talin introduced me to."

Monty nodded but pursed his lips when she wouldn't give him more details.

"I wish I could tell you, I really do," Quincy said.

He nodded, appeased. "Please take some time off to enjoy your Christmas from," Monty motioned to the key in his pocket. "I am sorry we did not have a chance to look at the second clue. Perhaps after the holidays?" Monty asked hopefully.

"Absolutely."

Monty smiled, pleased with her quick response and waved goodbye. Quincy hoped Monty would like the small painting of a puppy she had made and sneakily added in his pile of things outside the Main Hall.

Happier than she had been for a long time, Quincy decided to go up to her room with her box of sweets and read a new book from the library. The perfect way to start her holiday.

***

Quincy rubbed her eyes and stared at the ceiling trying to forget Christmas. She wished more than anything that she was back in her childhood home and that her father would come in any moment with hot chocolate. And for a strange reason she dreaded going downstairs, afraid of trying to replicate the wonderful feeling from the prior year. She continued to procrastinate by rolling over in her warm bed. Instead of thinking about the celebration downstairs, Quincy thought about the note hidden away in her night table.

The second clue.

After replaying the letter in her head, she finally decided to listen to Monty's advice and take a break. She needed his thoughts anyway, so why not take a short vacation from the impending doom of the universe. Or try to. At least for a few days? Quincy groaned and curled up on her side.

Eventually, curiosity won and she got out of bed to put on her robe and slippers. She walked down the passageways and poked her head into the family room. The scouts had already lit the fireplace, and had left her a candy cane on the mantle. Delightfully, Quincy opened the wrapper and licked the peppermint candy. She slowly made her way down the stairs and towards the Main Hall. She paused, horrified by the undecorated and shut door. Someone had pasted a notice on the door and Quincy had a sinking feeling it read, "Christmas has been cancelled due to an unforeseeable reason." Instead it gave a map to a room Quincy had not been to before. She committed the map to memory and walked towards her destination.

The map led her to a large room underneath Talin's home. The door had already been opened and Quincy heard laughter coming from the other side. She walked in and saw around twenty people drinking hot beverages and chatting. She looked around and wondered why she hadn't been in this room before. The dark wood paneled walls were engraved with trees from all four seasons. She looked down at the floor and its emerald green squares interlaced with cream colored ones. It reminded her of a chessboard. Quincy stopped near the magnificent fireplace with the faces of eagles adorning the corners of the posts. One of the small tables on the opposite side of the room, held a number of games and a basket of small boxes of candy. In the center, a beautiful fir tree decorated with candles and icicles shimmered, sending shadows and rainbows around the room. She looked under the tree and spotted different colored packages placed underneath. Another student passed Quincy a cup of hot apple cider and she watched the other people congregate near the tree. Everyone became silent when the headmaster walked in, wearing a festive hat. He smiled at everyone and clasped his hands.

"I believe we're all here. If someone would be so kind to pass me some delicious cider, then I believe we should begin. Professor

Valdez, would you be so kind to deliver packages to their rightful owners. Oh, Alexander, Megan, and Susan; would you please assist me?"

The three students jumped up, pleased to be chosen by name to help sort out packages to their rightful owners. As this happened, everyone else chose spots to open presents and play games.

After all the packages had been passed out, Quincy had four small boxes on her lap. She had not expected anything from Eloise since she had been busy and not feeling well of late. She recognized Monty's handwriting and opened his gift first. She smiled as she unwrapped a second charm for her bracelet. Her eyes widened from the details of the tiny clock charm. It would go nicely next to the clover. After, she opened a box of chocolates from Mrs. Adalin followed by a painting from Colin. The drawing of the sun looked so lifelike; Quincy imagined she felt heat radiating from it. The final present came from someone with nearly illegible handwriting. Cautiously, she opened the tiny box and a note with another small package fell on her lap. She read the letter and after a few attempts to decipher the odd hand she managed to read,

"Here's something that will always be there when you need it! Happy Christmas Quinn!

Delightfully,
D.F.

189

Quincy opened the brown paper to reveal a nail. She grinned at the piece of metal and Dwilight's decision to give this to her as a Christmas present. Despite her lack of "Creative Engineer tendencies," Dwilight parted with his special nail specifically for her. And more importantly, had remembered her on Christmas.

Quincy wished she had made him a Christmas present and felt sheepish she had not thought about it until now. She pondered a solution when her painting popped into her head. He had liked her painting of the night sky and she decided to wrap it up for him. She would slip out later in the afternoon to visit. Further thoughts were interrupted when the whole room became eerily silent. Quincy looked over to see what had caused the hasty hush. The same Third she had seen storming the headmaster's office last year, now stood awkwardly by the door. Instead of her usual high-heels, she wore black flats and a more casual attire with an oversized blue wool sweater. Her blonde hair flowed down instead of her usual tight bun. She looked painfully uncomfortable standing there. The headmaster stood up to face her, clearly pleased to see her. Quincy closed her eyes and searched for her name. Eleanor Morrow.

"Welcome! Come have some apple cider. I'm sure we could procure some cinnamon for you."

Eleanor took one step into the room, clearly tempted by the headmaster's offer but quickly pursed her lips. In a quiet but cold voice she replied, "No thank you. I'm sorry to have bothered you," and quickly retreated out the door.

The headmaster sighed and his face dropped from disappointment. "Please continue the festivities and don't wait on my account." He walked out the door and went after the Third.

After a moment of uncomfortable silence, Susan jumped up and waved her empty cup. "I want more apple cider! Who's in?" A handful of volunteers raised their own cups and the conversations continued. Quincy slipped out of the room to change into her warm riding clothes.

***

Even in the snow, Quincy had no problem saddling Consto and riding towards Dwilight with her picture wrapped in one of her pillow cases. She managed to smuggle it outside without being caught. She didn't want to think what would've happened if a scout caught her with it outside of her room.

The snow made the trip longer but she still managed to find Dwilight's treehouse without any difficulties. She left Consto under a protected part of the forest without much snow and then knocked on Dwilight's door. He grinned, delighted.

"Hot chocolate?" he offered when she had found a seat.

She nodded and took a sip of the unnaturally sweet beverage. She presented the pillowcase to him and he smiled warmly as he pulled her painting from it.

"I have the perfect place for this." He said as he hugged Quincy and placed it beside him.

"Tell me, how large is the tree in the Main Hall this year?" Dwilight asked.

"We aren't having Christmas in the Main Hall this year. We're in the room in the old tower underneath the top floor."

Dwilight looked impressed. "I wonder why."

Quincy shrugged and then told him about the decorations and what had transpired. She even mentioned the odd and unexpected visit from the Third.

"Well, that's why the celebrations took place there. It's her favorite room in the entire school." Dwilight said.

"You know her?"

Dwilight looked uncomfortable and nodded. "We were at school together. We share…a past. How did she look?"

"The same as last time I saw her. Tense, I think would be the best word."

Dwilight looked sad and excused himself to go check on his cooking. "I'm making a lovely pie for dessert."

Quincy wondered if it would taste as sweet as his hot chocolate.

Dwilight walked back in, "So tell me more," Quincy went back to the Christmas morning details including the headmaster's hat and tweed jacket.

"I quite dislike tweed." Dwilight said with a slight look of disgust.

"Dwilight, may I ask you a question?"

"You may always ask."

Quincy shifted her weight uncomfortably in the chair.

"Why are you alone on Christmas?"

"Alone? Present company excluded." He said teasingly. He tried to even out his hair to no avail. "My parents are unfortunately both dead, I am sadly no longer married, and I hope to never see my last living relation ever again. How is that for Christmas cheer?" Dwilight saluted with a glass decanter of alcohol before pouring some into his drink. He pretended to be amused, but Quincy saw through his façade noting the same pain and anger from the first day they had met.

"I'm sorry for asking," she said quietly.

He smiled sadly and shook his head. "Never apologize for asking. But, don't be offended if you don't get an answer. Now, be a dear and hand me my glove."

She handed him the worn-out glove and he opened the stove washing them both in heat and whiffs of apples.

She stared at the beautiful pie, sadly. "I don't think I have time for it to cool. I should probably take Consto back to the stable."

Dwilight nodded. "Prudent. I'll make sure to save you a slice."

Quincy waved and slowly made her way back to Oakley for Christmas dinner. When she made sure Consto was stabled correctly, Quincy placed her chilled hand inside her coat pocket and felt a small parcel. She frowned. When had Dwilight placed this in her coat, and hadn't he already given her a present? She pulled out the bag and opened it. Cinnamon cookies. She grinned as she walked back upstairs to her room. She nibbled on one as she curled up with a blanket. If felt like cinnamon stalked her. She closed her eyes and replayed the moments from the last year or so when she had smelled cinnamon and what memories in her childhood were tied to it. There were too many to count. Her mother often used cinnamon in her dough and placed dried cinnamon by Quincy and her sister's bedside table as well as the windows to keep the house smelling fresh. She had also placed cinnamon sticks in their hot chocolate and teas. The list continued on. Quincy frowned; her eyes still closed. What had been her mother's obsession with cinnamon?

***

Quincy leaned on the banister and waved when she saw her friends coming towards her with their luggage from the holiday break. Eloise appeared bright-eyed and it looked like she had managed to catch up on rest. Colin and Rusty walked up the stairs flanked by four girls from other floors who giggled behind them. One pointed at Colin and poked her friend. Quincy noted Genevieve wasn't with him. Behind the commotion, Monty noted Quincy and smiled. Quincy grinned before someone yanked her back, her arm painfully grasped by Eloise's umbrella. Before she could say anything, Eloise gave her a strong hug and held onto her arm.

"We need to talk." Eloise whispered standing on her tiptoes to Quincy's ear.

Quincy nodded. "Okay. When?"

"Tonight. After bedtime."

Quincy nodded again and Eloise released her umbrella.

CHAPTER TWELVE

ILLEGAL TRAVELING

Quincy blew out her candle and lay down on her bed. She left the drapes open and waited for Eloise to motion towards the family room. She wondered why she wanted to wait for lights out before talking to her.

But she had a strong suspicion it had to do with the Corocularum.

Slowly but surely, the rest of the girls trickled in, drew their drapes and blew out their own candles. Quincy yawned, wishing they would hurry up so she could talk to Eloise and go to sleep. After seventeen minutes, deep breathing and gentle snores drifted from the few roommates who kept their drapes open. Quincy heard a creak from the floorboards near her and she sat up quickly.

"Shh," someone hissed from the opposite side of the room.

"Sorry," another voice answered.

Quincy sat up in bed, surprised to see two people standing beside her. She stood up and followed the two shadows out the door. Once they walked out of the room, Quincy saw both Mikaela and Eloise. The three girls ambled into the family room where the embers from the dying fire left the room in odd shadows. The room had one previous occupant. Monty sat by the dying fire reading a book about the intricacies of Parliament for class.

"Do you have to be here now?" Mikaela asked clearly annoyed by his presence.

"I do not *have* to be anywhere." Monty closed his book and looked up at the three girls mischievously.

"We need the room for—,"

"No, he can stay." Eloise interrupted her sister. "He should hear this. He might know something I don't."

"Fine."

The three girls sat down around Monty.

"You all seem to know why we're here. Why, exactly?" Mikaela asked, narrowing her eyes at Monty.

He looked over at Quincy and motioned to her pocket. "Show us," he requested.

Quincy reached into her pocket and touched the device. "This?" she asked, pulling out the Corocularum.

"Let's get on the same page. Who knows what?" Mikaela demanded.

Quincy looked over at Monty and caught him staring directly at her and uncharacteristically biting his lip as if unsure what to say and how much to tell the sisters. Quincy took it as a hint to begin.

"You all know I found this thing when I was picking up Eloise's stuff, right?" After a couple nods, she continued. "So, when I opened it and thought about you in the Infirmary, it took me to where you were."

Eloise shifted in her chair before blurting out, "Is it true it worked for you?"

Quincy nodded.

"What was it like? Where did you go? How long did it take? How did you feel? What—?"

"Steady on." Mikaela told her sister putting her hand over her sister's mouth. "Why did it work for Quincy and not me or you, Eloise?"

Eloise mumbled incoherently and Mikaela took her hand away from Eloise's mouth.

"Not sure." Eloise said while wiping her mouth with her sleeve from her sister's germy hand.

Monty took off his glasses and wiped it on his robe. "A Corocularum is not known for its dependability. The inventor never built them in mass because of its finicky nature. It is notoriously difficult to construct."

"So how could you build it then?" Mikaela looked over at her sister.

"Believe it or not I can follow instructions." Eloise stuck out her tongue at her sister.

"You had instructions for that?" Mikaela pointed towards the Corocularum in Quincy's hand.

Monty cleared his throat. "This is where I jump in. I found the formula—"

"Blueprints!" Eloise interrupted.

"Blueprints," Monty continued rolling his eyes, "Anyway, I found them in an old book in the library and thought it might be of interest to Eloise. I also had a...feeling it would be needed."

Monty had not told them the whole truth that he had seen a piece of their future requiring Quincy to have it. He was embarrassed by his mutated Talent, so Quincy remained silent.

"Why did it transport Quincy and not me or Mikaela? I built it exactly like it told me," she frowned. "To be honest, I didn't think it worked."

"Again, there is no reason for why it works for one person and not the other." Monty sighed and leaned against the seat.

"Okay then, is this thing giving Quincy nightmares?" Mikaela questioned.

Quincy wished she would forget about it. She didn't want to tell her friends about her frequent nightmares and her terrifying stalker.

Monty shook his head. "Highly unlikely. The Corocularum, like its name, is affected by the desire of the heart and not the head."

Quincy released her breath she hadn't realized she had held and nodded. "See? An average nightmare."

Eloise huffed. "That's interesting and all, but what did it feel like?" She leaned in toward Quincy, her eyes wide with excitement.

Quincy tried to explain the strange feeling the Corocularum gave her but felt she fell short in her explanation.

"It's like when you fall asleep on your arm and it tingles. And then suddenly you're where you're thinking of."

Despite the short description, Eloise listened intently with a look of awe on her features.

"Well since it doesn't work for me it looks like it should be yours." Eloise looked disappointed at first but then smiled at Quincy.

Quincy quickly shook her head. "I can't take this from you after you worked so hard."

"Think of it as a belated Christmas present." Eloise grinned.

Quincy thanked Eloise and placed the Corocularum back in her pocket.

"Is that all for tonight, ladies? I am a bit tired from traveling," Monty yawned politely.

Everyone stood up and said goodnight. Quincy watched them all leave and decided to stay awake for a while longer next to the fire. She opened the Corocularum careful not to wish for anything and watched it blink through the different colors over and over again.

***

Quincy and Monty picked up hot chocolates at the Aquila Café and found a spot near the steps of the Back Library. The café had been filled to the brim and the darkened Star Room made looking at the letter impossible. Quincy handed Monty the clue and in his silky Irish accent read the poem aloud. After he finished, he frowned and took off his glasses to clean them.

"Quite a conundrum," he finally said, rubbing his brow.

"I'm glad I'm not the only one confused. Does anything make sense?" she asked.

"Very little I am afraid. If I recall the first poem correctly, it follows the same rhyme scheme."

At this, Monty looked over and waited for Quincy's agreement. After she nodded, he continued.

"There also seems to be instructions to what I am guessing is the Timepiece?"

Quincy nodded again.

"Is it possible to flip the dial?"

Quincy shrugged. "No idea."

"That might be a good question for Talin. Is there a way for you to contact him?"

She shook her head. "I know where he lives, but I'm not supposed to visit."

Monty pursed his lips. "Well then we must wait for him and then continue. I think I will need to give this some more thought before I venture any further. I have read some books on the topic of time, but I need to arrange my thoughts to make a cohesive discussion. Also, we need to find a map. Those numbers look like longitude and latitude."

Quincy felt silly she hadn't thought of that. "You're probably right. Let's meet this weekend and go look at maps?"

Monty nodded and followed her upstairs. They stopped outside the family room when Colin walked out the door, breathless. When he saw Quincy, he smiled.

"There you are. We've started a game of charades. Do you want to play?"

Quincy looked at the door eagerly and then peeked over at Monty. Monty raised his nose at the door.

"I crave the solitude of my own bed. You both entertain yourselves." He nodded at them and walked away. Colin scoffed and then grinned at Quincy.

"He has no idea how to have any fun."

"Apparently not," Quincy said, hurt he had left her behind so easily.

She followed Colin inside the family room and joined the group of roommates laughing at Rusty's imitation of what Quincy soon found out was Professor Agglebye.

***

Quincy wished she had worn warmer stockings in the classroom under the roots of the trees. She looked around and saw others also ill-prepared. Another student's face looked vaguely blue. Professor Hutchman had warned them three times, and next time Quincy would dress better. The professor droned on about some Grand Master who had created a mixture to protect wool from becoming stained and she fought to keep her mind from wandering. While the professor wrote notes on the board, she flipped through the pages to the next chapter. Finally, something interesting. A brief introduction of the Thirds. It's too bad it would take another year before delving into this particular topic in greater detail. She kept flipping through the pages until she saw a familiar picture. A younger version of the blond haired third. Her smile was contagious and her eyes danced. She still wore high-heels, but her loose hair gave her a carefree expression. Quincy looked down the list of Thirds when another name caught her eye.

Prieler.

She looked up at the picture, and there was a middle-aged man next to the blond-haired Third. He had a tight-lipped smile and stared directly into the camera. He stood uncomfortably straight with his hands behind his back. Frederick Prieler. Quincy looked closer at the picture and her arms prickled from the sensation of recognition. She had seen him get kicked out of parliament for breaking an important rule. Before she could ponder him further, the bell rang, releasing the students to their next class.

✳✳✳

Saturday mornings were the best. Quincy curled up on the overstuffed chair near the fire in the family room. She stretched, trying to find the motivation to move toward breakfast, but instead simply rolled over. The only plans for today consisted of studying and to visit Dwilight. She wondered if Monty would be interested in having hot chocolate and looking over the note a second time. As if summoned by thought, Monty came down the stairs and sat on the arm of the chair.

"I have what could possibly be a brilliant idea."

Instantaneously interested, Quincy looked up. "Oh? How so?"

"We seem to have hit the proverbial brick wall with the second clue. So, I suggest we do some experimentation."

"I'm curious to find out what your definition of experimentation is," she teased.

"Why? Do you expect me to say it is something along the lines of me reading a different book?"

"You said it, not me." She laughed. "What are you thinking?"

"Well, we have not had a chance to use Eloise's device."

"But I have; three times."

"Yes, but in our present. We do not truly understand the power of the Corocularum."

Quincy narrowed her eyes quizzically. "Are you suggesting we experiment with it in the past?"

"Or future."

Quincy liked that idea even less. "I think we should probably stick to the past. I don't know if the Timepiece works in the future. Time traveling is difficult enough without thinking about the implications of traveling *forward*."

Monty shrugged. "There is a way to find out…"

"Surprisingly adventurous of you," she teased.

Monty grinned. "Apparently I like a smidge of danger."

Quincy thought about Talin's reaction of them traveling. Would he be mad? Had she ever seen him truly angry? Still, these keys weren't going to find themselves.

She groaned. "Okay let's go, but not into the future."

Monty nodded. "Fair enough. Shall we?"

Quincy nodded and ran to her room to grab the Corocularum she had hidden in one of her socks. The two walked outside toward the Timepiece and made sure no one watched as they dodged the fence surrounding the clock.

She paused at the door and for what felt like the millionth time tried to decide if they should be doing this. Monty patiently waited as Quincy crossed her arms and chewed on her lip. She looked over in the direction of Talin's roost and when she did not see him flying towards her in reproach, she looked at the door.

"Are you ready, Quinn?" Monty encouraged.

Quincy nodded but before she could open the door Monty interrupted her. "Shall we use my key? If you get in trouble at least it will not be for using your key without permission." An unusually sly grin took over Monty's face.

Quincy couldn't hold back a laugh and nodded. Monty unbuttoned his jacket and pulled out the key from his pocket and placed it into the lock. She wondered what it felt like to take off the key. Her heart grew cold at the idea she may never find out. Hers, unlike Monty's key, could never leave her person while she still lived.

Monty had no difficulty opening the door and followed her down toward the Heart of the Timepiece. Once they were on the underground floor, Quincy ignited the glass ball in the center of the room and they stood around the sundial silently deciding where to go.

"We should probably go to a time we are both familiar with. Perhaps we should go to the same time as our last outing?" Monty suggested.

"Talin mentioned universal collapse if we were to accidentally cross ourselves. Or something along that line. Thankfully, the Timepiece will send us a few days before and after since I can't travel like Talin."

"So then let us use the identical date and allow the Timepiece to select for us?"

"Okay." She agreed and then turned the dial forward to go backward. After she had chosen the appropriate date, she pushed down.

"Do you want to go outside and watch? It's pretty magical…"

Quincy watched the blood drain from Monty's already pale face.

"I would rather not."

Quincy waited with Monty until they heard the Timepiece go silent for one moment and then begin to whir again. She felt vaguely nauseated until the ticking became normal again.

"I guess we're here?" Quincy hoped.

Monty nodded and slowly stood up.

"Are you alright?" she asked.

"I think so," he answered and slowly walked up the stairs. Quincy followed him outside to a cold and blustery day.

"We should have fetched our coats." Monty unnecessarily mumbled as Quincy shivered.

She pulled out the Corocularum from her pocket and left it on the palm of her hand. "Grab onto my shoulders. If it works and you're transported with me then we'll go together. If it doesn't work and you're still here, meet me in the Heart?"

Monty nodded his agreement. "Have you decided where to go?"

"Oxford. We were there the longest last time and I wouldn't mind seeing parliament again. It might help me for next week's exam."

Monty made a face. "Please do not remind me what I should be studying for."

Quincy rolled her eyes and grinned. "Like *you* need to do any more studying. Grab on."

Monty grasped her shoulders and tightly shut his eyes.

"Are you ready?" she asked.

"Do it," he ground out.

She opened the Corocularum and waited until the eye blinked and turned into a mirror. She looked deeply at her own reflection and remembered her first visit to Parliament until she felt the odd tingling sensation. Monty gasped.

Suddenly, the feeling ended and Quincy looked up. It hadn't taken her outside the Parliament building; it had transported them to the middle chamber. Without thinking, she grabbed Monty, who still grasped her shoulders tightly, and jumped into the large drapes hanging from one of the doors. She looked over at Monty whose eyes were wide from surprise. She wondered if hers mirrored the look on his face. She slipped the Corocularum into her pocket and waited. It felt hotter than the first time she had used it but cooler than the third time. She wondered if it had used twice the energy to transport both of them. Quincy hoped it would work a second time to take them back to the Timepiece and then home to their own time.

Monty gently shook her shoulder and with his head, directed her attention to the door next to them. She followed his face and saw the side of a man incoherently walking in. He stopped when he had reached the three magnificent chairs at the end of the room. One of the chairs was disturbingly empty.

Two of the Thirds stood up to face the man. Both wore the required black robes and white wigs. Quincy's eyes widened when she saw the Third on the left.

"It's Prieler," Quincy whispered urgently to Monty. He peered over and nodded.

Quincy saw two and wondered why the last Third wasn't in Parliament today. Shouldn't Eleanor Morrow be here?

The male visitor stood before the two Thirds with his hands clasped in front of him. His head and shoulders were sloped down as if carrying an invisible heavy weight. She caught a brief glance at the side of his face and saw dark circles under his eyes. His hands were inside his disheveled pinstripe suit and he had hurriedly put on the jacket because part of his white collar stood straight up. The shoelaces on his right shoe were undone and he landed on them every step he took. His pocket watch hung loosely from his belt and swung gently by his side. It looked like he had started to fix his hair but gave up halfway because part of his head had been combed flat while the other side stuck out in multiple directions. Quincy could not see the rest of his face but could feel the agony radiating from him. She wondered what caused him to appear like this. Prieler, the older and seemingly more senior of the two Thirds cleared his throat.

"Is it true?" Prieler asked in a formal Germen accent. The dejected man looked up to face his accusers and nodded. Quincy finally got a clear glance at his face. He wore a haunted expression and the room grew suddenly cold.

She knew him.

She knew his laughter, but there was no hint of amusement here. A younger version of the Oakley hermit hung his head again. What was Dwilight doing here? Quincy frowned. What could he have done for him to look like this?

"Dwilight Fairnight Grand Master Creative Engineer, do you have anything to add to the...incident," Prieler asked.

Dwilight's sallow eyes looked up at the speaker emotionless. He responded dully with a simple shake of his head.

Prieler looked saddened and turned his head to look at the other Third. "Tayo, do you agree?" Tayo slowly nodded in agreement. "Master Fairnight," Tayo said, "Officially, you have broken none of our laws. You were experimenting with unknown power and unfortunately it failed. You couldn't have known your invention would create the shadow monster that takes life. For this there are no words to best describe the pain we feel for you and the loss of your child."

After this pronouncement, Dwilight fell to his knees and sobbed on the floor. Quincy feared that rubbing her arms from goosebumps would disturb the curtain. *Shadow monster*. She shivered. The Noctem Umbrem had killed his child? No wonder he lived alone in the Oakley forest.

"We will not judge you for your failure." Tayo continued. "Your personal pain is consequence enough. We have unanimously decided to ban any use of nightmares for any experiment in any capacity. We require any and all information in regard to your experiments in this matter be turned over to us. From now on, any use of nightmares will be an offense with serious repercussions. Do you agree with our pronouncement?"

Dwilight gave a strangled "yes." After a moment's pause, he gained strength and stood up.

"With all due respect, since I'm here I'd like to take care of this now."

He pulled a piece of paper from his breast pocket and gave it to the scribe near him.

"This is notice of my resignation from my post as Grand Master Creative Engineer," the scribe read aloud.

The two Thirds and even the scribe looked flabbergasted.

Prieler broke the silence first. "We understand this is a time of emotional upheaval for you, but please. Please take time to think about this."

"I already have."

The two Thirds looked at each other and Prieler responded. "You are by far the best candidate for this position. There is no one worthy enough to take it."

"Give it to my brother. I know there's nothing he wants more."

Quincy jerked up in surprise. She recalled from Christmas, Dwilight mentioning a family member he didn't get along with. His brother? How could she know so little of her new friend? She wondered how much Talin knew.

The two looked at each other and at first said nothing. Finally, the older Third addressed Dwilight. "For now, we will give you a leave of absence and we will hold the position for you until you choose to take it back or until your time in this world is over."

"I'm flattered. Truly. But it's unnecessary. I'll never retake the position."

"We shall see. We wish you all the best, Grand Master Fairnight. We hope to see you soon."

Under his breath Quincy heard him say, "Oh, I seriously doubt it." He walked away and then stopped as if a thought had just come to him. "Pardon, but don't you need three votes to cement this request?"

"At this point in time, Ms. Morrow has also taken a short leave of absence and has relinquished her vote to be split amongst the two of us."

"So be it." He made a slight bow and walked towards the door. Quincy and Monty hid deeper into the curtains barely missing colliding with Dwilight.

Quincy's throat tightened as she looked back at his retreating figure. She felt guilty for eavesdropping on Dwilight's life. They continued to hide until everyone had left the chamber and the lights had been extinguished. Quincy and Monty stepped out from the drapes and used the Corocularum to come back to the Timepiece. Miraculously, it worked a second time but afterwards it burned. She quickly dropped it in her pocket and followed Monty into the Timepiece. He rubbed his head as if fighting a headache. After she re-entered her own time, her throat tightened from the intense sadness for her friend and knowledge she didn't want. Now she understood why Talin had warned her about traveling alone and potentially seeing something not meant for her. How was she supposed to act with him now that she knew his secret? He had created the Noctem Umbrem. How could he have created an invention so vile it had killed his own child?

"At least now you will be prepared for the section about Grand Master Creative Engineer Dwilight Fairnight? It is interesting that no one added that bit in our history book."

When Quincy didn't promptly respond, Monty frowned. "Is everything alright? Are you ill?"

Quincy numbly shook her head. "I'm okay," she mumbled. She couldn't explain how she felt because she didn't know herself. "Let's go back home."

Quincy pushed the gnomon back to their present day and hoped they had not lost too much time. After arriving, she sighed, relieved with the immediate knowledge they had only lost five minutes. It could have been much worse. Quincy's happiness was cut short by Monty's shallow gasps. She whirled around and saw Monty grasping the banister, trying to force himself up.

"I can't," he gasped. "I must get out of here. The walls are closing in," he sobbed. Quincy grasped his arms and helped him stumble up the stairs. She struggled up each excruciating step as he fought to stop shaking and she to not drop him. Once they had reached outside, Monty whimpered, "Oh, *ballsch*," and pulled them both to the ground shaking uncontrollably.

"Monty!" she yelled, but he didn't respond to her cry. She tried to move him to his side, but he unconsciously fought her. She couldn't help him during an epileptic seizure. Tears ran down her cheeks. In the distance, two people ran towards them. Nurses Watson and Dafoe had found them! Nurse Dafoe helped Monty onto his side while Nurse Watson grasped Quincy's shoulder. After what felt like hours, but in reality, seconds, Monty fainted. Dafoe grasped Monty in his muscular arms and walked inside. Nurse Watson gently patted Quincy's shoulder. "We'll watch over him, dearie."

Quincy watched them disappear and sat down against the backside of the clock and sobbed. Finally, when she thought she cried all her tears, she wiped her nose and sniffed. Once she had finished, she heard a polite cough near her. She looked up and saw Talin perched on the small fence surrounding the Timepiece. Seeing Talin made Quincy want to start crying all over again.

"You're lucky Marquam and I were waiting for you. Otherwise it would have taken much longer to get him medical attention."

"Do you think," she started. "Is he going to be okay?"

Talin slowly nodded. "This time."

She wiped her eyes on her sleeve and sniffed.

"Do you understand why I warned you about traveling? Especially without me?"

Quincy nodded.

"Time is delicate and the knowledge of it is sharper than the sharpest tool. It's a heavy burden to bear."

Quincy felt more tears run down her cheek.

"Ask your question, Quinn."

"I saw something I shouldn't have."

"Yes, you did, but what's your actual question?"

"How could Dwilight…? What happened?"

"It's not my story to tell and it's none of your business."

"What do I do now?"

Talin stood eerily calm as if he had been transformed into a statue. Quincy wished that he would shout at her or berate her or do something instead of talking to her in a calm and even voice.

"I can't answer that. Dwilight did nothing wrong. He made a mistake with unknown consequences. He pays for it every day and will continue to do so until he passes from this life. You can't judge him for his past actions."

Quincy nodded and looked at her toes. "What do you want to do with me?"

"I'm not your parent and I'm not your headmaster. I'm…not supposed to be doing this. Look, you made your choice. Like Dwilight you get to live with your choice and its consequences. I'm not going to punish you as an adult with a child. I'm not going to forbid you the Timepiece. I can't take your key away from you even if I wanted to. I will tell you this however. I warned you about time and traveling within it unattended. You were lucky this time. You and Monty. You do not play with time. One day you might open the door to the Timepiece and find yourself on the other side of it. What then?"

"Because I'm not a raven I could do damage?" Quincy responded sarcastically and immediately regretted her words.

215

Instead of lashing back or returning sarcasm with sarcasm, Talin simply sucked in air.

"I have better things to do than play games with a snotty sixteen-year-old. Please, by all means, be the end of your existence and time itself," Talin paused and stared icily at her. "Please. I beg you. Put me out of a job faster than my present course." And he flew off into the night leaving Quincy wanting to scream. She couldn't tell from the frustration, embarrassment, or the exhaustion from her constant state of confusion.

CHAPTER THIRTEEN

THOSE PESKY HUMAN EMOTIONS

Quincy woke up with swollen eyes and a clogged nose that stayed with her throughout the day. Monty hadn't been to any of his classes and she hadn't seen him at any of the meals. She took a sip of her soup and looked over at his spot. Its emptiness unnerved her. She reached into her pocket and looked at her exam one more time. She couldn't believe it. A perfect score. In Latin. She smiled and put it back in her pocket. She had to show Monty. As soon as they were released from dinner, she walked toward her room. To her relief, she saw Monty walking down the stairs. She ran towards him. "Hey, are you feeling better? Oh, and guess what?"

Monty turned towards Quincy clearly uninterested and annoyed. She stopped talking as she felt anger emanating from her best friend.

"What is it, Quincy?" Monty asked crisply. She noted his use of "Quincy."

"Oh, it's nothing important," she answered, surprised at his cold demeanor. "Is everything okay?"

Monty nodded and walked away. As soon as he had left, Eloise walked up and poked her in the calf with her umbrella.

"I don't think it's you. I don't know what his problem is, but I saw him right before dinner and he already seemed off. Maybe he's not feeling well?"

"Yeah, you're probably right," Quincy said while rubbing her sore calf. She sneezed and reached into her pocket to pull out a handkerchief. Instead, she grasped a pointy object and yelped. She put her finger in her mouth and sucked on the finger wound. The stupid thing hadn't been there at dinner.

"Are you okay, Quincy?"

Quincy stubbornly nodded.

"What happened?" Eloise asked.

"I poked myself," moaned Quincy.

"With what?"

Grudgingly, Quincy gingerly reached back into her pocket and pulled out her Christmas present from Dwilight. She swore to herself she had placed the nail in the box on her desk but it had somehow managed to find itself in her pocket. Eloise picked up the nail and her eyes opened up wide. Her mouth opened up in a large "O" and she cradled it in her hand as if it were a precious jewel.

"Quincy," Eloise said breathlessly. "Where did you get this?"

She hated to lie to Eloise, but she didn't want to ruin Dwilight's cover. "It was a gift. Apparently, it's a special nail?"

"Special? Yeah! Do you have any idea what this is? Who gave you this?"

"I got it from a friend I met through another friend, who has been helping with homework when I need help." Quincy grimaced. Thankfully Eloise had ignored her and pulled out a magnifying glass. "Brilliant! It's practically indestructible. No one can replicate these anymore."

"Do you want it, Eloise?" Quincy asked.

Eloise looked up at her in shock. "Quincy, you would give this to me?"

"What am I going to do with an indestructible nail?"

Eloise pursed her lips clearly tempted, but her face fell and she handed the nail back to her. "I appreciate you would give this to me, but I don't want to take your present away from you." Eloise looked longingly at the nail one last time and then smiled at Quincy. "Thanks anyway," she said as she walked outside. Quincy looked over to the library and wondered if she should go after Monty. She wanted to show him her paper and then go to the café to work on the clue. Quincy bit her lip and tried to make a decision. She knew she needed help. As soon as the thought came to her, she groaned. Gathering her books in her bag, she made her way to the East tower in search of Talin. He probably wouldn't even be there. She had no doubt he was still angry about yesterday.

She arrived in his easterly tower after ten minutes of debating whether she should turn back or not. Finally, she knocked quietly. After waiting for a response and not getting one, Quincy put her hand on the door handle and paused when Talin's cough interrupted her.

"Weren't you taught not to break and enter?"

"Hello, Talin," Quincy answered, abashed.

Talin mumbled a response and flew to her shoulder.

"I could use your help," she finally admitted.

"Why not ask the Irish kid for help?"

"He's mad at me, and I'm not sure why."

Talin sighed. "I know why."

Quincy looked at him with wide eyes.

"Part of this is my fault because I wasn't completely honest with you both." Talin cleared his throat. "When I told you not to travel without me, I did it to stop you from hurting yourselves. Time travel warps the human mind."

"Right, you already warned me. But I thought it was safe since I've traveled multiple times already."

"You're exempt."

"Me? Why?"

"How am I supposed to know? Your mind is wired for it. You know that thing where you always know what time and day it is?"

Quincy nodded.

"That allows your mind not to get confused when time-traveling. Your brain compensates for the change. A paltry .0001% of the entire population has this capability. Fewer even realize what it is. Aided by your perfect memory, you are the ideal candidate for time-traveling."

Quincy suddenly felt selfish. "Monty?"

Talin shook his head.

"Then why did you let him come with me for the first clue?" she asked, anger turning her face red.

"Hear me out first. You get three to five freebies before there is any permanent damage. I know you needed support, so I allowed Monty to come with you knowing he would have other chances to help in case of an emergency. I didn't think you two would go without me." Talin frowned.

"Then he can go a few more times?"

Talin shifted his weight from one talon to the other. "In theory, yes. But he had such a violent reaction last time that I wouldn't suggest it. It's as if he's already time-traveled."

Quincy frowned. "How's that possible?"

Talin shrugged. "I have a theory. I need to run it by a friend."

"Is that why Monty's mad at me? Because he time-traveled?"

"It's not so much mad at you than it is mad at himself."

"Himself? Why?"

"Because you listened to his idiotic idea. Suddenly things became real for him. It's no longer a story in one of his books."

Quincy's eyes widened. "So how does he know about this?"

"We had a conversation last night."

Quincy felt horrible she had unintentionally put Monty's life in danger.

Talin sighed. "Give him time. Now, let's see your letter."

Quincy opened the document which he quickly scanned. He groaned when he had finished. "This is why you people shouldn't be allowed to time-travel."

"Are we traveling by Timepiece?"

"So, it would seem," groaned Talin.

"Are we going now?" Quincy asked, the hope and excitement elevating her mood.

Talin mumbled unintelligibly to himself. "Unfortunately, not now. I have business elsewhere."

"You're leaving Oakley?" Quincy asked in disbelief.

"Contrary to your idea that I follow you around 365 days a year, I do have a life. A semblance of one, but one at least."

"When do you want to go?"

"I'll come and find you."

Quincy wondered how long she would have to wait.

"Oh, and Quinn, go see Dwilight."

Quincy grimaced and nodded.

***

She looked so ill. Her face so deathly pale. It made his heart ache. He switched to a moment where she looked at him and laughed. Her arm

222

linked with her best friend. Eerily, the other girl faced a similar problem herself. These fragile humans.

He hated this more than anything. Immortality; the greatest curse.

"Who's there?" she wheezed.

"It's me," he murmured.

She looked at him, relief flooding her features. She coughed again, leaving blood behind in the handkerchief.

"You're here."

He nodded and moved closer to her.

"I'm dying," she stated, not questioned. He nodded. No use lying to her. She already knew.

"Now?" she whispered, fear overtaking her features. He shook his head. "Soon, but not now."

She grasped his hand tightly. "Please don't let me die alone."

He closed his eyes, seeing the moment of her death. "I can promise you, Kate, you won't be alone."

She breathed a raspy breath out and nodded. "Thank you," before turning her attention to the wall next to her. He didn't have to ask who wailed on the other side.

"They've taken him from me," she whimpered. "Afraid he will get sick too. But I barely got to hold him."

"Your son is fine, Katelyn," he said softly. Her eyes watered and he gently brushed her tears away. "But I need your help for the older Montgomery. Because he's too close to Quincy, it's playing with my ability to see clearly. When was the last time you time traveled?"

"Me?" she asked. Confusion clearly written on her features. "Why me?"

"Please, Kate, answer my question."

She coughed again, and frowned. Trying to think. Recognition dawned on her features. "It's been about eight months since I've traveled." She struggled to sit up to face him. "Why are you asking me this. Is Montgomery alright."

"Yes, yes. He's fine," he lightly grasped her shoulders and helped her back down onto the pillows. "He had great difficulty time traveling and now I know why. He's already traveled a few times with you, hasn't he?"

Katelyn nodded. "Before I knew I was pregnant," her face fell. "I hadn't even thought about that."

"There's our answer then. On multiple accounts" he smiled. "And now we know." He stroked her hair.

"I'm sorry," she whimpered.

"Sorry? You have nothing to be sorry for."

Katelyn reached for her necklace and pulled on the ribbon holding the clover key to her neck. "Will you please make sure this gets safely to my son?" She turned to her side and looked over the mantelpiece where her polo stick hung over the fireplace. "That too?"

Talin nodded. "I have already done what you asked."

Katelyn smiled. "Good. Remember your promise to me."

He nodded and dissipated from the moment. Time for one more difficult conversation. Quincy and Montgomery would be the end of him.

***

"Hello, Talin. To what do I owe this pleasure?" Dwilight asked staring up at the open window in his lab.

"Believe me," Talin mumbled. "It's not a pleasurable visit."

"That bad?" Dwilight questioned, putting down his wrench and sitting at his work table.

"Tea?"

"No, thank you," Talin replied. He flew in and landed on the work table. "You have a smudge of soot on your cheek, again," teased Talin."

Dwilight grinned and shrugged. "Nothing unusual. What's your unpleasurable news?"

"I have to warn you about Quincy's time-traveling. She happened to visit the day you attempted to give your resignation."

Dwilight's face dropped. "Oh. That's…unfortunate."

"Yeah, 'oh.'"

Dwilight sighed and opened a drawer from his workbench. He pulled a bottle of scotch. "I'm going to need something stronger than tea."

"Figured you would. I'll take a sip as well."

"Well, the proverbial cat is out of the proverbial bag."

225

"She's going to want to question you. Or be embarrassed about it."

"A curious mind like hers should question. I appreciate you warning me."

"That's not all of my bad news."

"There's more?" Dwilight sighed.

"Yes. I've tried to keep you out of this as best as I could, but I can't any longer. Your brother is using your key."

Dwilight swore. "You warned me he would. I didn't think he would attempt anything. What does he want?"

"To change the past."

Dwilight rubbed his forehead.

"What do you want me to do?"

"The key is yours, legally. You must try to get it back."

"And if he doesn't want to give it up?"

"We have to try." Talin replied.

"Am I going to have any luck with this?" Dwilight asked.

Talin shook his head. "At this point it could go either way. But I sincerely doubt it."

"You offer him too many chances," said Dwilight, bitterly.

"And I don't for you?" Talin said, the feathers over his eyes raised.

"Fine, I'll set up a meeting."

CHAPTER FOURTEEN

THE FAIRNIGHT KEY

Quincy yawned from another horrible night of sleep. In last night's nightmare, she saw Dwilight, but when she ran up to him, it wasn't him. When she tried to run away from him, he restrained her until the Noctem Umbrem came for her. She shivered again. Quincy grabbed her coat and walked out into the family room. She waited for a moment, hoping Monty would know she wanted to talk to him. After five minutes, she shook her head and walked outside to the stables. She rubbed her swollen eyes and gave Consto a death glare. The horse stopped mid-bite and allowed her to place the saddle over his back. They slowly plodded towards Dwilight's tree house while Quincy occasionally reached out to grab at petals on the trees. When she arrived, she sucked in her breath and knocked. Dwilight's head poked out of one of the windows above.

"Come in!" he hollered cheerfully at her.

Quincy walked in and took a seat in her customary spot in his living room. He offered her a cinnamon cookie.

"How did the Latin exam go?"

"Much better." Quincy handed him the 100% paper and he beamed.

"Excellent. In honor of your exceptional paper, I think we should go for a walk."

Quincy hesitated but followed her tutor down the stairs. Dwilight closed his eyes and took a deep whiff of air.

"I smell spring."

Quincy nodded.

The two walked down one of his small footpaths towards the river that fed the waterfall over Oakley. Occasionally, each would pick a flower or leaf and add it to a bouquet in Dwilight's hand.

"I know you want to talk to me. Do you want to do it now?" Dwilight gently prodded.

She sucked in a breath of air before answering. "Have you ever made a mistake?"

Dwilight burst into laughter. "Practically every day."

"A serious mistake."

Dwilight grew somber. "I have. What is it you want to know?"

"How do you deal with it?"

Dwilight sighed and cupped his hand in the river and watched it slowly drip out.

"I'm the wrong person to ask I'm afraid. I disappeared into a forest and now live alone in a tree. Well, mostly alone," Dwilight said with a sad smile in Quincy's direction. "My best advice would be not to run from it. Problems and mistakes don't disappear. They remain, often as shadows in your heart."

Quincy shivered as Dwilight mentioned shadows.

"Do you want to talk about it?" he asked.

Quincy shook her head. "I wish I had listened."

Dwilight nodded. "Is there anything I can do to help?"

"Can you create a device to make me un-see something?"

"I'm very good. But not that good."

"I'm sorry," Quincy whispered.

"Why? Because you let curiosity get the better of you? Are you sure you have no interest in Creative Engineering?" Dwilight grinned at her. "I can't fault you for that."

Quincy looked up quickly. "What do you know?"

Dwilight sighed and started to walk again. "Everything. What Talin didn't say, I managed to fill in the blanks. I am usually fairly intelligent," Dwilight said ruefully.

"What do you mean?"

"Let's start from the middle. My favorite part of a story. Each Creative Engineer has interests or obsessions that ask questions seeking answers we must find out. For some it's illusions, for others it's movement. Time never called to me in that regard."

"What's yours?"

"Power."

Quincy found it difficult to imagine Dwilight wanting power over others. Dwilight caught her frown and waved his hands.

"Not that kind of power. Actual power. Like the heat from the fire. A sort of energy. I wanted to invent a force that could be a source of power. I apologize if this sounds convoluted. It's difficult to understand and to clarify. Even to a room filled with Creative Engineers."

Quincy laughed. "Sounds like it."

"Anyway, back to my story. My adopted uncle used to tell hair-raising tales of time travel and its many gifts and dangers. You see, he was trying to train my brother and I about something important, but I had no interest. My brother, however, became obsessed with it. He believed he could use it for his purposes. The *dunderheid*, you can't tame time." Dwilight scoffed. "It's a pity I couldn't have been bothered. For character reasons, my uncle decided I would be the better fit for his gift."

"Gift?"

Dwilight pointed to Quincy's chest. She instinctively put her hand protectively over the key.

"Exactly," he replied.

"You have one?" she gasped.

Dwilight grimaced. "Sort of. Even though he meant it for me, my brother has taken ownership of it. It should have been yours when you were ready for it."

Quincy's eyes widened. Dwilight had a minor key! Now three of the five keys were accounted for. She noted Dwilight's use of "should" and "when you were ready." What was his brother doing with it?

"We should talk about what happened yesterday," Dwilight prodded again.

Quincy gulped. "Stupid bird," she growled.

"Try not to be annoyed with Talin. He had every right to prepare me."

"Prepare you?"

"You saw the consequences from my greatest mistake. Not quite the visual I would like you to have of me. It's important you know the whole story so you can understand why I did what I did." Dwilight sat down on dry bit of ground underneath a tree and beckoned Quincy to join him. "In my quest for harnessing power, I tried to hold on to the powers I knew. For example, fire is too hot to contain long term and has to burn *something*, solar is inconstant, wind too fickle, etcetera. My brilliant idea harnessed the power of dreams. However, I found its power too potent to contain in any device, so I went to what I thought could be the next best thing."

Dwilight put his hand over his mouth and breathed in deeply.

"I used my device to harness the power from nightmares and used it on myself. For a moment, I thought it worked. The power created a source that took shape in front of my eyes. Then it turned and looked at me. It was me, but the darkest part of me. Our nightmares are often coated with what we fear the most in all the world. After losing my mother the way I did, I feared I couldn't protect my family. It personified my fright and the shadow drifted off to the nursery before I could attempt to banish it."

"The Noctem Umbrem," she whispered.

"Just so. I had created my goal. I had created my power source, but it did the opposite of my desire. Instead of creating power to aid humanity, I created a monster and it formed energy by taking it."

Quincy shivered. She didn't want to hear this, but she knew she needed to.

"It gained power from what we fear the most, the stuff of nightmares," continued Dwilight. "To defy me, my creation took my greatest fear and used it against me. I came at it with fire, but it no longer mattered. My two-year old had no defenses for the nightmare and it snuffed out her very life. And just like that, she was gone."

Quincy wished she could say something to comfort Dwilight, but she knew there weren't words for this. She offered his handkerchief and he smiled at her.

"So, you left and came here?" Quincy slowly asked.

"And that's where you find me here today."

"I'm sorry I saw—what I saw."

"I appreciate your apology. It is unnecessary, however. As you now know, we are all guilty of making mistakes. I hope, in the future, you will be more careful about where you go. Or the past?"

Dwilight smiled at his pun. Rules are to protect you. Especially Talin's. He doesn't always do an excellent job of explaining them."

Quincy groaned. "You're telling me."

"Let's drop this subject now, hmm?"

Quincy nodded. "Thank you."

"Let's go back for some tea, shall we?"

When they walked back to his tree house, he gestured to a chair and disappeared into his kitchen. She looked over at his side table and peeked at some of the various blueprints, linen napkins with notes, and maps. She paused when she looked at a map. There were numbers on the edges. Dwilight came in and swept the papers to the side to place the teapot on the table. She grasped the map and gave it to Dwilight. "What does this mean?"

"It's Britain."

"Yes, but the numbers."

"Longitude and latitude?"

"Exactly! Do you know where this is?" she asked as she wrote down the numbers from the second clue.

"51.5194° N, 0.1270° W," he pondered aloud. He walked over to a bookshelf and pulled out a large atlas and his spectacles from his pocket. Quincy looked over his shoulder as he flipped through the pages before stopping in England. He pointed to a large dot. London.

"This is where your coordinates lead."

Quincy stared at the map. How was she supposed to find a circle of stars in a huge city like London?

***

Wilbright stared at his pocket watch. Late again. No respect for anyone else's time. But he had always been that way. His head elsewhere. He sighed and took a sip of tea as he took on his surroundings. Their mother had loved this teashop. Hidden away in a corner of a busy shopping center, they could drink their tea in peace. She had made an effort to do the yearly Oakley shopping with them, even at the end when ill. This had been their treat after shopping. They'd split a pot of tea and dipped the white powdered cookies she and his brother had loved so much.

His twin brother sat down in front of him and he noted his uncomfortable shivering.

"That's what happens when you cut yourself off from society," Wilbright spat. "You can no longer live in it."

"I'm surprised you realize that, given the tiny fact you have always separated yourself from the general population. Too good for everyone else, Wil?" Dwilight rebutted.

This was going well.

"You requested this little *rendez-vous*, what is it you want?" Wilbright asked. "Last time we spoke, you informed me we would never meet again."

"I had never intended to do so," Dwilight admitted. "But Talin requested it."

"Talin," Wilbright spat. "What does he want, now."

"My key," Dwilight replied, his face infuriatingly even.

"*Your* key." Wilbright coldly laughed. "You left *your* key in the family vault. You said you wanted nothing inside of it. So, it's *my* key now."

Dwilight stared at him angrily. "I've heard what you've been doing with *my* key. I can't condone your actions. You could have killed someone."

"You've been gone for too long, go back to your treehouse and your blissful solitude. Where you can relive your mistake over and over again."

Dwilight shook his head. "I'm not living in the past; I'm hiding from it. At least I'm not living in a state of denial as if it never happened."

Wilbright hissed at his brother. "I'll never understand what people see in you."

Dwilight shook his head. "This is why people like me better than you."

"Are you finished insulting me?"

"Are you ready to give me back *my* key?"

"Never."

Dwilight stood up. "Fine. If things go badly, you'll have yourself to blame."

"Enjoy going back to your silent graveyard, little brother," sneered Wilbright.

"Little by seven minutes hardly counts. Enjoy going back to your empty estate." Dwilight jabbed back and left the teahouse.

Wilbright growled and finished his tea. This would be a problem if Talin managed to pull Dwilight back on the chessboard. A problem he hadn't foreseen. Wilbright didn't have a line on his precious board for this. He rubbed his forehead and the headache attached. It couldn't be helped any longer. Time to speak to Prieler.

***

Prieler stood at the window digesting the information. Wilbright's news should be bothering him more, but at this moment, he didn't care. He stared at his meal: an apple, a hunk of bread, and a steaming piece of meat completely disinterested.

"Eat it," Iblis demanded. "You need it to stay alive."

"I don't feel hunger," Prieler answered. "Or much of anything."

Iblis' eyes narrowed. "You must eat. I need you alert. What we're doing is of utmost importance."

"Is it?" Prieler mused. "I can't remember why anymore."

Iblis ground his teeth, frustration causing sparks to emanate from his body.

"After this, you're going to have to take a break from the Noctem Umbrem."

"After this?"

Iblis nodded. "Send Wilbright to follow the girl. Have him take a case of the Nocti."

Prieler took a bite of the apple. It tasted like nothing in his mouth. He forced himself to chew and swallow. "Fine. But what about the other twin?"

Iblis snapped his fingers, watching the sparks flicker from them. "I'll take care of it. Give Wilbright the Nocti and send him after her."

CHAPTER FIFTEEN

ALTERNATIVE LONDON

Quincy ate her oatmeal while pretending to listen to Eloise chattering on about a new umbrella she was designing. Occasionally, Quincy would nod and smile. She looked over and tensed up when Colin sat next to her. Since Monty had not sat with them over the last five days, Colin had appropriated it. Especially now that Genevieve sat on the opposite end of the table. If she wasn't so anxious about Monty, she would have thought more about why Genevieve wasn't around, but honestly, she didn't care right now. That realization should have surprised her and she should be happy Colin chose to sit closer to her.

"So, are you going to do it?" Colin asked.

Quincy shook the cobwebs from her mind. "I'm sorry, what?"

"Pooooolooooooo," moaned Rusty, elongating his face his hands so the sound came out strangely.

"Tryouts are this afternoon," Colin answered stuffing an apple in Rusty's contorted features. "Did you still want to do Polo?"

Quincy crossed her arms on the table and dropped her head down to place her chin on her arms. She had completely forgotten about Polo, the tryouts, the upcoming signups for the Equospatium, and everything that didn't have anything to do with keys, schoolwork, and her frosty friend.

"I take it you're trying out," she teased Colin. "How about you, Rusty?"

Rusty shook his head. "Unless I can duplicate myself. I'll already be in the band stands," he shrugged.

"Why can't non-band students sit in the band stand?" Eloise pouted.

"Because you're not in the band?" Rusty replied, shrugging.

"That's okay, Eloise." Quincy smiled, stealing one of her grapes. "If I don't make it, you can sit with me."

"So, you're going to try-out?" Colin beamed.

Quincy chewed thoughtfully. "I don't know how well I'd do with Consto."

"Have you thought about trading horses?" Colin asked trying to be helpful. But Quincy's frown forced him to laugh awkwardly. "Or not."

"I like my horse," she retorted. "Even if he's impossible to ride." Quincy laughed and Eloise not needing any encouragement, also burst into giggles.

"At least he's pretty to look at." Eloise added.

"True," Quincy agreed. "Which is absolutely important." She rolled her eyes and laughed again. Her mood sobered when she noted Monty walking in the room. He grabbed a sandwich to go and quickly left again. This had happened for over a week, and she was over it.

"Okay, does anyone know what's going on with Monty?" Quincy asked.

Everyone shrugged or looked suddenly busy stirring oatmeal and hot chocolate.

"Honestly," Rusty finally said, "We haven't seen much of him in the dorm. Rumor has it he's been in and out of the Infirmary when he's not in the library."

Quincy's heart plummeted. He was still sick.

"Okay, well thanks for the info. Please let me know if you hear anything else?" she asked.

"Of course," Rusty replied. "But if you don't know anything, I doubt anyone else would."

Quincy noted a sour expression from Colin, but his face quickly evened.

"See you later." She waved.

"See you at tryouts," Colin yelled after her.

Quincy walked outside, hoping to clear her head. As her frustration wore off, she shivered in the crisp morning air. Her shoulder involuntarily tensed as Talin landed.

"Cold?" Talin inquired.

Quincy nodded. "Hello, Talin."

"You look unhappy."

"Monty is still mad at me."

Talin nodded. "Give him time."

"I've done that."

"Give him *more* time."

Quincy narrowed her eyes. "Fine."

"I have something to cheer you up. Are you ready to go?"

"Where?"

Talin rolled his eyes. "For the second clue."

"Now?"

"No time like the present," yawned Talin.

Quincy nodded eagerly and walked inside and down into the Timepiece. Now familiar enough with the room, she no longer paused walking down the stairs. She stood in front of the sundial waiting for further instructions. When he didn't give her any, she put her hands on the dial. "But, Talin, how can we travel if it says not to twist the dial?"

"It doesn't want you to travel forward or backward."

"Well then, what does it want me to do?"

The raven sighed and flew to the top of the dial.

"Push the dial underneath to release."

Once Quincy had done so, he continued. "Now take hold of the tip where I'm currently perched and push until I say stop."

Talin flew to the lit candelabrum, and carefully perched from one of the leaves. Quincy touched the top of the dial and felt it give way. She pushed and it creaked, rusty from being unused. Slowly, the entire dial flipped and it revealed an identical dial underneath it.

"Keep going until the other dial clicks."

Quincy followed his instructions until she heard the click of the second dial connecting.

"Good. Now it's ready. Push."

"Wait. The coordinates point us to London. Will the Corocularum work wherever we're going?"

Talin shook his head. "No, it won't work there. But you don't have to worry about getting to London," he winked. "Let's go."

She pushed the dial down and the entire clock groaned its objection. "What did I do?" Quincy asked, panicking.

"You followed the instructions."

"Where is it taking us?" She yelped.

Quincy felt her heart leap into her throat and for a brief moment had the sensation of floating. She felt herself take a head dive as if following the same motion of the dial. Finally, her rotation stopped and she landed on her chest, flat on the floor. She slowly stood up and rubbed her sore arms.

She froze when she looked up. This wasn't the heart of the Timepiece. Instead, she found herself in a glass box inside four clock faces. Clocks with hands.

"Talin, where are we?"

She whirled around, but the raven had disappeared.

"Talin," Quincy called out in panic.

A hand reached for her shoulder and Quincy squeaked and jumped from the surprise. She whirled around and faced a man.

"You!" Quincy pointed at him.

She immediately recognized him. His black hair and dark eyes stared directly back at her. He wore black slacks and a matching dress shirt with a feather sticking out from his hat. He had been the man in parliament. And the man who had followed her in London the previous year. How could he have not aged a day in thirty years?

"Save it. We have to get out of here now," he hissed.

"Wait, what?"

The man grabbed her elbow and dragged her out of the room, ignoring her protests. Quincy tried to pull back, but the man in black deflected her easily.

"Where are you taking me?" Quincy asked breathlessly as they ran down flights of stairs.

"Trust me, this can wait."

The man swore suddenly and grabbed Quincy, pulling her to his chest. He jammed his hands over her ears, and before Quincy could push him back, she heard clanging above her. The clock rang out the time and she felt her heart stop as it reverberated in her chest. It kept clanging the hour and she fought the desire to faint into his arms. After an eternity, the bell went silent, leaving only the echoes. She strangled a sob as she dug her face into his chest. In her ear she heard a soothing sound from the man above, bringing her out of her reverie.

"Who are you?" Quincy whispered.

The man in black sighed as he looked down at her. "I have many names. You've heard a number of them. Which one do you prefer?"

Quincy gasped as she realized she recognized his voice. She leaned in to him. "Talin," she dropped her head on his shoulder. Suddenly all the emotion from the past week came back and she sobbed into the velvet jacket. Talin let her cry for a minute before gently disentangling her.

"But you're human?" she demanded.

He grasped her shoulders and shook his head. "Yes, and no. You are well aware I have Talents like you. Nod if you understand me"

She nodded.

"Good. We need to move right now, Quinn. The bell rings at every quarter of an hour."

She nodded and followed Talin down the rest of the stairs. Once they were on the ground floor, Quincy let out a sigh of relief. Even Talin regained life in his pale cheeks.

As she caught her breath, she looked over at the raven, now a man. His dark eyes were the same, but little else reminded her of the raven. How could he be both a man and a bird? She narrowed her eyes at him. He had been the man in Oxford. From the past. And the man on the eagle. Talin looked over her as if reading her mind.

"It's a long story," he told her with a strain in his voice. "I don't have time to explain this to you. Remember your regret seeing Dwilight's story?"

Quincy nodded slowly.

"This is the same case. This is not your story. Not yet."

Now that Quincy had taken a moment to breathe, she overheard a peculiar roar from the nearby street. She looked up and saw odd light that didn't flicker.

"Where are we?"

"We're in London."

Quincy shook her head furiously. "Impossible. I've been to London. I don't remember the odd roaring sound or this clock."

Human Talin rolled his eyes at her. "You've been to London what, twice? Besides, I said London, not *your* London."

"Well then, whose London is it?"

Someone politely coughed behind them and they turned to see a man in a three-piece grey suit pointedly staring at them.

"Forgive me for interrupting, Sir Tempus. You weren't expected today."

"Wasn't I? Are we not meeting today?" Talin asked.

"The house isn't meeting until next week."

"Oh, right," Talin said, smiling nonchalantly.

The other man peered at Quincy with confusion written on his face. Talin saw him observing her. "This is my niece," he added.

The man grasped Quincy's hand; his eyes wide.

"It's such a pleasure to meet the family of Sir Caleb Tempus." He took another long look at Quincy before turning back to Talin. "I hadn't realized you had any."

Talin pursed his lips. "We have business in the city today and I wish to show my niece around."

"Oh, of course." The man bowed and disappeared.

Quincy followed Talin inside. "What's the name of this building?" she asked.

"We're in the houses of parliament. It's the government building for this version of London. Don't worry too much if you're confused by what you see. This parliament is completely different from the one you were recently tested on in class. Stay close to me and don't stop moving."

Quincy followed Talin outside and took a step into the street and froze. A horseless carriage drove straight towards her. A piercing cry came from the carriage and then it attempted to screech to a stop. It saw her too late and it couldn't stop before it hit her. Right before the bizarre carriage ran her over, strong arms grasped her around the shoulders and pulled her away.

"I told you to watch your step," he hissed in her ear.

Quincy had no doubt this was Talin. She watched the back of the now retreating metal box. "Where's the horse?" she gasped as the black machine crossed into another street.

"It doesn't need a horse to move. Remember the lift at school for the Infirmary? It's similar."

"You mean there's a person hiding in the front moving it?"

"I said similar," Talin sighed. "The driver is pushing pedals which starts and stops the vehicle."

Quincy looked at another moving blue box-like object. "Is it magic?" she blushed and closed her mouth after registering her comment.

Talin rolled his eyes. "No such thing. Remember?" He paused before continuing to berate her. Instead he slowly smiled. His smile looked rusty to Quincy, as if he didn't do it often. "You could call this engineering, magic. These people certainly thought so when these automobiles graced the streets for the first time."

"Automobiles? Are those the horseless carriages?"

"That term is a bit old fashioned. People here call them cars. Want to take one?"

Quincy shook her head furiously. "No thank you."

Talin smirked. "Fair enough. Let's go. Seriously, stay close to me."

She nodded and stayed in Talin's shadow.

The two walked down the streets and Quincy stared in awe at the changes between her London and this one. This city had metal monsters that looked like someone had taken two of the metal carriages and stacked them on top of each other. Red boxes lined the streets and people talked to themselves with odd tiny boxes. Talin explained people spoke into the small books they held to their ears and talked to someone else who also had one. So, they were not mumbling to themselves. She eavesdropped on some of the conversations and giggled.

"Josie's picking up the kids from school—For dinner—Sure, let's heat them."

A shrill whistle made Quincy cringe and walk even closer to Talin. She hated the screeching of the horseless carriages.

Quincy gaped at the fashions. People dressed in pants purposely cut and falling apart and wore tights underneath them. Others wore colors that gave her a headache. Some people wore odd things on their heads and handbags of all shapes and colors. Talin motioned toward a passageway leading underground.

"Eagles?" she asked.

Talin shook his head. "They don't have those here. Well they do, but they're not the same size you're used to. We're taking an underground train."

She smiled, relieved that she didn't have to get on a "car." After changing what Talin called "lines" once, they walked up the stairs and into the London evening. "Where are we, exactly?"

"You'll see," Talin replied as he gestured down the street. Quincy shivered and pulled her coat tighter as they walked into the night. She followed Talin, marveling at his long strides, and quickly became winded trying to keep up. Talin paused, allowing her to catch her breath before pointing to a large building. "There's where your coordinates lead."

"The British Museum." Quincy read the large red sign. She watched families and other visitors leave the building. "Are we too late?"

Talin snorted. It sounded strange coming from a nose instead of a beak. "I'm never late."

They walked closer to the building and waited until the day staff left. Finally, Talin waved her over to a side door and gestured to the lock. "After you," he grinned.

Quincy wondered if her key would work in this universe, and nervously giggled when the lock released. "What would you do without me?" she grinned.

"Fly in."

"You can be a raven here too?" She asked.

"All the rules apply across timelines. For me, anyway."

"How many timelines are there?"

Talin placed a finger to his mouth to silence her and gestured for her to follow. They walked past rooms and different exhibits.

"Do you know where you're going?" she whispered.

He nodded and walked through a staff door.

An older man looked up and Quincy paused mid-step. The man saw Talin and grinned. "Caleb Tempus, as I live and breathe." He stood up and shook hands with Talin. "One day you must tell me the secret to your eternal youth."

Talin, or Caleb to the man, chuckled. "I could tell you, but you wouldn't like the answer."

The older man shook his head, smiling. He turned his gaze to Quincy.

Talin cleared his throat. "Forgive me, Owen. This is my niece, Quinn. Quinn, this is Owen Masters, one of the curators here."

Quincy and the curator exchanged handshakes.

"Not that I don't enjoy our impromptu meetings after hours, but what can I do for you, Sir Caleb." Masters asked.

"We're on a scavenger hunt and we were given the coordinates here."

Master's eyes widened. "Curious. It's a bit of a needle in a haystack situation. This is a fairly large museum," he laughed.

"Tell him the line," Talin requested.

"51.5194° N, 0.1270° W, which is where you will go, to find a circle of stars to see how they glow." Quincy answered from memory.

"A circle of stars." Masters mumbled. "A circle or a globe?"

Quincy's eyes widened. Of course. A celestial globe. Her father's specialty was the celestial heavens and he had always kept one in his office.

"Do you have any currently on display?" Talin asked.

Masters rubbed his chin. "We do, actually. It's currently displayed in our Babylon exhibit."

Talin's eyes widened. "Oh, indeed? Would you mind showing us?"

Masters shook his head. "Not at all."

Quincy followed the two men out of the room and around the museum. She let them catch up as she silently walked behind them. Quincy tried to look at the passing history from this timeline, but they walked too quickly for her to learn anything. Quincy shivered, and rubbed her arms. For some reason she had goose bumps up and down them.

Finally, they stopped in a room with more artifacts and in front of a metallic globe.

"Hopefully, we found it," Quincy said, taking a closer look at the globe. "Now what?"

"Excellent question," Talin groaned.

Quincy looked over the strange and illegible writing engraved on the base and hands of the globe. "What language is this?"

"It's Arabic," Talin answered.

"I see your linguistic skills are still intact." Masters laughed.

"Just like my good looks," Talin teased.

Quincy took a closer look at the inscriptions, delighted that some of them looked recognizable. Her father would have known all of their names. The thought of him made her heart tighten and she breathed deeply, focusing in on one of the pictures. "Which constellation is this?" She asked.

"*MUL.UGA.MUSHEN.*" Masters replied. Talin coughed and turned his head away from them. "Today we call it *Corvus*."

"The crow?" Quincy asked.

"I'm glad to see Latin is still being taught. But in Babylon it meant *raven*."

Quincy turned to Talin's back. "The raven, huh?"

"Yes, indeed. The raven was an important creature in ancient Babylon. Adad, the Babylonian deity of the rain, favored the constellation." Masters said. His pocket chimed and he pulled out a small device and excused himself. Talin sighed, clearly relieved.

Quincy watched him leave. "He trusts you."

"Hmm." Talin mumbled, not listening. "The rhyming loon. I'm finished with this game." Talin sighed and closed his eyes, becoming eerily still.

"What are you doing?" she whispered as she walked up next to him.

"Cheating," he replied. After another moment, his eyes flashed opened and he whirled around to face her. "Did you see every piece of this?"

Quincy nodded.

"Are you sure."

"Ye-es. Why?" Quincy shivered again; this time, she felt the hairs on her neck rise. She tried to turn around but Talin grabbed her shoulders. "Don't look behind you."

She didn't need to. The overwhelming stench of bleach told her what she wanted to know. She shook in his grasp. The Noctem Umbrem. "How is that here?" she whispered.

"Someone brought it with them," Talin hissed. She looked up in his eyes and shook from fear, more afraid of Talin than the silhouette creature behind her. Talin's eyes were no longer dark. They had turned a dark blue like a terrible storm brewed within. She felt the air inside change and she involuntarily whimpered. Talin's eyes instantaneously turned back when he saw the terror on Quincy's face. He pulled her around so his back faced the horror but he stood in front of it, bodily protecting her. His face softened and he spoke to her in a warm tone. "It's going to be alright."

"Oh, uncle. You're such an excellent liar," a cold Scottish accent interrupted. Quincy looked next to her and saw a tall man with a pointed nose and mostly silver hair walk toward them. He smoothed his tweed vest and stared directly at her. She sucked in her breath. She faced the exact copy of Dwilight Fairnight save the hair. She drew closer to Talin.

"Finally, Quincy Harris in the flesh," the Scottish man said. "I was beginning to wonder if you truly existed."

"Here I am," she whispered. "Who are you and what do you want?" she jabbed, hoping she sounded braver than she felt. She felt Talin grasp her shoulders tightly.

"Me?" he replied. "You don't know me? I have to admit I'm disappointed."

"Quincy," Talin interrupted. "Meet Wilbright Fairnight. Yes, he does look quite a bit like his twin brother, does he not?"

Twin brother. Quincy took another look at Wilbright and noticed some tiny differences between the two of them and relaxed. Not her Dwilight.

Wilbright growled, clearly offended by the comparison. Quincy had heard the name before. She quickly thought back until the name popped up. Blood pumped through her ears and her hands shook from the uncontrollable anger. She stood before the monster who killed her father and her baby sister. Before she could plan a way to punch him in the face, Talin grasped her even tighter. He slowly shook his head.

"You haven't answered her second question," Talin jeered. Quincy wondered why Talin purposely angered the dangerous man.

The Noctem Umbrem slid toward Wilbright and she quickly got her answer. Talin purposely drew the silhouette, and its danger, away from her.

Wilbright stopped when he saw it and he gasped. "But how?"

"You didn't bring it?" Talin said, completely emotionless.

Wilbright shook his head. "Why would I ever want *that* one." Quincy wished she knew what he meant. She stared at Talin who slowly shook his head. She felt Talin's shoulders tense over her arms. Quincy peeked around and saw the Noctem Umbrem seemingly staring at her. It shimmered and it took a different shape. Suddenly her mother appeared in front of her. She looked scared as she reached out toward Quincy, her eyes pleading.

Talin reached into his pocket and threw a pocket watch at her mother. She gasped in horror as the watch came into contact with the woman, turning it back into a shadow. It stayed in the corner of the room seemingly unsure what to do next.

"Wil, tell me now, and tell me truly, are you playing with nightmares?" Talin growled. Wilbright paused and slowly shook his head. "*I* am not."

Talin breathed out a sigh of relief. "There are few things more evil than that technology. The things it will do to you are unspeakable. The creation of those requires your very essence. The more one makes, the more they begin to lose. You pay a high price for the power in those."

Quincy's eyes widened as Wilbright's gaze momentarily softened. He nodded once. "I understand."

"Good lad," Talin answered back in a strangely kind voice. Quincy bit her lip until she tasted blood. Why be nice to the man who had ruined her family?

Wilbright grasped the edges of his tweed jacket tightly against his chest and he looked behind him. "I'm sorry," he said.

"For what?" Talin asked. Talin's question was soon answered. Five more silhouettes sauntered into the room, answering Talin's question. The Noctem Umbrem slid towards them.

Talin swore. "Wilbright, what have you done?"

"You could have made this so much easier, uncle. Instead you forced me to travel. Forced me to follow you here."

"You don't think I can't take all of you?" Talin sneered.

"True. But at what cost?" Wilbright turned his gaze at Quincy. "She has to be alive, true. Alive being such a loose term."

Talin howled angrily. He looked at Quincy, his eyes dark blue again. "Quinn, I want you to run."

She looked at Wilbright and the approaching creatures. She shook her head. "I'm not going to leave you."

He grasped the sides of her head. "Love, I need you to run. I will find you. Now go."

The term *love* rang in her head and she took off in a sprint away from them. She dodged the exhibits looking for a way out. A flash of dark red from a reflective surface forced her to pause momentarily. An unearthly scream brought her back to reality and she ran even faster until finally she saw an exit sign. She pushed the door open and a roaring siren screamed and echoed around her. She ran outside and into the cold London night. The strange lights and moving vehicles cast eerie shadows on the street. She had no idea where she was going, but knew she couldn't stop. A loose piece of sidewalk tripped her, forcing her on the ground. Her lungs screamed from the adrenaline. She painfully pushed herself against a storefront and looked behind her. No one had followed her.

An older couple wearing a suit and a nice dress stood in front of her. "Everything alright, dearie? Are you all alone?" the woman asked. Quincy paused. Not sure what to say. "No, she's not. She's with me," another voice said. She looked up and saw a man staring down at her. After a moment of using her memory with a random list of faces, she recalled his name. "Mr. Bauer." she said with relief. The owner of the London bookshop from her timeline. How could he be *here*? He smiled and helped her to her feet.

She nodded. "How are you here?" she asked, turning to Mr. Bauer. He grinned and pointed to a cup in his hands. "I'm here for coffee." He helped her walk to the alley behind the store and pushed open a seedy-looking door next to the coffee shop.

"Uh, where are we going?"

"Back to our own timeline," he answered as he pushed open the door. "I like the coffee here much better." She followed him inside and nearly cried from relief when she recognized Mr. Bauer's Bookshop in her own timeline. He helped her to the front of the store and made her a cup of tea. She sipped on the hot beverage, embarrassed by her shaking hands. "Want to talk about it?" he asked. She quickly shook her head.

"It's alright. You're back now. Does my sister know what's going on?"

Quincy shook her head again. "Can she please not find out?" She hated to think of what Mrs. Adalin would have to say if she had heard about her traveling.

Mr. Bauer slowly nodded. "It's your business. Do you know how to get back to school?"

Quincy reached into her pocket to make sure the Corocularum hadn't fallen out in the kerfuffle. Her shoulders slumped with relief when she felt the cold metal device. "Yes, I have a ride home."

Mr. Bauer nodded. "Good. Take your time and finish your tea." He stood up and pretended to be busy on the other side of the room. After she had finished, she limped to him and gave him back the teacup.

"Thank you for rescuing me."

Mr. Bauer smiled. "It's not every day I get to play a knight in shining armor."

Quincy smiled and turned to him.

"Those people. They're…they're real people, aren't they?" She felt silly saying it out-loud. Of course, they were. They had lives, and feelings, and desires. Just like her.

Mr. Bauer nodded. "Exactly like us."

Her shoulders sagged. She felt utterly spent. She took one more look at the back of the store. She hoped Talin could take care of himself.

CHAPTER SIXTEEN

MEANWHILE, BACK IN LONDON...

Talin watched as five more of the monsters slinked in behind Wil. Quinn shook in his hands as she saw them slowly slink towards them. His immortality gave him immunity from their effects, but not so for her or his nephew. He narrowed his eyes at the boy and fought to keep his anger in check. He swore and grimaced as he felt her flinch. He leaned in closer to her ear. "Quinn, I want you to run."

He watched her turn her gaze from him to Wilbright and the approaching monsters. She shook her head. "I'm not going to leave you."

He sensed her fear, but she still wanted to stay with him. His temper dropped as he grasped the sides of her head. She needed to leave. She didn't need to see this happen. "Love, I need you to run. I will find you. Now go." He saw a flair of recognition flash through her eyes. *Good. As long as she left.* A scream pierced the air and Talin turned around. Three more shadows had joined the others.

261

Talin turned to Wil and saw fear in the boy's eyes. Finally, Wilbright realized he wasn't in control. Talin took a closer look at the new creatures. One of them had a strange glow about it, like Dwilight's Noctem Umbrem. This new one had taken a human life, making it unnaturally strong. Talin's heart sunk. The scream. Masters. This timeline shouldn't be involved in this fiasco. At least his old friend hadn't been able to see the Noctem Umbrem. The humans in this timeline would chalk it down to a heart attack.

The thought only fueled his anger. A siren pierced through the air. He felt the corners of his lips rise. Quinn had made it out. One down. He turned his gaze to the other. "Wilbright," Talin said, trying to keep his voice even. "It's time for you to leave."

"But—," Wil tried to speak.

"No. Go. Take the clock back, and don't come back to this timeline again." Talin narrowed his eyes at Wilbright. "I will break my oath if you do, and I will kill you myself."

Wilbright stared back at him fear registering in his eyes.

"And remember what I said, don't mess with the nightmares." Talin growled.

Wilbright looked like he wanted to say something, but he quickly lost or forgot it as he sprinted out the door in the opposite direction of Quinn. *Good.* Talin thought. Fewer spectators. A wet drop fell on his head. Hopefully nothing else would be ruined today. Talin breathed out and willed his body to change forms, finally releasing his temper. Talons were much easier to wield...

CHAPTER SEVENTEEN

WHAT'S YOUR NAME, AGAIN?

Quincy walked outside into her London and looked at the sky. 7:17 PM. Polo tryouts had been over for one hour and seventeen minutes. She could feel disappointed later, but now, she had other problems to deal with. Quincy pulled out the Corocularum from her pocket. As much as she wanted to travel directly to her bed, her anxiety for Talin won. She opened the device and stared down at the eye. It blinked as it instantaneously transported her outside of Talin's rooms. She knocked on the door, but nothing stirred within. She sat in the doorway and leaned against the door. She wondered if he would show up as the raven or the man.

Love. He had called her love. In a tone she knew before. *Love.* She closed her eyes and fighting the exhaustion, sorted through her memories. She finally stopped at the face of a man with a dusty cap and hay on his worn jacket.

Cigfran.

How had she not figured it out? Cigfran was Talin. Or was Talin, Cigfran? Her eyes watered and she squeezed them shut trying to stop the tears. Cigfran, the keeper of the neighborhood stable and the one thing that had made the foster home bearable. But he had left. And then Talin had arrived. She jumped when she felt a weight against her. She looked up and saw Talin in his human/Cigfran form sitting next to her. Other than the dusty clothing and odd accent, it was obviously him. He took off his soaked jacket and groaned.

"What happened to you?" She gasped.

"Hello to you too," he mumbled.

"Are you okay?"

He slowly nodded. "It will take more than a handful of Nocti to finish me off."

"Nocti is plural?" It wasn't the question she wanted answered, but she had no idea how to start.

Talin grinned, despite himself. "Ask. You won't hear anything I'm about to tell you until you do."

Quincy couldn't help but laugh. "Probably true," she paused deciding what to ask first. "Are you Cigfran or Talin?"

Talin laughed. A warm laugh. A Cigfran laugh. "Smart girl."

"Not smart enough for how long it took me to figure it out." She frowned.

"Don't insult me. I work hard to blend in and disappear in plain sight. Between C and Wilbright, they forced my hand in the other timeline to reveal my human self, otherwise you might never have figured it out." With the mention of Wilbright his face fell.

"Is he actually your nephew?"

Cigfran nodded. "Adopted, but yes. Both boys."

Quincy understood his protectiveness of Dwilight. "But he knows you in as," she wanted to say Talin but decided on something less tricky. "As a raven."

"Indeed. Dwilight saw through me. Wilbright never did. Until today." Cigfran released a torrent of air through a sigh. "That's going to be a fun conversation at some point," he groaned as he leaned back. "I'm too old for this."

"So, then why did your nephew kill my parents?" she clenched her fists and fought to keep her voice neutral.

He sniffed and turned away from her. After a moment, he turned his gaze forward, but Quincy could see his eyes were dark blue and the hairs on her arms raised. "I'm not completely sure. But I am sure *he* didn't purposefully kill anyone." he said. He grasped her shoulders so they were face to face. "I know it doesn't make you feel any better, and it shouldn't. There aren't words to be said, or gestures given that will ever make you feel any better. I know that, and I hope he does as well." He released Quincy and they both turned their gazes forward. Her throat tightened, leaving her with an urge to either cry or scream, but she didn't have enough energy for either emotion. This wasn't Talin's fault. It's not like he had any control over his nephew's or her fate. Talin, or Cigfran? Quincy frowned.

265

"So, are you Talin or Cigfran?" she quietly asked.

Talin/Cigfran turned to her and stared until she broke his gaze, uncomfortable.

"Both. And neither," he winked. "Like I said, I answer to many names."

"So, what's your real name?"

He tapped his nose. "That would be telling."

She rolled her eyes. "Fine. Keep your secret."

"I will," he laughed.

Quincy chewed her lip and stared at him. "What do I call you now?"

He shrugged. "Whatever you're the most comfortable using."

She thought about it. They both felt like two completely separate names for completely separate people. How could she use either one? She shrugged. "I'm not sure."

He stood up and stretched pulling off his soaked jacket. He twisted the jacket, watching the water drip. "It will take hours before it dries," he groaned. He turned to look back at her. "If you ever have to fight a Noctem Umbrem without me," he clenched his fists and tightened his jaw, "Use the elements. Water, fire and light. They hate it. Do you understand?"

Quincy nodded.

"Good girl."

Quincy struggled to get up and winced when she put her foot down.

"Want some help?"

She shook her head. It felt strange hearing Talin asking her if she wanted any help, especially since it came from Cigfran without a strange accent. She shook her head. "I'm going to take my time going back to my room."

He nodded and she slowly walked down the stairs. Once she had reached the bottom floor, she found a corner without anyone nearby where she could cry her confusion out in private.

***

Quincy walked into Marquam's office and plopped down in her customary seat. She looked around the room but couldn't find the headmaster. She closed her eyes, lulled by the ticking of the countless clocks around her.

The noise coming from the clocks gradually quieted until one clock remained. She sat up and turned to search for the ticking clock. She found the small, wooden, coo-coo clock hanging in the corner by one of the headmaster's bookshelves. She walked behind his desk and took a closer look at it. What had happened to all the other ones? The clock struck the hour and the small door in the top, flung open. A red hawk sprang through the opening and taunted her with an "I'll find you. I'll find you. I'll find you."

Quincy?

Quincy woke up, still curled up in her chair in the headmaster's office. She shivered from the realistic daymare.

"Is everything alright?" the headmaster asked.

She nodded, rubbing her tingling shoulders. "I'm fine, thank you. Just tired."

"Are you well enough for your exam?"

Quincy paused, a wave of cold fear hitting her. What exam? After a moment of wild thrashing around her memory, she recalled the map. "Yes, I think I'm ready."

"Excellent. Now, let's test that memory map we keep postponing." Marquam pulled out a large piece of parchment paper with gaps in parts of the map. Quincy noticed most of the visible parts of the maps had names while other pieces were noticeably vacant with a line where the name should be. "I would be a terrible professor if I didn't test you on *something* pertaining to your Talent," continued the headmaster. "Draw the absent bits of the map and label the missing names. Take your time. I would rather you be right than to hurry through this process."

Quincy nodded and closed her eyes imagining the map. She struggled trying to keep the image in her head with her eyes opened, leaving the whole process tedious and slow. The headmaster stopped her after half an hour. He glimpsed her work and nodded approvingly.

She held her breath, waiting for his grade.

"Well done, Quincy. You didn't quite finish, but what you did do is correct. I see we are going to need to work on keeping your eyes open while you use your memory."

Quincy smiled, relieved she had passed.

"Now, do you feel up to discussing the letters and the traveling?"

She nodded, quickly catching Marquam up, hoping she had given him the important details.

The headmaster clasped his hands together. "Your first clue took place in the past, correct?"

Quincy nodded.

"And the second in the present."

Quincy squirmed in her seat. "I guess it's considered the present, but not ours."

Marquam nodded. "I take it you noted the similarities and differences."

Quincy nodded again.

The headmaster smiled. "I'm quite jealous, you know? I wrote my final paper on the other timeline. Now, back to your riddle. What were you supposed to see or do in both?"

"The first one was to grab a black feather. I saw it, but I didn't get it. Strangely enough, it could have been the same feather that came with the second letter. The next riddle had me look at a celestial globe. But it didn't request I get anything. I'm not even sure what I was supposed to learn. Honestly, none of it makes any sense."

"Did you notice anything in particular on the globe?"

Quincy shrugged. "I have the whole globe in my memory, but nothing stood out. Except for the raven constellation," she grinned.

The headmaster didn't share her amusement. Instead, he clutched his hands together and leaned his chin upon them.

"You father studied maps, didn't he?"

Quincy nodded.

"Do you know anything about the history of that particular constellation?"

Quincy shook her head. "Not that I instantly recall." She frowned.

"My father would have known. What if he told me at some point?"

"Possible. But it's dangerous to try. It's a lot of time to pass through to find a moment. Eventually, it will be possible for you to do so, but your Talent is still young. Unless a smell, or a specific memory is called upon, I would be wary of memory travel. In the future, we can see if you can manage what we like to call a 'word search,' but it will take time and skill to learn."

"That would make things easier," Quincy groaned.

"A goal for you to work towards. In the meantime, there are many reasons why we have an extensive library here at Oakley. Your homework will be to read through the constellations you saw on the celestial globe and to see if you find any connections with the riddles."

The library. Monty's domain. *Space*, she reminded herself. She was giving him space until he felt ready to talk to her. She winced. Unfortunately, she had barely visited the library in the last month since everything had happened. Regrettably, Monty couldn't be the reason why she didn't do her homework. And she knew she had to, because the book about stars she had chosen at the beginning of the school year didn't have enough information to satisfy the headmaster.

"Okay, I'll work on it over the weekend." Quincy left the Back Library, wondering how Monty would react.

Outside of the Main Hall, Colin waved to get her attention. She forced a smile and waved back.

"Hello, Quincy!" Colin grinned, his smile momentarily catching her off guard.

"Hey," she smiled back, his grin infectious.

"What are you doing Sunday afternoon?"

She hadn't thought past the library. "Nothing I can think of?"

"Great!" His smile grew wider and then locked awkwardly into place as his cheeks turned an unnatural pink. "Would you like to spend some time with me?"

"You want to hang out in the art room?" Quincy asked.

"I'm thinking more like away from school. We could take our art supplies and draw and paint outside? Weather permitting of course."

Quincy smiled; this time completely genuine. "I'd like that."

"Fantastic." He laughed and bounced away. As an afterthought, he turned around. "I'll see you Sunday!" he hollered before bounding away.

"Oh, my goodness, Quincy," Lindy gasped, grabbing her shoulder.

"Colin asked you out."

"Are you sure that's what he did?" Quincy asked, hoping she sounded as incredulously as she felt.

"Yah, duh!" Lindy laughed and linked her arm into Quincy's. "We need to find the perfect outfit."

***

On Sunday morning, Quincy stood on the threshold of the library, her fists clenched. She couldn't wait any longer. She anxiously rubbed her arms. Why did she feel so anxious about going inside? Monty didn't own the library. She narrowed her eyes and strode purposely inside. She walked up to the desk and asked for the section of space and celestial bodies. Miss Grastorf pointed her in the opposite direction of Monty's usual corner. She sighed, relieved. She needed to stop being so silly. What were the odds of seeing Monty in the massive Oakley library?

Not in her favor.

She recognized the light-blonde head. She ground her teeth and searched the aisle for the reference book. She stared at the empty gap where the book should have been. Who else would have taken it? She looked around and frowned when she saw Monty and what he held. *A Detailed Guide to the Stars and...* Monty's fingers hid the rest of the book's title. She walked over to him and recognized the glassy, blank stare of his seizures. She waited for him to come back, not bothering to mask her anger. Why completely ignore her but be holding on to the one book she needed? He didn't randomly pick out this book. Monty didn't do random. "Why that book?" she whispered.

His eyes flickered, recognition crossing his features. His eyes narrowed as he found the moment he had already seen. An argument they had yet to have? She didn't care if he already knew the outcome, she would get her chance to yell at him. Unfortunately, and as usual, he spoke first. "Despite your current thought, the entire universe does not revolve around you," he spat.

She stared at him, aghast, but then the anger rushed back. He knew the fight they were going to have and he chose to say it anyway.

"I could say the same thing about you," she growled. "Especially since you clearly have no interest in my activities whatsoever," she pointed to the book in his hands. "I'm giving you time and space but why are you still mad at me?"

His cheeks reddened and he thrust the book into her hands. "Take it, I am finished."

"Enough!" an angry voice cut through. They both turned and faced the angry librarian, her gaze frosty and her arms crossed. "Take your lover's spat outside."

"She was leaving," Monty said, his voice now insultingly even.

Quincy shook her head at him. "Unbelievable." She stomped to the front desk and handed the book to Miss Grastorf. "I'd like to borrow this one, please."

Miss Grastorf looked at the book and then at Quincy. "Sorry dear, this is a reference book and must stay inside the library."

Of course, it did. Quincy smiled tightly and left the book in the re-shelve shelf. She would look at the book tomorrow. Instead, she stomped outside into the sunny day. As she stepped out into the sunshine, a thought struck her. Dwilight had recognized her starry night painting. She wondered what her chances were that he had a book on stars in his own library?

She decided against riding, hoping a long walk would clear her head. After nearly an hour, she arrived at her destination. She knocked on the door and above her a cheery voice called out, "Come in!"

Quincy slumped on the chair out of breath.

"Did you walk here?" Dwilight asked.

"I did."

"Impressive!" he said delighted and handed her a glass of water. She quickly took a sip and thanked him gratefully.

"What might I do for you on this lovely day?"

"Do you have a book on constellations? Or ancient Babylon?"

Dwilight ran a hand through his spiky hair. "Definitely have one on constellations. Not sure about Babylon, though." He stood up and motioned for her to follow. "Follow me to my library. It's a disaster, but do come in."

She walked in and paused in awe at the room. The walls were covered in notes, blueprints, and maps. There were small tables all over the room covered with odd bits and creations. At the end of the room, a large bookshelf took over the wall. Dwilight sorted through the books placed in the bookshelf in no particular order. Finally, she heard an "Ah-ha!" and a slam as he pulled out a large book on a less-busy table.

"You're in luck." Dwilight said as he paged through the glossary. "There's a section here about the constellations of Babylon."

Dwilight pulled up a chair for her and left to make tea. She looked through the names of Babylon version of the modern-day constellations. Quincy wondered how many similarities there were between the other Babylon and her own. So why did 'C' want her to travel to the other timeline? Maybe the globe no longer existed here? She gently placed her finger over the raven constellation and flipped through some of the others. So enthralled by the illustrations, she hadn't even realized Dwilight had left her tea. She took a sip of the now lukewarm tea. She groaned, wishing she knew what "C" wanted her to know from the other timeline. "It doesn't make sense," she groaned, placing her head on her elbows over the table.

She heard a scrape of a chair as he pulled it next to her. She sat back up and let Dwilight take a peek. "What are you looking for?"

"A circle of stars to see how they glow," she replied. "Or globe. And why they're important."

"I have no idea what it means." Dwilight blinked.

"You're not the only one," she sighed.

Dwilight crossed his lanky legs in a crisscross fashion and leaned closer to her. "My mother was a magical woman. Unique in every way. It's why my father was so taken by her the moment they first met. In my youth, she used to grab a shawl and my hand to disappear into the local village. We would play a game pretending to be first time visitors to the village and miserably lost. I admit I found it confusing. What were we looking for? For what purpose? After getting annoyed by my incessant questioning, she finally said, "What you think you're looking for isn't what you were meant to find. It's about the journey.""

Quincy frowned. "I'm not sure what that has to do with what I'm looking for."

Dwilight shrugged. "I'm not sure it does. I remember after she died, it finally made sense to me. It was her way of spending time with me. I don't remember what we did or why we had gone out that day, but I do remember the quality time we spent together."

Dwilight smiled, his eyes staring off into the distance. Without looking at her, he continued. "What if the object you're supposed to find isn't an actual thing, but a moment? Or a memory?"

A memory. What if she knew the answer already? Quincy thanked the hermit and quickly left. When she placed her hands in her pocket, she grasped a cookie placed in a folded napkin.

* * *

Quincy walked from the treehouse and stopped at the Templum. She sat on one of the swings and stared at the forest above, the midday light left odd shadows through the branches. Her father would know everything about the stars on the globe. He would have recognized the connection. At some point he might have even tried to talk to her about it. She decided to replay a few moments with him talking about his beloved stars. She missed her father so much, it would be nice to see him again, even if only in her memories. Besides, she had a few hours before her afternoon plans with Colin. She closed her eyes and stopped the day before her father had died. She replayed moments of her father talking about the stars, a tedious project because he spoke of little else. He had done it often enough that she hated to admit she had often tuned him out. Now, she would give anything to have a new conversation with him droning on about the mythology of some star or other. As she rewound her memories with her father, she tried to filter them through with the words: *globe, Babylon, Corvus, MUL.UGA.MUSHEN,* or even *raven*. She hoped she was doing it correctly and wished they had covered this type of memory search already.

She decided to be careful instead of going too quickly and risking getting lost, so the whole thing felt both tedious and heartbreaking. Something in the corner of her eye forced her to pause. Quincy and her little sister Emily, were sitting down on the floor in a similar position much like how she sat now, on a summer's evening, months before the accident. In the window, over her father's shadow, something stared at them. She felt her younger version shiver, but at the time didn't understand why. She hadn't registered seeing the monster, but her memory had caught enough of a glimpse of it that her older version could see it in detail.

The shadowy hand of a Noctem Umbrem tried to reach them. Despite the open window, the silhouette couldn't get inside. Older Quincy stood up to get a closer look at it. She recognized it as the spiky hair shadow from Miss Heatherwoods and the terrifying one from London. She looked around the window frame and gaped when she saw what hung from the frame. A sprig of dried cinnamon. Did cinnamon stop the Noctem from entering the room from the window?

She looked back at herself and shook her head. How many times had she seen the Noctem Umbrem and had not understood what she saw? She turned to face her father. Her poor father who had died for nothing. Whose Talent of perfect memory hadn't saved him. She tried to push herself from the moment, but instead she started it again. Now she watched the Noctem try to force itself in but was thwarted. She felt sick and couldn't differentiate it coming from her past self or present self. She needed to go back to the present. She fast forwarded her memories until she lost focus. In her mind, she screamed, trying to take control. She saw moments from all over her memory. From her childhood, from her last year at Oakley, none of them in any specific order. Finally, she forced herself out of her memory stream into a memory of no particular meaning. She was in a bed staring up into the faces of her parents. She looked side to side. It looked like a cradle. So, her memories went back into infancy.

"Are you sure we have to leave London?" her mother asked. The sadness in her voice broke Quincy's heart.

"Yes," her father replied. "Between your key and Q, we're sitting targets. It's better for us to leave and hide in another country." He kissed her forehead tenderly and moved her light brown hair away from her face. "It's safer this way."

Her mother nodded. "I know," she whispered as she gently brushed baby Quincy's cheek with a dried sprig. Quincy felt the roughness against her new face as she breathed in the smell of cinnamon for the first time.

"Did you know cinnamon is used as a barrier against evil spirits?" her mother whispered to her father. He laughed quietly. "Evil spirits?" he gently scoffed. Chelsea rolled her eyes. "Don't tease my upbringing." she narrowed her eyes at him. "Besides, I am well aware your family has used cinnamon as a memory anchor for several generations."

Her father grinned and stared back down at baby Quincy. He gently booped her nose. "I hope you'll have perfect memory like me. Remember, my tiny Q, cinnamon will always take you back."

Baby Quincy yawned and closed her eyes. She quickly opened them and found herself sitting back in the Templum staring at a shaker filled with cinnamon, held up by Katelyn Prendergast.

CHAPTER EIGHTEEN

PROPERTIES OF CINNAMON

Quincy flung her arms around Katelyn who laughed. "You're alright now," she said, patting her back.

Quincy nodded and Katelyn handed her the cinnamon shaker.

"I'm so glad to see you. How are you here?" Quincy asked.

Katelyn waved her clover key in front of her as if silently saying *Duh.*

"I know *how* you got here." Quincy rolled her eyes, grinning. "I meant more of how you *knew* to be here."

Katelyn stared at her; confusion written on her features. Her face changed and she grinned. "You sent me a letter. Or you will send me one." Katelyn handed her the letter.

Quincy scanned the contents, frowning. The signature on the note said "QH," but it wasn't her handwriting. It asked Katelyn to be exactly here, at this time, with cinnamon. Quincy groaned. "I am so sick of all of this time traveling."

Katelyn groaned as well and sat down on a bench in front of the swing. "You're telling me."

"I'm sorry you wasted a trip for this."

"Waste? For this?" Katelyn said, incredulously. "I'm told it's a terrible fate to get caught memory traveling."

Quincy nodded. "I think I understand why my father loved cinnamon candy."

Katelyn laughed. "So many questions finally answered."

Quincy leaned back against the wall and sighed. "I'm so tired of all of this. Why do I keep getting clues which make no sense?"

Katelyn frowned. "What are you looking for?"

"I went to another timeline to look for a star globe. I saw it but it didn't show me anything. At least anything obvious. Some stuff about ancient Babylon, but a version slightly different than ours. I think. But they both had the same constellations." Quincy leaned over to Katelyn. "Do you know how many timelines there are?"

Katelyn shook her head. "Not for sure. I assume three since it keeps repeating itself. Over and over again." She rolled her eyes. "But then you had to fix my death in this timeline so could there be timelines within timelines?"

Quincy rubbed her forehead. "But it looks like there are some major similarities and differences between each of them. At least the two I've seen. So weird, you know? Seeing people from the other timeline. Like us, but not us. All with lives of their own."

She felt her throat tighten and her eyes water.

"You wondered about your other version, didn't you?" Katelyn asked. "That's a natural question."

Quincy nodded. "What if she had never left London and her parents and sister were alive. What if she didn't have weird key problems? What if the other Quincy is a completely normal teenage girl."

"Then she wouldn't be you. She would be her own Quincy." Katelyn shrugged. "And that Katelyn would be her own Katelyn."

"But what about Talin?" Quincy murmured.

"What about him?"

"I don't think Talin has other alternate versions of himself. I think it's all... Talin." Quincy felt the hairs on the back of her neck rise.

"Are you saying there's one Talin?" Katelyn asked. "Across all the timelines?"

"Why else would 'C' have sent me to the other timeline so I could see a star map? My father studied star maps, so I didn't need instructions to understand one. What if "C" wanted me to see the raven constellation?"

"Sure, fine. But why?" Katelyn asked.

Quincy shrugged. "I'm not sure. But Talin wasn't happy about being forced to admit he has human forms."

Katelyn stood up and stretched.

"Walk me back to the Timepiece?" Katelyn asked. "I'm supposed to be cooking dinner. Hopefully, I'll make it back with plenty of time to spare. Let's see if time is nice to me today."

***

Quincy waited until Katelyn closed the Timepiece's door before dashing off towards her room. Lindy had chosen the perfect outfit to paint outside while still remaining stylish. She quickly tied her hair back and grabbed her art satchel. Colin met her at the family room door in khaki pants, and a gray shirt with permanent smudges from his charcoals. He had combed his hair to one side. "Ready?" he questioned.

"Lead on," Quincy smiled.

Colin and Quincy walked away from the main buildings of Oakley chatting about small things from classes, horses, and the upcoming Polo matches. Of course, Colin had made the team.

"Next year, is the big tournament. They haven't officially announced where it's going to be held yet. So many schools in one place! I wonder what it would be like," he speculated, a dreamy expression taking over his face.

Quincy forced a grin. She didn't have to imagine. She had accidentally attended the Polo tournament last year while saving Katelyn. "Yeah, I bet it's something," she muttered.

Colin misunderstood her reaction. "I'm so sorry you're not on the team. Hopefully, you can make it to tryouts next year?"

"Yeah, hopefully," Quincy shrugged. "It's probably better I focus on school work, I can enjoy watching you instead."

Her cheeks heated. She hadn't meant it that way, had she? If Colin noticed her turmoil and embarrassment, he kindly didn't say anything. Instead, he gave her a warm smile. "Thanks, but it would be more fun if you were on the field."

"I'd like that, too. At least I have the Equospatium coming up soon so I might finally get a chance to show off." She laughed.

"If you can stay on your horse," he teased.

She shook her head and grinned. "Low blow, sir. Low blow."

Colin stopped near the cliffs close to the waterfall. "Is it fine to stop here?"

When she nodded, Colin pulled out a blanket from his art bag and invited her to sit down. He pulled out his pencils and sketched one of the flowers in the rocks.

"*Jasione Montana*," he quoted. "Commonly known as 'Sheep's-bit' from the Campanulaceae family." He stopped drawing and looked at Quincy sheepishly. "It's early this year."

Quincy smiled, genuinely surprised. "Artist, horse lover, and flower enthusiast," she gently teased. "What next?"

He laughed. "It's called a botanist. One who studies plant life. My father was one. A great one. Could talk about flowers all day if my mother would let him."

"Is that what you want to do? Draw and study flowers?"

284

Colin put down his pencil and gently touched the flower. "Not anymore," he sighed, longingly. "My mother has other ideas for my future."

Quincy frowned. "She gets to decide for you?"

Colin shrugged. "It's no use disappointing my mother. She always gets what she wants, in the end." He laid down on the blanket and sketched the clouds with lighter pencil lines. "Don't look so sorry for me. I don't care much about it anyway. Besides, no matter what happens, I'll always have art."

"That's a good way to look at life," Quincy replied.

"It's how do they say it? 'It is what it is.'" He shrugged. "How about you? Any idea what you want to do after Oakley?"

Quincy shook her head. Surprised how sad it made her feel. It's not like she had much of a choice since she had put on the key. "I'm not sure what I want to do."

"How about being a Third?" he teased.

"Sure, why not?" she laughed.

Colin moved his paper to see her properly. "I bet you'd be great."

"Aww, thanks," she laughed. "I don't think I would like it. Too much notoriety for my taste."

"What, you don't want to be a topic of gossip and conversation while every move you make is completely scrutinized?" He questioned; his sarcasm muffled from the paper.

"No, thank you." She groaned.

"Genevieve would like it." Colin mumbled; loud enough Quincy could hear.

"Is that why she doesn't sit by us anymore?" she carefully asked. "She doesn't even talk to the rest of the floor."

Colin sighed, carefully putting down his artwork and rolling over onto his stomach. "Yeah. Something like that. I know she wanted to date me because of my money and connections. And honestly, she was pretty boring."

"So how did you know that's what she wanted?"

"Just a feeling. Why? Do you want to paint with me because of my money and my social connections?"

Quincy burst out laughing. "No, I'm painting with you because I'm hoping some of your art Talent will rub off on me and I can pick up some tricks!"

Colin uncharacteristically giggled. "Good answer."

A dark cloud blocked out the sun and a large raindrop fell on Quincy's nose. "Oh, no!" she gasped.

"We'd better run for it!" Colin yelped when another drop fell on his art book. He quickly scooped up the blanket, grasped Quincy's hand, and they ran towards the Main Hall.

***

Quincy stared down at her hands firmly clutched on the arms of an ornate chair. A cursory glance told her she thankfully wore clothing. For some strange reason she felt a sense of relief from this knowledge.

286

"Miss Harris?"

Her head flew up to face the voice next to her. It was one of the Thirds from her travels. Tayo, she quickly recalled. He spoke again but this time, in Latin? He continued to question her, all in Latin. She turned to her right and her eyes widened as she recognized Prieler. He too, questioned her, also in Latin. She felt panic begin to choke her. Why weren't they speaking in English so she could take part of this conversation. And why was she sitting in a Third's chair? She turned to face the audience and when she saw them, she screamed. Nocti made up the entire audience and they phased in and out of human form and into their shadowy silhouettes. She pointed at them.

"Don't you see them?" she cried.

The two other Thirds stared at her; confusion written on their faces. As if she spoke a completely different language.

"We have to run," she tried again, this time in Latin.

Tayo shook his head. "Mememto mori," he answered.

Finally, she understood him. "I don't want to die," she screamed as the Nocti encircled the chairs. Their shadowy hands reached for her neck and she felt the pressure as their fingers squeezed...

✳✳✳

Quincy woke up coughing. She touched her throat and it felt oddly warm. She groaned, hoping she wasn't getting sick. She lay back down on the bed and stared at the ceiling. A nightmare in Latin. Strange.

CHAPTER NINETEEN

THE EQUOSPATIUM

Quincy stared at the calendar posted near the door in her dormitory. She traced over the dates. Five more weeks before school ended for the year. How was she going to get through everything she needed to finish before heading back to New York? She noticed someone had written "Finals Week!" in red with a crying face next to it. Quincy needed to spend more time with her books than day-dreaming about the next clue. If she got it. What would happen if it came during the summer? Would it wait in the mailbox slot until she arrived for the next school year? Is it possible for the clues to expire? She crossed her arms and shook her head. Wasting time with this again.

"Finals," Eloise faux-sobbed. "We'll never make it."

Quincy pretended to smack her shoulders. "I think you're going to be fine."

Eloise's lips trembled. "Language arts will be the death of me." She sighed over-dramatically and fainted on Mikaela's bed and on top of Mikaela, who had somehow managed to fall asleep.

"You're such a numpty, you melodramatic drama queen!" Mikaela growled, shoving her sister off her bed.

"Kettle, kettle!" Eloise screeched. She grabbed Kalleigh's pillow and brought it down with surprising force onto her sister's head. With lightning quick reflexes Quincy didn't realize Mikaela had, the older sister jumped up and grabbed her own pillow. "And now you're dead. Any final words, wishes, or pleas?"

"I'm too young to die!" Eloise squealed, running into the bathroom.

"You should have thought about life before you woke me up, you twerp!"

"Five more weeks, it's five more weeks," Mon-Aye grumbled next to Quincy. They shared a wince from the crashing door.

"Yeah, five more weeks." Quincy echoed. Not enough time. She grabbed an apple on her nightstand and decided to take a break and visit Consto.

Consto stuck his head out of the stall and to Quincy's pleasure, nickered a hello.

"You can smell apple, huh?" she asked and offered the snack. Consto happily took the offering and smacked his lips contentedly. She gently patted his nose, careful not to place her fingers too close to his mouth. Best not ruin the moment. She waved the bridle. "Want to ride?" When he didn't screech at her, she saddled him and led him out. After mounting him, she took her hands off the bridle. "Okay, Consto. You lead today."

Consto didn't need to be told twice and barely gave Quincy time to grasp the pommel of the saddle before he took off with breathtaking speed. *Maybe we could enter the speed event for the Equospatium this year.* She pondered.

***

Quincy hoped she hadn't made a mistake writing her name on the list for the speed race for the Equospatium this weekend. She didn't have a clue to deal with at the moment, and she wanted at least one moment of feeling like a normal girl with normal girl problems. If Consto didn't want to race, then they wouldn't. She shrugged it away and walked to her Language Arts class. On her way, she paused at the Post Office. She had stopped visiting daily two weeks ago, but why not try today?

"These are strange letters you've gotten this year," the attendant commented as he handed her the now familiar writing. Quincy felt the blood drain from her head as she grasped the letter.

"Yeah it's a weird pen-pal thing. Sort of." She grinned. She waved the letter. "Thanks!" Quincy quickly placed the letter in her bookbag and squashed her desire to skip class. Too soon with finals to do that. She groaned before jogging to class and towards Colin who motioned her to follow. "I'm coming," she waved back.

"Are you ready to knock everyone flat in debate today?" he questioned.

"We're about to find out."

***

Quincy managed to make it through the rest of the day mostly paying attention. The letter in her bag pleaded to be read. Finally, she escaped from dinner and ran to the Aquila Café. She managed to find a corner table and sipped on her hot chocolate while skimming the letter. She briefly looked up, half expecting Monty to be there. She hated her disappointment when he wasn't. Forcing him out of her mind, she ran through the clue.

I hope you have learned so that I may adjourn
Our lessons.
Your choices have voices that changes and arranges
Around you.
When you are finished, I know I must diminish
My power.
Do not be forlorn for where you were born and go
to Hawthorne where you will be warned to not scorn
lest you mourn.
You will need to remember the day in November
when your heart became your chart and made you depart,
to a place of safe.
To win my favor, you must be braver in order to see,

Tomorrow's morrow.
Find the dial and filled with guile,
travel ahead and for the moments unread.
Three clicks should finish my trick,
Find the man with hair quite white,
Who will lead you to the light.

Great, she groaned. Another one. This better be the last one. Glancing through the letter, one sentence in particular stood out to her. *Travel ahead for moments unread.* So, the Timepiece could potentially go *forward* in time from her present day. She carefully placed the letter back into the envelope and into her bag. She needed to speak to the headmaster. What had she done to earn the third clue? How had she solved the second riddle? She met Colin on the staircase and politely passed on Colin's invitation to study together claiming exhaustion as the culprit. It hadn't been a lie, but when she curled up in the covers, it took her hours to fall asleep.

***

Quincy forced herself to place the letter in the back of her mind, at least until the Equospatium weekend finished. She needed to focus on Consto if she wanted to make it through the speed race. The first was scheduled for this afternoon and the final race tomorrow, if she placed. Eloise ripped open her curtain, and her excitement fell when she saw Quincy already awake and dressed.

"I wanted to surprise you," she pouted.

Quincy laughed. "How about next year?"

Eloise's face lit up. "This is your first Equospatium, isn't it? You weren't feeling well last year…"

Quincy coughed. "Yeah, great memory."

Eloise giggled. "Maybe I have a second Talent!" She jumped up and continued ripping open curtains to grumbling neighbors.

After all the girls had received their "war" makeup in the form of a green "3," they all trampled down to breakfast. Quincy forced herself to eat a breakfast sausage and drink some orange juice. Today would not be a good day to lose consciousness on the speedy Consto. She shuddered, imagining falling from that speed. If Consto would even run for her today. She grabbed two apples and waved to the table. "Eloise, save me a seat?" Eloise nodded and waved a Floor Three flag at her.

An hour later, Quincy heard the stadium bell ring, opening the Equospatium. Most of the students participating in the tournament were on the stadium trotting once around the floor with their mounts in ribbons. Quincy didn't want to force anything on Consto that would leave him annoyed before the afternoon race. Instead, he munched happily on her apple offering while she tried to contain her anxiety and excitement. Quincy stayed in the stables, watching the board near the entrance warning riders of the current event and the following one. Quincy's throat tightened when she watched a stable groom write her event. They were next.

Quincy grabbed her equipment and gently rubbed Consto's nose. "Will you please try this with me?" she murmured. When Consto didn't scream or attempt to kick her, she led the horse outside and to the starting line. Quincy looked up at the clear blue sky. The perfect day to be outside. She felt Consto quiver underneath her.

"Good luck, Quincy!"

Quincy looked over and smiled at Colin. He looked so confident and calm on his horse. "Thanks, you too."

She looked at the spectator's area near the line and felt a jolt of happiness. She would recognize that perfect posture anywhere. Monty stood next to Eloise who leaned over the barrier with her banner flying over. An official had to gently push her back. Colin laughed at her exuberance.

A shrill whistle released the horses and they all dashed down the raceway. All but one.

"Consto," she cried. "Please, not now."

Consto sniffed the ground. She heard snickers and laughter from the audience. She couldn't smack his backside and kick him any harder, otherwise he would happily throw her. It was better to remain mounted than to hit the ground in front of the entire school. She released the reigns and crossed her arms. "Fine. Do what you want."

After the invitation, Consto took off. She barely had time to grasp the bridle before he thundered down the raceway. Her mouth opened wide as she passed the stragglers. Within moments, they were already in the head of the line of galloping horses. She hardly recognized Colin at the speed in which they ran. She laughed as the wind whipped past her. Was she flying? Quincy lowered her head closer to Consto to keep from falling from the speed. Colin sped up to keep the place, but it only emboldened Consto. With a shriek, he gained even more speed and shot past the forerunner. But instead of stopping at the finish line, he kept going and zoomed into the forest. He ignored any of her physical and vocal requests to stop and kept galloping.

"Consto," she screamed, but it did nothing to deter him.

Quincy stopped trying to control Consto when she noticed the horizon of the direction he rode towards. Smoke.

CHAPTER TWENTY

FIRE AND RAIN

B lack smoke billowed and curled in the distance. Consto didn't relinquish his speed until they were in eye distance of the fire. She shivered, recognizing where they were. He had taken her to Dwilight's treehouse engulfed in flames. She quickly jumped off Consto and rubbed his nose. "Stay away from the fire," she begged. Consto stamped his feet and bolted from her into the forest. Not what she had meant. Now stranded, she quickly banished her frustration as a burning book fell next to her.

"Dwilight," she screamed. When he didn't answer, she shook her head. She pulled off her jersey and wrapped it around her face. She pushed open the door and carefully made her way up the tree. Thankfully, the flames had not reached the staircase, but they had started on the door. She quickly gazed over the kitchen and noted his absence. She hoped he wasn't trapped on the other side of the treehouse, because the bridge connecting the main house to his bedroom already burned. Silently pleading, she opened the door towards his lab. She ran past the flames licking the walls and stared in horror at the slumped figure over his workbench. She grabbed him and pushed him over. Placing her hand over his neck she drew closer to him. She felt a faint pulse.

"You have to wake up," she screamed. She noted a number of empty bottles in front of him. "Did you drink all this today?" she cried and pushed him again. She felt tears pooling at the corners of her eyes as sweat collected and fell from her forehead. She could never lift him, much less drag him down the stairs. She looked around the room, trying to find liquid to douse the fire, but looking at the flames, she couldn't stop it. She coughed and put her arm over her mouth. She didn't want to die like this, but she couldn't leave Dwilight behind either. Before she could make a decision, a crack of what sounded like thunder shook the entire tree house.

Thunder? But the sky was completely clear not even an hour ago. Was the noise from the fire? In answer to her question, rain pelted the treehouse until water seeped through all the cracks in the building. Had she lost her mind from smoke inhalation?

A figure in black burst through the door, flames running over his arms and hands.

She pointed. "Fire," she cried. She burst into a fit of coughing. The figure looked at his arms and quickly wiped the flames away. He came over and pulled up Dwilight. She heard a groan as he lifted the hermit over his shoulders. He drew his face closer to hers.

"Quinn, can you walk?"

Talin she nearly wept with relief. She quickly nodded.

"Good. Follow me," he demanded. Quincy grasped the back of his jacket and walked behind him. Rainwater continued to pour in, dousing the flames. They walked out the front door and Talin motioned towards a tree. Consto waited patiently next to it, completely soaked from the rain. Quincy ran to the horse and leaned against his head. "Thank you," she whispered, her eyes watering. Her throat ached and she fought to keep from coughing. Quincy stared at the charred treehouse, in awe that the whole structure hadn't fallen. Only smoke remained from the rain. A groan interrupted her as Talin placed the incoherent man on top of Consto. "Now you," he gestured to Quincy. She quickly mounted behind Dwilight.

"You're going to need to hold him," Talin said.

"What about you?" Quincy asked.

"Too much weight for Consto to carry. Poor creature is already exhausted," he said, his voice gentle. "I'll take care of myself."

Quincy gasped as human Talin effortlessly morphed into a bird and flew in circles around them.

"Fly," he called to Consto, and the horse galloped towards Oakley.

***

Consto stopped, panting near the entrance of the Main Hall. Talin landed on his human feet and pulled Dwilight from her grasp.

"Where are you taking him?" Quincy croaked. Her throat raw and ached when she spoke. She jumped down from the exhausted Consto.

"He needs to go up to the Infirmary," Talin groaned, hoisting Dwilight over his shoulder.

"Can you do it alone?" Quincy asked. She gently rubbed Consto's nose. "I'm worried about Consto."

Talin nodded. "Go. Meet me after."

Quincy agreed, holding the door and gestured them in. She walked next to Consto leading him to the stables. "So heroic," she murmured. She wiped him down and made sure he had water and food. "I'll be back later with an apple," she murmured. Consto knickered and dug his head into his water dish. Coughing, she ran after Talin and Dwilight. She didn't stop until she ran past the Infirmary door. "I'm with..." she paused unsure what names to use. "I'm with them." The nurse understood and gestured her to follow. Quincy followed the nurse past the student Infirmary and into a door at the end of the hallway housing larger and more private rooms. Nurse Watson stopped at the end and knocked on the door. "Come," Talin growled from inside.

The nurse's shoulders tensed, but she opened the door. Quincy followed the nurse inside the room. Dr. De Aguiar pumped oxygen into Dwilight's mouth, her focused features not acknowledging their entrance. Next to the doctor, the hunky Nurse Dafoe gently cleansed his burns. Despite everything going on, she finally understood Alba's and Mon-Aye's obsession with his hands. As he helped the doctor move Dwilight over to reveal his back, Quincy failed to stifle a gasp. "Is he going to be alright?" she whispered seeing the burnt skin.

Talin nodded, emerging from a shadowy corner of the room in human form. "Some burns, but he'll live."

"Too soon to tell," the doctor hissed. "Honesty is the best policy with his family."

Talin walked closer to Quincy, rolled his eyes and pointed to his head. "My Talent is not completely gone, yet."

Quincy smiled and wiped the tears accumulating from the corners of her eyes.

"Now is not the best time to be here," the doctor stared her down. "You can visit after I've saved his life. And I want you checked before you leave." She turned to Talin. "You, too," she demanded. "Go."

Talin nodded and followed Quincy outside. Their shoes made horrible squelching noises from the rain. She looked at his fire-damaged clothes, still drenched. The skin underneath the charred fabric was unburned. Talin cleared his throat, "I'll wait for you outside."

The nurse sat Quincy on a bed and helped her take off her shirt. Quincy winced as it left her skin. She had been burned as well, though not nearly as badly as Dwilight. With the adrenaline leaving her body, Quincy began to feel the pain. Nurse Watson put ointment on her wounds and placed gauze gently over her body. She handed her a cup of water and some pain medication. "Take this and go straight to bed. And stay there until you feel better." She gave further instructions about putting on more ointment and visiting for a checkup. Quincy nodded and slowly walked out of the Infirmary, Talin close behind her.

He gently placed his hands around her head. "How are you feeling?" he asked.

Quincy shook her head. "I have no idea. Alive, at least."

The corners of Talin's lips raised. "Good." He looked surprisingly alert, as if he could still fight another fire, but his eyes told her a different story. He looked even more weary than she felt.

"I'm glad you were there today," she whispered.

"Me too," he said with relief. But for some reason he sounded guilty. He kissed the top of her head. "Thank you for going into the fire to save him. Now go to sleep. And stop running into danger." He wagged his finger at her and forced a smile. She nodded. "You too," she croaked.

He nodded, morphed into the raven, and disappeared into the rafters. She painfully made her way up the stairs almost bumping into Mikaela.

"Blimey, Quincy. What happened?"

"Talk later," Quincy groaned. "Bed, now."

Mikaela nodded. "Here, lean on me."

Quincy felt her eyes water from the pain but kept focusing on each step, deeply thankful Mikaela didn't ask her any more questions.

"If I ever have to bury a body," Quincy wheezed. "I'm calling you."

"You'd better," Mikaela laughed hoisting Quincy into her bed. "Don't fight me, but I'm leaving your drapes open in case there's a problem.

Quincy nodded and curled up in bed.

✳✳✳

Fire came towards her in every direction. She couldn't hide from it. She ran deeper into the forest, but a creature of flame lumbered after her lighting the forest around her. She couldn't stop. If she did, she would be caught. She wasted a moment looking back and stifled a scream. Its face looked like a Noctem Umbrem. It reached out towards her and hissed. "It's useless to run. Why put yourself through this misery when you could be done now?"

"No!" Quincy screamed. Rain fell from the sky above and dropped onto her forehead. Something grabbed her shoulders and she whirled around to fight...

✳✳✳

"Shh, you're okay," Lindy cooed.

Quincy looked up and saw the whole floor surrounding her. Eloise gently lifted the washcloth from her forehead.

302

"What happened?" she coughed.

Alba handed her a glass of water. "Fever. Go back to sleep."

Quincy nodded and closed her eyes, falling gently back to sleep to the quiet humming.

CHAPTER TWENTY-ONE

A CLOUDY FUTURE

Quincy rubbed her face into her pillow grimacing at her sweat-filled sheets. For the first time she could remember, she didn't know the time and she didn't care. The sound of a shrill whistle floated through her window indicating the start of another race for the second day of the Equospatium. She would care more later when her fever broke. She smiled despite the pain. Consto had practically flown yesterday, even having started dead last. Hopefully one day she could feel victory again. The true victory came from the speed in which they made it back to the Infirmary. Even if she couldn't play polo competitively, she wouldn't trade Consto for any other horse. She groaned hearing a thump on her bedside table.

"Hello, Talin," she mumbled, mostly incoherently from her pillow.

"He'll live," Talin answered her next question. "I will, too."

"You're doing the thing Monty does," Quincy rolled over to face him.

"In my defense, I was doing it long before he was. Though I knew what you were going to ask without having to look." He chuckled.

Quincy groaned forcing herself to sit up.

"You look rough." Talin said rudely matter-of-fact.

Quincy noted his grumpy personality in full show today.

"Yeah, I don't feel great, either. Thanks for pointing that out."

Talin softened. "I'm sorry you're missing the festivities."

Quincy smiled. "Worth it. But yeah, I'm sure the freak rainstorm and the smoke didn't help me much." She sneezed into her blanket and grimaced. "I hear they had to cancel most of the afternoon events from the pouring rain."

"Hmm," Talin mumbled.

Quincy frowned wondering how much he would tell her. "Talin, rain seems to appear with you. The first time I met a Noctem Umbrem, in London, and probably other times too. Is controlling the rain one of your Talents, as well?"

Talin cleared his throat. "More or less. Amongst other things."

"Fire too?"

Talin groaned. "Do you have to know?"

"Is it something I shouldn't?" She narrowed her eyes.

Talin turned into his human form and sat at the edge of her bed. Quincy pulled her blanket tighter to her. She still hadn't decided how she felt about this person being simultaneously Cigfran and the mysterious man in black.

"It's a long story. It's *my* story. No, fire isn't my dominion, but I can master it."

She licked her lips and swallowed. "That's the other bird's power, isn't it?"

Talin paused for so long Quincy figured he wouldn't answer her. After a long while, he sighed again and mumbled to himself. "So, I'm finally having this conversation." He paused again before slowly nodding. "Yes." Answering both questions. "His name is Iblis, and he's the true villain of the story. Long before Wilbright, and long before Prieler."

Shivers ran down her body. "Prieler? The man we saw in Parliament?"

Talin nodded. "I believe he's the one sending the Nocti to pester us."

Quincy's throat tightened. "Why?" she asked hoarsely.

"Iblis preys on humanity's weakness. He smells it reeking off all of you. He saw Prieler's desire for greatness, and Wilbright's lust for someone not his. He's become adept at it over the centuries and he uses it to his advantage and everyone's detriment."

"Why?" she frowned. "What does he want?"

"Who knows, anymore? We have not spoken in a long time. Pretty sure he wants the complete destruction of the remaining two timelines."

Quincy choked from her coughing. Talin handed her the cup of water on her desk.

"But, why?" she gasped, wiping the excess water from her lips.

"We spent too many years amongst you," said Talin, leaning on his knees. "Your human traits rubbed off on each of us. For good and bad." He shrugged. "For Iblis, he fell victim to desire. To the point where he would sacrifice anything and everything for it when it was denied him. For me, I hated the immortality, watching friends die and move on when I could not. For Gabrielle..."

Talin paused and Quincy felt her heart pound. She had never seen this from Talin. Pain contorted his features and her heart pounded from the fear of seeing it.

"For Gabrielle, she prized humanity's passion and ability to love and to be able to sacrifice oneself for it. She didn't even pause when she did it to save us all. To save me."

Quincy whispered. "She's dead, isn't she?"

Talin nodded. "So that I would live and through me, all of you. Iblis didn't like that. The realization she chose all of you and me against him left him...bitter." He shook his head.

Quincy stared at him, as if seeing him for the first time. "The three birds, the Raven, the Hawk, and the Dove."

"Just so," Talin responded.

Quincy shook her head, struggling to digest all the information with the fever. "So, what's next?" she mumbled, the exhaustion hitting her.

"You wait. You get better and work on your final clue from C. Meanwhile, I'm going arson hunting."

"The fire wasn't an accident?" The blood drained from her face.

He shook his head. "Definitely not."

"Iblis?"

"Possibly." He stood up and stretched his arms. "Probably." He turned to her and smiled. It looked unpracticed but it still brought warmth to her heart.

"You did well, Quinn. Thank you for running in after him. It...surprised me." He took off his hat and rubbed his hand through his jet-black hair, or was it? As the light touched it, she imagined she saw multiple colors in the black.

"I hate being surprised, Quincy. Don't do it again." He narrowed his eyes at her. He looked down at his head and pulled out the feather held by the black ribbon encircling the hat and handed it to her. "My feathers are coveted. Once a Creative Engineer believed time residue hid within the plumage."

"Is it true?" she asked.

Talin shrugged. "Possibly. At the very least you can bargain it. Unfortunately, I can't see what you do with it."

"Can't see because of me?"

"Probably because of your key. It interrupts everything." Talin rolled his eyes and placed his hat back on his head. "Rest. You're going to need it."

"Thanks?" she replied, but if he had heard it, she didn't know. He had already flown away.

CHAPTER TWENTY-TWO

GOING ALONE

Quincy and Eloise swung on the swing reading through note cards and quizzing each other back and forth.

"My brain is mush!" Eloise wailed and coughed as a rose petal fell into her open mouth.

Quincy giggled.

"You're no help," Eloise cried, spitting out the petal.

"You both are so loud!" Mikaela growled.

"At least none of you have to finish your Year Four Oakley final," Kalleigh groaned.

"How's that going?" Quincy asked.

"Slow. I have to show how my Talent can better society and pass on the Oakley prestige and blah blah blah." Kalleigh giggled.

Quincy chewed on her pen. Her memory Talent had definitely been placed behind the importance of the scavenger hunt for the key this year. The headmaster had been easy on her. Probably more than he should. She stared up at the roses in full bloom winding themselves around the Templum. What would she say if she had been a Year Four? What could she do with her Talent to better humanity? Quincy rolled her eyes. She could try to do one better. She could save it.

Eloise frowned. "What's wrong?"

Quincy forced a smile and shook her head. "Nothing, I'm tired of studying."

"Me too," Lindy laughed. "Let's go swimming in the river?"

The Third Floor girls all jumped up and skipped back to their rooms. Quincy included. She could have one afternoon for herself away from studying, birds, Talents, and saving the world.

***

The break had been exactly what she needed as she dodged a wet ball from Alba to Lindy and managed to keep her wet towel from falling to her ankles. Instead, it hit Mon-Aye's head. She narrowed her eyes and threw it back.

"Ladies, don't you remember my advisory class?" Professor Agglebye admonished. "Balls are to be thrown *outside*."

"Sorry, professor," the girls chorused.

Quincy laughed and waved as they continued toward the dormitory, still throwing the ball back and forth. As she ran up the stairs, her heart raced from the exertion. She leaned against the railing to catch her breath and waved her friends on. For some reason, she felt dread roll over her in waves. She continued up the stairs and ran into her room, pulling the curtains around her. She had waited long enough. She pulled out the third letter from her desk and read through it again. She recognized Hawthorne as the street in Portland where she grew up. She would be traveling back home but in the future. She quickly dressed and went to hunt down Talin. She couldn't travel forward without him anyway.

***

"Wait. Alone. As in by myself?"

Talin sighed. "You do know the definition of 'alone,' don't you."

Quincy narrowed her eyes at the insult. And at the suspicion he had been surprisingly easy to find in his tower.

"But you told me at the beginning of the year not to travel by myself. That I needed an anchor to make sure I get to the right time."

Talin nodded. "True. And I wasn't lying when I said it. But I've traveled with you mostly to keep an eye on you. The truth of the matter is you've anchored yourself, even without meaning to. With your time management Talent, you can get there, or rather then, by yourself."

Quincy pursed her lips.

Talin sighed. "Ask it."

"Your Talent, can you see ahead?"

Talin switched his weight from one talon to the other. "Sometimes it's there."

"Is it possible to travel into nothingness?"

Talin shook his head. "I'm sure the Timepiece would stop before it happened."

"You hope."

"I hope."

"Is this why you're letting me go alone?"

"Would you like me to go with you, Quinn?"

She shook her head. "No, if you think I'll be fine. I want to do it."

"I do. You already know where you want to go, and you can follow instructions, right? Three clicks?"

Quincy nodded.

"Good. Go when you're ready." He saluted her with a wing. "Safe time travels," and he flew off, leaving her alone. She walked outside toward the courtyard and stopped in front of the Timepiece. No time like the present. If things were truly getting worse, it would be better to time travel to the future now. She placed the key into the lock and walked below.

CHAPTER TWENTY-THREE

TO THE FUTURE

Quincy closed the Corocularum and placed it delicately in her pocket. She looked around Hawthorne Street and stared at the storefronts, feeling a strange sense of familiarity but also a sense of being out of place. She recognized few of the storefronts. She pulled her thin coat tighter against herself as the wind blew at her. The cold and gray day in the city made her realize how badly she wanted a hot drink and wish she had worn a warmer sweater. Quincy followed the instructions from the note until she walked into the diner down the street. Quincy looked at the heads of all the diner's occupants, recalling the final part of the clue,

> *Find the man with hair quite white,*
> *Who will lead you to the light.*

Quincy walked by older gentlemen with white hair, hoping one would recognize her and call out to her. After looking for five minutes, she sat down at the counter.

"What'll you have, sweetie?"

Quincy reached into her pocket and remembered she hadn't brought any dollars. She sadly shook her head.

"Nothing, please."

As the waitress took a step away, a warm voice stopped her.

"She will have a cup of hot chocolate with raspberry syrup if you please."

She looked over at her benefactor shocked he knew her favorite drink.

His well-kept white hair grew wispy over his eyes, but had been kept short in the back. He reached up and brushed the hair over the top of his glasses that partially hid his friendly blue eyes. He was thin, barely healthily so, and sat on the corner with his hands clasped. Quincy guessed his age to be around his mid-forties. She looked at him quizzically.

"Our mutual friend let me know you would be here to visit me today."

"The gentleman who has been leading me on this wild goose chase?" Quincy questioned.

"Something to that extent."

Quincy felt more reassured and slid over to sit next to him. The server brought her the drink and she took a sip.

"Thank you."

"You are welcome." He gave her a slight sideways smile then turned his gaze towards the front of the diner. He had a slight accent Quincy couldn't immediately decipher.

"Whata 'bout you, hun?" The server grinned at the man.

"Tea, if you would be so kind. Herbal."

The server smiled and left them alone. He turned his attention to Quincy.

"By now I am quite sure you have a decent grasp upon time and its quirky rules."

"I think so, what do you mean exactly?" she narrowed her eyes at him. "Why?"

"This is a possible future," he gestured around him. "This place might not even exist for you."

"Is this a good future?"

At this, the gentleman laughed. "Well I think so," he reached into his pocket. "Here, I have a message for you."

Quincy grimaced and in response the gentleman cocked an eyebrow.

"I'm sorry; I thought I was done."

"Ahh, I understand the disappointment all too well. It never seems to be over when you think it is." He handed her the note.

Quincy accepted it from him but before she could read it, he gently placed his hand over hers.

"You have plenty of time to look at it later." At the mention of time, he looked mischievous, but then grew serious. "Before you read it, I need your full attention for a moment. This is going to be the hard part of the message." Here the gentleman paused as if deciding whether or not to continue. He looked unhappy but grudgingly continued.

"In your fairly distant future, someone is going to betray you. And it is going to be someone who is close. It will hurt you deeply. I am terribly sorry."

Quincy felt chills down her spine. "Who? Who is going to betray me? Why?"

"You know I cannot tell you. It is imperative that you make your own decisions so you do not disorder this future. It is one thing for the future to do so to your present, but another for me as a possible future, to try to change your present."

"That makes no sense."

The man rubbed his temple. "I do not have a better way to explain this to you."

"You know who's going to betray me?"

The server interrupted the conversation by leaving the steaming cup of tea in front of the man. He unclasped his hands and Quincy saw his hands tremor as he grasped the cup.

"Your future, my past." He smiled sadly. "But yes, yes I do."

"Could you possibly give me a hint?"

The gentleman cocked his eyebrow once more. "I wish I could. I truly do."

Quincy saw pain in his eyes before he continued. "I apologize. This future is something you are working towards, so I cannot help you with details."

"Then why tell me at all?"

The gentleman bit the corner of his lower lip.

"Because the future threads looked better when I told you to be warned than when I did not."

"You see the future?"

The gentleman looked her in the eyes and gave her a small smile. "To some extent."

"My best friend does that. Kind of."

"Does he now?" A slow smile spread from the corners of his mouth.

"Yeah, but he can't control it."

"Everyone needs to work on their gifts. None of them work correctly from the beginning."

"He doesn't think anyone else has his Talent."

"It is certainly unusual."

Quincy stared at her hot chocolate, a frown covering her features. She missed him. And she hated how much she did.

"He will come around." the gentleman said softly. "He is still young."

She looked over at him and for the first time truly saw him. She knew those blue eyes. Her eyes burned and she rapidly blinked to hide any evidence of watery eyes. He handed her a handkerchief and despite herself, she laughed.

"So, you do learn to control it?" she whispered.

He winked. "That would be telling," he grinned and stretched. "Do not let him have coffee," he laughed warmly. Quincy loved the sound. He looked down at his watch and then at her. "Time for me to go. Besides, you have finals to finish."

Quincy groaned and stood up.

"Oh, and Q?" he asked. Quincy looked back at him. *Q?*

"Please be gentle with him."

Quincy watched Monty's future walk outside and her brain swarmed with questions she wished she had asked him. She finished her hot chocolate and found a bench outside. She wanted this to be done. Angrily, she tore open the clue to read the spidery handwriting again.

You thought three would make you free,
but you were mistaken.
You've worked hard in this regard,
and I am pleased.
One last riddle of me in the middle
of your desire.
It's time to go home to the time of your own,
and with this feat, it's time to meet
me soon.
Be safe and do not wait,
I will not be late.

Sincerely,
C

Quincy fought the desire to tear the letter into tiny pieces, but instead placed it back in her pocket. She walked towards a private corner of the street and used the Corocularum to take her back to the Timepiece and then home. She turned the dial to go backward to her present, dreaming of her warm bed. She heard the familiar clicking noises until suddenly everything stopped. Her eyes flew open and she looked around. She hadn't left the Timepiece, but her internal clock was askew. Her heart began to pound. She didn't know the time or when she was. Cold sweat pooled on her temple and she pinched herself. Definitely alive.

Cautiously, she walked up the stairs and opened the door to outside the clock, fearful to find out where she had been taken. Did she break something? She walked out the door and shivered in shock. She couldn't hear a sound. Not a bird chirping, or laughter, or even wind through the trees and the Oakley buildings. She paused when she saw the most curious thing she had ever seen; a flock of birds, frozen mid-flight. She whirled around and saw large trees no longer in existence. What had she done?

"It's not what you've done, but more so what I've done."

Quincy whirled around and looked behind her. A man leaned against the Timepiece. He wore a plum suit and towered above her. She narrowed her eyes at him. "It's you."

"Yes, it is me. If that's who you mean."

"Why aren't you rhyming?" Quincy asked skeptically. The man's laughter shook his body.

"Why don't you follow me and I'll explain."

Quincy narrowed her eyes at him. "Why should I trust you?"

"My dear, I can hardly harm you. Here, see." He reached out for her and she gasped as his hand went through her.

"You see, I'm a memory, a simple shadow of myself."

"What do you mean?"

"I'm technically dead. I died ages ago. I copied myself until you were ready to meet me and ready for this." He dangled the key towards Quincy and she reached up to grab it. Her hand went through the key.

"Tut tut my dear. It's not quite that easy, I'm afraid. But you're close."

"How can you be dead, we met back in September. That was you, right?"

"Indeed, one of my last traveling adventures. For me it was over seventy years ago."

Quincy gaped at him.

"How old are you?"

"Old enough," the man winked.

Ugh, she shook her head and changed the subject. "You said *one* of your last adventures? How many times have you time-traveled?" she asked.

The man paused as he thought about it. Finally, he shrugged. "I stopped counting after the twenty-fifth time."

"You're like me!"

The man patted her head. "No, my dear, I wish I had been. Alas, not so fortunate."

"What do you mean?"

"Why do you think when we met, I rhymed like a mad man?"

"Why?"

"Because I'm quite mad don't you know? Let's continue this inside, shall we? Please follow me if you wish to receive the original key."

Quincy grudgingly followed the man into Oakley, knowing she had no choice. At least he couldn't physically attack her.

Quincy's eyes widened when they walked in. It looked like a typical school day in Oakley, except for the frozen life around her.

"Welcome to Oakley in 1888."

Quincy followed the man into the back hall and past the Back Library. Except these were the glory days of the library. All the lights were on and countless students congregated inside, all of them frozen in their last action.

"Why aren't they at the library in the Learner's Citadel?"

"My sweet girl, the Learner's Citadel won't be built for another twenty years."

Quincy continued to follow him up the stairs until they walked towards a room.

"Why are you taking me to the storage closet?" Quincy asked.

"Storage? Now it isn't."

The man in purple walked through the open door and took a seat next to a frozen roaring fire. Quincy tensed when she saw two young boys in the corner looking at blueprints. She looked over the room at the covered walls filled with posters of clocks, dials, keys, and timelines.

"What is this room?"

"Students with dreams of ingenuity are given rooms in which to build, experiment, and study. This is my room and my brothers."

Quincy stared at the two boys who looked nothing alike. She recognized the immaculately well-kept younger version of the man. But not the other with his shirt partially untucked and ink smudges on his cheeks from his fingertips.

"Not naturally born. We're technically step-brothers. We both shared a fascination with time. As you can see," he said while gesturing to their work. Quincy looked closely at one of the blueprints and saw four clock faces on top of each other with no hands.

"The Timepiece," Quincy said in awe.

The man looked disappointed. "That's not what it's supposed to be called. The name is the *Chenoweth Clock.*"

"Yeah, no one calls it that." Quincy shrugged.

"Unbelievable. No credit for the years of work."

"Wait a moment. C? Chenoweth?" she asked turning around to face the man.

"At your service," he said, taking off his hat and bowing.

"*The* Marcus Chenoweth?"

"Is there another?" Chenoweth asked.

"Not that I know of," Quincy admitted.

"Phew, I don't like the idea of being replaced," he grinned. "I believe you want my key, do you not?"

Quincy nodded eagerly.

"Excellent. Please take a seat."

She felt odd moving one of the smaller chairs to face Chenoweth.

"How can they be frozen and how can I be able to move this chair?"

"Not to worry, we boys were delighted to see that chair move across the room."

Quincy sucked in her breath. "I've changed the moment?"

"Nonsense, you made sure it happened. I have seen every possibility and choice from this moment, which is why I decided to live here."

"In this moment?"

"Exactly. I'm a shadow living in-between this moment. You could restart my clock and watch what is transpiring in this room as it happens. But I wouldn't be here, and you are here to see me. At least the last remnants of me."

"May I ask you something?" Quincy requested.

Chenoweth nodded. "Certainly."

Quincy pointed back to the blueprints. "How are we in this moment if you're only building the clock now? It doesn't exist yet."

Chenoweth grinned. "Exactly! Well done. The Chenoweth clock isn't bound to the usual rules of time. Because of the Heart, it is its own entity. So, it can travel backward or forward. Do be warned, it will appear whenever you go. It's fine now, since I've frozen time.

But if you actually traveled here on purpose, the school would see a clock that doesn't exist yet."

"That's convoluted."

"Thank you."

"Why did you choose a time-traveling machine that's so visible?" Quincy wondered.

"Eh, mistakes might have been made," shrugged Chenoweth. "Too late now. Let's address this. Are you ready?"

Quincy nodded. "What do I need to do?"

"I love a good riddle, if you haven't already figured out. So, I've comprised your three clues into riddles to make sure you were paying attention. I'm afraid you can't miss a single one, or I will send you back keyless to your present and wait for the next keyholder. As you well know, you can't finish your quest without my key."

She nodded, wishing Talin or Monty had come with her.

"Okay, how do I start?"

"We have already begun." Chenoweth's eyes twinkled mischievously.

Quincy twisted her fingers nervously.

"Answer me this. In the past, why didn't Prieler's position last?"

Quincy remembered the discussion with the headmaster regarding the failure of the Third. Quincy thought this question was too easy. Was he tricking her? The two stared each other down as if they had a chess board placed between the two of them. Uncertainly, she answered the question. "Pride."

"In detail."

"He thought himself above the rules because of his position."

Chenoweth smiled, pleased. "Hmm, textbook answer, but nevertheless true. Question two. "Who, or rather what, is Talin."

Quincy gulped and squirmed. "He wasn't happy with you forcing him to reveal information."

Chenoweth grinned. "Good. It's only fair you know exactly what you're dealing with. He was never going to share enough information with you. It could be detrimental to all existence."

"You're not fond of Talin." She said, a statement not a question.

Chenoweth shrugged. "It's not that I don't like him, he's miserably strict about those who wish to time-travel." He looked disgusted.

"It's not necessarily a bad thing." Quincy said, cautiously. "You said so yourself your mind shouldn't time-travel."

Chenoweth nodded. "True, but I wouldn't give up anything for it. You take your Talent for granted, my dear."

Quincy crossed her arms. "You weren't asked to save the universe."

"Fair statement. Let's continue, shall we? Talin, if you please."

"Talin is one of the three guardians."

"What does he control."

"The rain, I think."

Chenoweth nodded. "I had suspected as well. What *else* does he control?"

Quincy chewed on her lip and stared at him. "I think he watches over time."

Chenoweth rubbed his chin. "Yes, I'll accept that answer."

Quincy leaned over, sighing with relief. She looked at him, frowning. "Why the whole thing with the celestial globe and the other timeline? Why make it so much harder?"

"Because I wanted to remind you of your own emotional attachments and to understand all those feelings are mirrored on the other side. There's more at stake than this timeline."

Quincy nodded. "I understand."

"Good."

"So, you placed two clues in one. Isn't that considered cheating?"

Chenoweth gave her a sly smile. "A small ruse. You should thank me." He winked. "You're welcome."

Quincy fought against rolling her eyes at the man before he had given her his key.

"Now, for your final riddle. What will be your downfall?"

"My what?" Quincy sat straight up, gaping. What kind of question was this? How could she know?

She shook her head. "I don't want to know."

Chenoweth's face fell. "Not at all?"

Quincy crossed her arms and shook her head. "Not at all."

"That is…unfortunately incorrect," Chenoweth said.

Quincy's heart plummeted. The moment felt like hours as she stared in horror at the man in plum. How could she have come so close to fail at the end? Anger overcame her fear and she frowned at Chenoweth.

"No. It's not wrong. I don't know the answer. I shouldn't know the ending of every major choice I will make or my future downfall. I should prepare myself, but what would be the point of living in the now if I already know where I'm going to fail?"

Chenoweth released a breath and he smiled. "Well done." He nodded approvingly. "Well done indeed."

Quincy's eyes widened. "What now?" she asked.

"You're finished."

Quincy slumped in her chair, relieved the ordeal was finished. "Why all of this? Why not give me the key right away?"

Marcus Chenoweth leaned in closer to her. "You are not the first major key holder you know."

Quincy nodded. "I know my mother was one. Why didn't she get your key?"

"She declined my quest."

"Why?"

"She knew she wasn't ready. Two people have touched my key, its creator and myself. I didn't want to give it to just anyone. I would hate for you to make it this far but find yourself ill prepared."

"But how do you know I'm prepared?"

"I don't. But I wanted to make sure you understood how your decisions affect not just you, but the remaining timelines. This is not an easy task, and we are small pawns being used in a larger war between time and law. Do you understand?"

Quincy nodded somberly. "I think so? Do you truly believe that?"

"I do. Now for my key. When you arrive at your own time, take the other door upstairs into the clock faces. There is a plaque with my name and a dedication. Push the letters to spell out 'clock' in order."

"That's it?"

Chenoweth nodded and gestured towards the door. Quincy nodded. "Okay, but may I ask you one more question?"

"Please."

Quincy pursed her lips. She knew she would regret it if she didn't ask. "Do you know who is going to betray me?"

The laughter left Chenoweth and he looked down at her.

"I do not. For there are too many choices ahead for me to know."

Quincy looked at the towering man and felt a pang of sadness.

"Is this it? Will I see you again?"

He grinned mischievously. "Only time will tell." His face dropped. "Once you have received the key, this recording of me will disappear. Please do not try to find me again." Chenoweth looked around the room sadly until his face stopped on the two young boys in the corner.

Quincy looked closer at the two boys. "Who is your brother?"

Chenoweth winked at her. "Spoilers." He ignored her and sat back down near the fire.

"So, are we done?"

"Having a bit of a letdown already, are we?" Chenoweth asked.

She didn't like his tone of voice. "Nope, I'm good to go." She gave him a tight smile and walked outside to the Timepiece that technically did not exist yet. Timepiece or the Chenoweth Clock? She shrugged. It would always be the Timepiece to her. Sorry, Chenoweth. She paused at the clock and looked up. How did she even get here? Another question for Talin. Not that he would tell her.

She walked down the stairs and calculated her present date and dreamed of home. After a few minutes, the Timepiece commenced its ticking back to its normal routine. She carefully locked the door on her way out and walked to the other side of the Timepiece. She turned the key to the entrance of the brain of the Timepiece and walked up the claustrophobic steps until she ended behind the clock faces. She peeked out and remembered being inside the clock of the alternate London. She looked around and stopped when she saw a large plaque on the floor near her feet.

MARCUS CHENOWETH
TO OAKLEY
A small piece of time.

The Timepiece, Quincy smiled. She looked over the letters spelling out "clock." She pushed down the *C* in Marcus, the *L* in Oakley, the *O* in Chenoweth, and second *C* in Chenoweth, and finally the *K* in Oakley. The plaque groaned and a small slit in the 'L' in Oakley gave way. Quincy peeked inside and saw a glimmer of silver. The third minor key had been hidden in the Timepiece all along. She picked it up and held it to the light. There were slits in the eye like a clock. She brushed her fingers in the key hole, noting the multiple circles within the eye. Much like the faces of the Timepiece. She carefully placed it in her pocket and walked back to her room. Possible Future Monty's words haunted her.

"Someone is going to betray you completely. And it is going to be someone who is close. It will hurt deeply."

Quincy slowed her pace from the courtyard. Instead of going to dinner, she walked right past the Dining Hall and took the stairs towards the Third Floor. Who could betray her so much it would "hurt deeply?" On the steps Quincy almost bumped into Colin.

"You don't look well. Are you sure you don't want to go towards the dining hall?"

"I'm quite sure, thank you." Quincy replied crisply to Colin as she walked around him up the stairs. She didn't know who she could trust. She went straight to bed and feigned sleep when the girls came up from dinner. Quincy closed her drapes and threw the covers over her head when she heard them trampling up the stairs. She did not feel like talking to Eloise or Mikaela. Right at that moment, Quincy realized she wanted to talk to Monty more than anyone else. But Monty was still mad at her and future Monty's voice tugged at her. *Someone who is close...* What if the headmaster or even Talin could betray her? How could she trust anyone now?

CHAPTER TWENTY-FOUR

ACED AND FAILED FINAL EXAMS

*S*he was back in Portland. The smells of roasting coffee and fresh bread wafted past her. She turned around, half expecting to see her family behind her. Instead, random individuals meandered around her. She frowned. Where was her family on this unusually beautiful spring afternoon? She saw her father walk past one of the buildings nearby.

"Dad! Wait for me," she called out, but he continued on as if he hadn't heard her. He walked past a corner so she ran after him. She reached out to clutch his elbow when he turned into a black silhouette, and faceless, turned around to confront her. A Noctem Umbrem. Eerily, it still kept the shape of her father. It reached out toward her and she took a step back. A stone wall stopped her from escaping.

"Be careful who you trust," it hissed in an unnatural voice but still reminded her of her father's. It grabbed her and she tried to scream as it sucked the life out of her...

Quincy jumped out of bed, grabbing a candlestick to protect herself. When she remembered she was back at Oakley, she sheepishly put down the would-be weapon. She grabbed her coat and put on her boots to walk outside. She stood in front of the Timepiece and let the raindrops fall on her face. The echoes of the rain drowned out any noise and she closed her eyes, letting her heartbeat normalize.

"Rough night?"

Quincy opened her eyes and stared at the barrier. Talin perched on one of the posts and shook the rain from his feathers.

"Definitely not an easy one," she answered.

"Most of the time, nightmares are your subconscious trying to deal with problems. Or so I've been told."

Quincy shivered, she hated to admit how much the Nocti terrified her. "What is a Noctem Umbrem? Dwilight told me how he accidentally created one, and Prieler has been making them, too, but what are they, exactly?"

Talin shifted his weight from one talon to the other. "They're the darkest part of a person's soul. The thing most terrifying to you."

"But why did it turn into my mom at the museum?"

"That's one of life's greatest ironies. Sometimes the ones we love the most can be our greatest nightmare. You're terrified of losing

335

your mother, aren't you?" Talin asked. Quincy nodded, dread tightening her throat.

"Well, there you are," Talin continued. "They emulate that fear so they can feed off it."

Quincy shivered. "They're evil."

Talin paused. "Yes, and no. The Noctem Umbrem, or night's shadows, are *you*. Our fears and our nightmares don't necessarily make us evil. If you take away courage, love, and empathy, you have created a nightmare. But the process of making one is truly evil. In order to create one, you must give it a piece of your soul. The more powerful your nightmare, the more powerful the Noctem Umbrem. Without taking a life, they fade away. Except in the case of the one shadowing you. Once they've taken a life, they're a greater problem to deal with."

"Why do I keep dreaming about them?"

"Because they're terrifying," he stated.

"I don't like seeing them. Especially in my childhood memories."

"Of course not. No one wants to tarnish a memory with those. Speaking of childhood memories, what was it like being back in Portland?"

Quincy shrugged. "Weird. I miss it. But what I really miss is my family being there. Without them, it didn't feel like home anymore."

"It's the ones we love that make it home." Talin said.

"Talin, may I ask a question?"

"You know the rules," he rolled his eyes. "You may ask, but I might not answer."

His comment sounded strangely like Dwilight.

"Do you know why we left Portland for New York?"

"Because they were looking for a key—,"

Quincy shook her head, interrupting him. "I don't think so anymore. Do you know why we *really* left Portland?"

Talin coughed, clearing his throat. "Yes, I do. But you're not going to like the answer."

"Tell me."

"For some reason, Dwilight's Noctem Umbrem keeps finding you. And after, Prieler and his entourage are not far behind. They hoped the sheer amount of people would be able to hide you."

Quincy's throat tightened. "We moved because of *me*." She shut her eyes and clenched her fists. Now she knew why they had left so quickly. She had thrown a tantrum for weeks and had been completely ridiculous to her parents. And they had done it to protect her.

"They didn't want you to know. They wanted you to have a childhood for as long as possible," Talin soothed.

Quincy wiped her nose against her sleeve.

"I apologize for changing the subject, but may I see Chenoweth's key?"

Quincy paused and stared at Talin. Or Cigfran, or whoever he was. If Quincy couldn't trust him, then who could she? Quincy pulled out the key from her pocket and handed it to Talin. He gingerly balanced his weight on one talon while grasping the key in the other. He shook his head. "What did you think of Chenoweth?"

Quincy frowned. "I'm not sure how I felt about him. Something about him seemed...off."

Talin snickered. "You mirrored word for word what people felt about him. It's why he wasn't elevated to a Master Creative Engineer. Even he manages to generally annoy me."

"Everyone annoys you," stated Quincy.

Talin snorted. "Mostly."

"Why did he annoy you in particular?"

Talin cleared his throat. "I like my secrets. I don't like people finding them out."

"About your importance in the other timeline, or that you're also Cigfran?"

"Yes." He rolled his eyes. "And more which you'll figure out eventually. I prefer to stay behind the scenes. Running everything from a safe distance. *Safe*." Talin snorted again. "As if such a thing exists in my life."

"I'm sorry, Talin."

"For what?"

"For having to watch people you care about grow old and die."

He nodded soberly. "Thank you. But I figured out the secret to protect myself."

"Oh?"

"It's better not to care." The corner of his lips wavered into a smirk.

"I was trying to be nice! You're so mean!" she laughed.

"I know. When you're as old as I am, you're allowed to be crotchety."

Quincy rolled her eyes.

"Changing the subject, do you want to hold on to two keys?" Talin asked soberly.

She shook her head. "No, I don't want to. But I don't know where to put it and I don't know who to trust. Will you hold on to it for me?"

Talin shook his feathers dry. The action reminded her of a shiver.

"No thank you. I held on to Montgomery's key in my perch for far too long. But I can tell you it will be safe with the headmaster."

"Are you sure?"

Talin nodded. "From what I can see, anyway."

"You know who's going to betray me?"

Talin shook his head. "Like I said, I can't see your future, if I had known, it's been lost."

"You don't remember anything? Nothing at all?"

Talin shook his head. "And it's not only you anymore. After you came back from your Portland trip, I can't see anyone's future more than twenty years."

Fear tightened Quincy's throat. "What happens if you stop seeing or being able to travel at all?"

"Not something you need to worry about. By the time that happens, no one will still exist to comprehend what's going on."

Quincy shivered and for the first time, realized her feet were soaked through to her socks. "We have to find the next key."

Talin nodded. "Sooner rather than later. You're on the right trail. Have Monty keep looking into that break-in at the Swiss bank."

Quincy's heart pounded. "Why aren't we going after it now?"

"Because you're legally required to go back to Miss Heatherwoods and your inventor needs to learn how to pick locks."

"My what?"

"Your little purple friend is going to learn how to pick a lock and it's going to take her a couple of months to master it."

"You've seen it?"

Talin chuckled. "Eh, sort of. My Talent isn't completely useless."

"But what about these?" Quincy shook the key at him. "I thought these could open any lock?"

"True, but these aren't your typical locks. There was a reason it created such a scandal when the bank was broken into. But enough talk. You have finals tomorrow and we would both hate for you to faint before you could take your exam."

"Ugh," Quincy faux-groaned. "Not nice."

Talin saluted and flew off.

∗∗∗

Quincy sat down and pulled out her pencil from her messenger bag. Her shoulders sagged, relieved. She expected Latin to be a more difficult exam, but skimming through the questions on the first page, she instantly knew she would be fine. She had forty-five minutes to complete her exam, but barely thirty minutes later, she finished the last question. She hadn't even needed to memory travel. She quietly put down her pencil and brought it up to the professor. He raised one eyebrow at her paper and silently took it, placing beside him. She walked back to her seat and saw a few Year One faces look up in horror and then back down at their exams. Quincy sat down and closed her eyes, feigning sleep. Finally, the professor rang a small bell at his desk, forcing everyone to bring their exam papers to him. Quincy stopped herself from skipping out of the room.

The rest of her exams flew past and she felt confident with all of them, despite her constant yawning. Between the traveling and studying, she could sleep for a week. Her last exam was with the headmaster and she had no idea what his exam would be like. She sat down in his office and toyed with Chenoweth's key in her pocket. She hated holding on to it. It felt so dangerous to have something so important she could easily lose. She laughed to herself. She finally found the one good thing about her key being stuck to her.

The headmaster walked in and sat down in front of her. "Ready?" he asked.

"I have no idea."

The headmaster grinned and placed a jar of cinnamon on his desk. "For your final, I want you to pick a specific memory. The date must be from January 1st from the year of your choice. Don't go back too far. But it must be longer than five years."

Quincy nodded, grabbed the cinnamon and closed her eyes. The cinnamon smell wafted through her nostrils and she allowed herself to wipe every current memory until all of her recent memories washed over her, rewinding throughout the year. Finally, she stopped. A younger version of herself sat in front of a Christmas tree, bawling her eyes out.

"Quinn, sweetie," her father said drawing her into his lap. "Why are you crying."

Quincy sniffed and dug her face into his shirt. "I don't want it to go away."

"You don't want what to go away?"

Quincy pointed to the tree. "I don't want to take down the ornaments."

"Why not?"

"Because Christmas will be over and then I have to go back to school. It will be a whole year before it comes again. I'll be so *old*." She burst into a fit of tears.

As an older Quincy, she noted for the first time her father stifling laughter from her dramatic crying. But he managed to hold himself together so that younger Quincy never caught on.

"It's okay to be sad when we say goodbye to things," he said as he took down one ornament from the tree. "But many of these good things will come again. Sometimes we need to let things go so we can make new memories." He gently pried her away from his chest so they could face eye-to-eye. "It's going to be okay, Quinn. You're going to be fine. There will be good moments, and bad moments, and some in-between. But through all of it, my sweet, don't stop being *you*."

Quincy paused. For some reason, it felt like he spoke to her now instead of her child version, as if he had already known.

He kissed the top of her head. "Now, it's way past your bedtime. Say goodbye to tree. You'll have a new tree with new memories next year."

"Goodbye, tree," small Quincy said, sniffing as she tried to hug the spiky tree.

"Goodnight, Quincy."

"Goodnight, Daddy."

✳✳✳

Quincy allowed herself to be led back by the cinnamon and found herself staring at Marquam. She quickly recounted the visit without going into too many details.

"Which brings us to my final question. Or rather my first. Why do we study our past?"

"It's so we don't forget it. And to help us decide which path to take."

"Well done." The headmaster smiled, clearly pleased. Quincy sat back in her seat, feeling both relief and exhaustion.

"You look tired," he noted. She nodded. "I definitely need a nap."

"Don't let me keep you then."

She stood up and paused, pursing her lips.

"Was there anything else?" he asked. She nodded and pulled out the key from her pocket, placing it on his desk.

"Is that—?"

She nodded. He smiled grasping the key and pulling it closer to him. He shook his head. "Marcus Chenoweth. I would have enjoyed meeting him."

"Enjoy is not the word I would use," she replied. He took one more look at the key before offering it back. She shook her head. "Would you be willing to keep it with you? I don't trust it with me at Miss Heatherwoods."

He nodded, smiling and obviously pleased by her request. "It would be my honor."

She sighed in relief, glad to be rid of it.

"I'll hold onto it until you want it back."

"Thank you." She stood up and grabbed her bag. "And now I'm going to sleep."

"Rest well."

She turned around to answer, but the key's details had his full attention, so she quietly left his office.

***

Quincy chewed on her bacon, not tasting the flavor. The exhaustion from the clues and finals had left her feeling numb. The obnoxious popping of chewing gum interrupted her reverie. She turned around to face the office assistant who handed her a note. The assistant saluted and left. Quincy stared down at the handwritten letter.

Miss Harris,
Please meet me in my classroom promptly after breakfast.
—Professor Thomasin.

The Latin Professor. Quincy's heart plummeted. Why? She had felt confident about her exam. She put down the rest of the bacon and decided to walk to the Learner's Citadel to wait outside the classroom for judgment. The professor met her there a few moments later.

"That was quick, Miss Harris," he motioned inside. She followed him to his desk and he handed her an exam. She recognized her name on top of the page. She looked below it and didn't see any marks on any of the pages.

She frowned at her paper and then looked up. "What did I do wrong?" she asked.

The Latin professor smiled tightly. "Absolutely nothing. Completely flawless. I would have chalked it down to cheating, but I recalled your Memory Talent."

Quincy nodded.

"Even though there are so few of you, all of the Talent schools report the same thing. Did you know most memory students test out of Latin at the end of their second year?"

Quincy shook her head.

"I'm surprised you had such difficulty with this class last year."

Quincy crossed her arms over her chest and tightened her shoulders from the embarrassment.

"Well, I don't see any need to keep you with the Year Ones next year for Year Two Latin. Instead, you'll start as a Year Three with the rest of your year."

Quincy grinned; her humiliation quickly placated.

"Don't be too excited. You'll have some catching up to do. Once you have, though, you'll probably graduate Latin at the end of the first term, since you seem to have finally caught on to the basics of your Talent. I suspect languages will continue to become easier and easier for you. Many Memory Talents choose to go on as translators. If I were you, I would start to think about whether or not you see a future for yourself in this. I imagine, with your Talent, you could be a phenomenal translator. If this interests you, I would be happy to place you with my advanced students in a crash course for general languages."

A translator. What could her life be like? Was she even allowed to plan her future? She could travel, be free. She grinned at the professor. "Thank you, sir. I would like that."

"Good. If you pass the final exam for Latin in December, we will talk again. Such a pity the headmaster didn't assign you to me right away. You would already be so much further. *Infortunatus*. Marquam knows best, we hope."

Quincy's eyes widened at this new piece of information.

"You may go," he released her. Quincy walked outside and stared at the sunny window. Translator. It sounded like a nice dream. But never more than a dream. She still had two missing keys and a door to open. If she existed long enough. She shivered and walked out.

Colin paced outside, a smudge of blue paint on his cheek.

Quincy smiled and Colin looked up. "What's so funny?" he asked.

She pointed to his face. "You have paint on your cheek."

Colin laughed and tried to unsuccessfully wipe the wrong cheek. Quincy laughed too and rubbed the dried paint off the correct spot.

His cheeks reddened. "Thanks."

"Any time."

"So," he paused. "Have you already been asked out for the banquet?"

Quincy's throat tightened and she shook her head. Colin grinned. "May I have the honor of asking you to banquet with me tonight?"

Quincy laughed. "Your honor? You sound so formal."

Colin laughed sheepishly. "How about pleasure instead of honor?" He looked so hopeful Quincy laughed. "Yes, you may have the pleasure of taking me to the banquet."

He smiled victoriously. "I'll meet you at the family room at 5:45?"

"Sounds great."

"Brilliant. I better go and make sure all the paint is gone."

Quincy waved as he fled. Why wasn't she happier? Colin was kind, and good-looking, and artistic. Any girl would have been ecstatic to have been asked. So why wasn't she? She slowly walked back to her room. Upstairs, dresses were being traded and tossed around. Kalleigh pinned Mikaela's hair up and groaned when two more girls jumped in line. Quincy dug through her trunk looking through her clothing. She finally decided on the blue one she hadn't worn last year. Eloise twirled next to her in a princess style purple dress, she sat grinning. "What do you think of my new dress?"

"It's definitely purple. And fluffy." Quincy laughed. "Do you even own dresses in any other color?" Eloise toyed with a strand of purple hair. "Of course. I have a black one. For funerals and the like."

Eloise jumped up and tried to copy Kalleigh by placing Quincy's hair up in a similar fashion. "So, have you and Monty made up yet?" Eloise mumbled. Quincy shook her head. Eloise sighed. "So, are you going alone tonight?"

Quincy shook her head and smiled. "Colin asked me to go with him."

Eloise ear-piercingly squealed, and the rest of the room groaned. *Sorry*! Eloise mouthed silently to the room. Genevieve slammed the bathroom door shut and the whole room shuddered.

"Just ignore her," Eloise murmured. "You didn't do anything wrong."

Quincy knew that, but it didn't make her feel any better. Their roommates cringed after the scene and went back to their own outfits. Kalleigh looked over and groaned. "Oh, my goodness, Eloise." Kalleigh grabbed a brush and lovingly pushed Eloise to the side. "I'm here to save your reputation, Quincy."

Eloise stuck out her tongue, giggled, and left the room while Kalleigh pulled out pins and fixed Quincy's hair.

***

Quincy took a bite of the savory roast beef that should have been wonderful, but instead it tasted bland. Despite the fizzy drinks and the abundance of her favorite foods, she wasn't enjoying herself. Colin met her at the family room door and his eyes bugged seeing her. She had borrowed earrings from Lindy while Kalleigh and Mikaela had done her hair and makeup to perfection. He told her how beautiful she looked and she complimented him on his handsome outfit. Which he was completely true. He wore a green tie offsetting his eyes and his new gray suit looked ironed and tailored. He offered his hand and walked her down to the Main Hall.

Banquet felt silly to her. Dinner felt like any other except this was the last meal they would share with Kalleigh. Some of the Year Threes and Fours were heading off to Oakdale to celebrate in town. The Year Fours would celebrate now being allowed to enter the Oakley Arms Pub. But for Quincy and her year, everyone would be going to the café for drinks or upstairs, to the family room.

"A hello to Quincy Harris!"

Quincy looked up to see Eloise waving her arms to get her attention.

"Are you alright?" Colin murmured, gently tapping her on the shoulder.

Quincy forced a smile and nodded. "I'm worn out from finals."

"We're thinking of grabbing drinks in the café to take away and then games in the family room." Eloise said.

"Unless you want to go for a walk around the grounds?" Colin mumbled. Quincy smiled at him, flattered. But Monty's empty spot had ruined any chance of a fun evening. He couldn't even bother to show up tonight.

"Games sound nice, and so does a walk," she turned to face Colin. "But honestly, I need some rest before I leave tomorrow. Eloise shrugged and turned to yell at her sister at the end of the table. Colin looked down at his own meal and then up at her, obviously forcing a smile. "Of course."

"Spending time with you sounds lovely, raincheck?"

Colin nodded again. This time his smile genuine. "Would you allow me to at least walk you back?"

Quincy smiled, relieved. "I'd like that, thank you."

They finished their dessert and the Headmaster gave his final farewell to the graduating students. "And please remember, the eagles will be leaving promptly," he wagged his finger at the graduating class. "So, don't have too much fun tonight." After everyone finished laughing, he released the student body with his hand, and everyone left for their final night activities. Colin and Quincy slowly walked back toward the third floor, him talking about his summer plans and her trying to be as vague as possible. Eloise and Rusty rushed past them to grab his trumpet.

"I'm going to join Rusty, and Eloise to get hot chocolates. If you're sure you don't want some."

"I'm sure, but thanks for asking." At the bottom of the staircase, Colin kissed her on the cheek and quickly walked away. She stared at his back, dumbfounded. Kalleigh walked past her and she must have seen Colin's kiss, because she turned back to Quincy and grinned. Quincy numbly walked upstairs. She dodged multiple students, of all floors, milling around the staircase enjoying their last night at Oakley before the summer holiday. Quincy hid behind a taller student not to be caught by Eloise who giggled at Rusty's joke. Quincy rolled her eyes. She had heard the joke about this same animal four times now and had not found it funny the first time.

Quincy closed the door to the dorms and sighed, the sigh turning to a yawn. It felt silly to go to sleep so early on her last night of freedom before Miss Heatherwood's, but she was exhausted. She heard sniffles in the corner of the room and couldn't help but investigate. Genevieve wore plain clothes and Quincy painfully realized that she didn't recall seeing her at the Banquet. Genevieve wiped her eyes and looked at her angrily.

"What? Bored? The attention of two boys isn't enough?" Genevieve hissed.

"Excuse me?" Quincy gasped.

"You already have an Irish lord, why did you have to take Colin, too?"

"I don't *have* anybody," Quincy sputtered.

"It's not like you're rich, or influential and your Talent isn't really that great. What do they see in *you*?" she cried. "You're practically an orphan."

Quincy felt like she had been kicked in the stomach. "I have no idea what you're talking about," she gasped.

Genevieve stood up and wiped her face. "All because I took the horse you wanted. How petty," she spat.

Quincy gaped. "This is about choosing our horses from *last year*?"

"Isn't it?"

Quincy shook her head. "I love Consto. I wouldn't want any other horse."

352

Genevieve deflated and shook her head, confused. "So then why did you take Colin?"

"I didn't take him!"

Genevieve slapped her and Quincy gasped holding her hand to her warm cheek. She had endured much worse from Amanda, but the attack coming from an Oakley student shocked her.

"I hate you," Genevieve screamed and rushed towards Quincy. Before she could physically attack her again, Alba and Mon-Aya grabbed Genevieve's arms.

"Enough, child." Alba hissed. "You've had your tantrum."

Quincy stared at the girls before turning around and fleeing the room. She ran down the stairs and crossed over the hall towards the staircase near the headmaster's library and ran up the stairs, taking them two at a time. A difficult task in a dress. She thought about stopping at the storage closet wondering if Chenoweth would be hiding within. She dismissed the thought and ran towards her sanctuary. She swung open the door and fell onto the plush floor of the Star Room. She gulped in air trying not to burst into tears. Her second gulp failed and she subsequently sobbed, curled up in a ball, holding her smarting cheek.

She would give anything to be eight again. To sit at her father's feet and have her hair stroked by her mother. Quincy felt the key slip down to her shoulder and she repressed the urge to scream. More than ever she wanted to rip off the key and throw it off the top of the waterfall behind Oakley. She wished she hadn't given the third key to the headmaster so she could release her anger, throwing the other key instead. These keys had brought pain and loss. It had taken her friends, family and her happiness and had given her nothing in return.

Quincy heard a polite cough from the opposite side of the dark star room.

"Who's there?" Quincy timidly asked.

"It is only me," Monty answered softly.

"Oh. It's you. How long have you been here?" she asked coldly. "What time is it presently?"

Quincy rubbed her eyes and sat up. "10:04."

"At night." Monty said neither as a question or as a statement.

She sniffed, wishing she had pockets for a handkerchief in her dress. Her cheeks burned from embarrassment. She vaguely saw Monty slowly sit up as well. He pulled out a white handkerchief out of his pocket and with a shaking hand offered it to Quincy. She smiled despite herself.

"Hmm, night indeed," Monty mused out-loud. "I have been here since noon."

"You were here all day?" Why was he talking to her again, and why had she bothered to ask?

"Seizure." He sighed.

Quincy looked at him in alarm despite her anger.

"It was not a difficult one," Monty said soothingly. "I chose not to be around people for it."

"You missed the last banquet," Quincy said, as emotionless as possible.

"Lucky me."

She could hear the sarcasm dripping from his voice. "Why 'lucky you?'" She felt her cheeks grow hot again this time from frustration.

"You went with Colin did you not?"

Quincy's eyes widened at his bitter tone.

"Yes."

They both remained silent until she couldn't bear it anymore and burst out, "Because you weren't there. Because you haven't spoken more than one syllable to me in months. But if I had known you weren't feeling well, we could have stayed here or in the library, or somewhere else."

"Truly?" Monty whispered.

"Truly," she answered, but felt her forehead grow warm, surprising her how angry she felt. "You ignored me for three months because of *tonight*?" Her voice grew louder, "Three months!" she nearly yelled at him. Now she wished the room was better lit and Monty closer to her so she could see his face.

"I am so sorry," he whispered.

"Why? What did I do?"

"It is not you," Monty said, his voice trembling. "It is me," his voice broke. "Because I cannot help you." He tossed an object angrily at the wall and it bounced, landing near her. She reached over and grasped the object, already knowing what he had thrown. She rubbed the design of the clover on the eye of Monty's key.

"I cannot time travel with you. I cannot protect you," he paused, his next words in a whisper. "I am completely worthless to you. I will slow you down."

Quincy heard the catch in his breath. She wondered how hard he fought not to cry in front of her.

"Are you serious, right now?!" she cried. "I don't care about the stupid key. I missed *you*!" A tear streaked down her cheek. "I thought you were mad at me."

"At you?" Monty questioned.

"Yes, because you got sick from traveling."

"I am so…embarrassed."

"I don't need you to bodily protect me. I'm not a damsel in distress in some tower somewhere." Her voice lightened. "Besides, I could have used a partner in our final paper for our history class." Her anger dissipated and she giggled manically.

"What is so funny?" Monty begged.

"Well, I am a damsel, and I am in distress. Stupid key. At least you get to take yours off and throw it against walls."

Monty laughed uncomfortably. She tossed it back to him.

"So, you found the coordinates?" he asked.

She quickly caught him up with her adventures. She kept the meeting of his future self a secret and the knowledge of Cigfran being Talin. She hadn't cleared her own thoughts about that yet. She told him everything else and he listened with rapt attention, not saying a word but occasionally nodding or making a small noise of surprise, or frustration for her. After she had finished, she saw him shake his head. "Unbelievable. Chenoweth orchestrated these events this entire year from the past."

"Yeah, unbelievable," she agreed. They stayed silent for a minute, pondering things when Monty cleared his throat. "Are you terribly mad at me?"

"Not a lot, but definitely a bit."

Monty laughed.

"What's so funny?" Quincy demanded.

"I failed my Independent study."

"*You* failed?" Quincy asked him incredulously. "How can you fail Independent Study?"

Monty scooted next to her until she felt his shoulder with her own. Her own shoulders sagged from the relief. She hadn't realized they had been tensed. Now that he sat closer, she could make out his facial expressions.

"The headmaster tried to warn me, but I did not understand." Monty laughed at himself again before continuing. "I had what is called a grand mal seizure three months ago the same night we returned from the past. For some odd and unknown reason, it showed me tonight. I saw you with Colin and did not see myself. I felt angry and resentful. I had never seen a moment so distantly in the future before. And after Talin told me I could not travel again, I felt so frustrated. I told the headmaster I saw this future transpire months ahead and he turned most of my assignments towards this direction to see what would come to pass. You see, I *made* tonight happen." his voice grew small. "I wasted precious time."

"*Ddefnyddio'r amser yn ddoeth,*" Quincy quoted, giggling.

Monty forcibly sighed and mumbled, "School motto, strikes again." They shared a laugh and went back to comfortable silence.

Quincy thought about how a small moment of the future had ruined their evening and had hurt both of them for months without reason. What if she did the same thing? She decided to admit what she feared the most. "You remember I mentioned a person I met in the future? The one who gave me the riddle."

"And...," he encouraged.

"He gave me some information. He told me someone close to me would betray me." Quincy crossed her arms tightly across her chest and squeezed her eyes shut. "I guess I'm afraid it would be you."

Monty nodded. "I can understand that anxiety. Especially after how I behaved towards you. However, you have more than one close friend."

"I know," Quincy answered miserably.

The two silently sat next to each other.

"How would you like to go about this?" Monty finally asked.

"I don't know," she answered quietly.

"Might I make a suggestion? Do not make the same mistake I made. I lost a couple months of friendship where I could have helped you on the hunt for the key. I would not have been so miserably…alone." He sniffed. "In addition, we lost valuable time. I could have enjoyed this evening instead of sitting here alone, pouting. Do you truly wish to do the same to protect yourself? I created my own misery because I had the foresight of seeing it. Are you going to take at face value something someone from a possible future told you?"

Quincy pondered his statement. She refused to so easily dismiss the warning from the future, but at the same time she didn't want the fear to rule all of her relationships.

"I'll find a middle ground."

"Wise decision in this situation, I believe." He paused and she felt him squirm. "Quinn, I am sorry for ignoring you and even worse, for dismissing you."

"Thank you. I'm sorry for making you time travel."

Monty grinned. "I am not. How many may boast they have visited the past."

"You won't have any lasting effects, right?"

"No. Not this time, Talin believes I have one more before there is irrevocable damage." Monty looked disappointed. "I probably should not go again."

"You'll have to be happy with being the brains back at headquarters."

Monty rewarded Quincy with a contagious smile.

"Other than Independent Study, how did the rest of your classes go?" she asked.

Monty slid his glasses down his nose and looked pointedly at Quincy.

"Well, we all can't be geniuses." Quincy giggled.

"True. How did you fare?"

Quincy groaned. "Irony rules the day. I'm pretty sure Latin ended up being my best exam."

Monty's eyebrows rose. "Truly?"

"Truly. Apparently once I learned the basic rules, it came naturally to me."

"Ironic indeed."

Quincy faux slapped Monty's shoulder and they sat comfortably looking at the night sky until their yawns became too contagious. Monty opened the door to let Quincy out and she turned around to face him. He gasped and gently caressed her cheek.

"What happened?" he whispered.

Quincy shook her head. "Genevieve had a bad day," she said simply.

Monty sighed. "Jealousy."

"Over what?"

Monty sighed. "You in the blue dress. Even with the smudged makeup, I have no doubt you were the prettiest girl on the floor."

Her cheeks reddened. She wasn't sure from him noticing her smeared makeup or his compliment.

"Thank you. Listen, you can't *ever* abandon me like that again. Promise?" she begged.

Monty nodded. "I promise."

A FUTURE?

"**C**heckmate."

Quincy frowned staring at the chess board. Dwilight pointed. "You need to look on all sides before you move." He admonished.

"I'm never going to learn this game," she moaned.

Dwilight grinned. "It's been a week. It takes years to learn. Some would say decades." He winked, and then grimaced from the bandage. There would be some scarring on his back and head, but he had lived. She noticed more white patches amongst the brown and the gray in his hair. She tried not to make the connection with his twin brother.

"We'll have next year?" she questioned.

He shook his head. "It's going to take some time for the treehouse to be rebuilt, and in the meantime, I have a parliament to look after."

362

"You're going back?" Quincy gasped.

He nodded. "In a month or so, after these bandages and stitches are removed. It's time. And someone will have to face my brother," sighed Dwilight.

"Are you ready for that?"

He shook his head. "Probably not. But it needs to be done."

Quincy felt a rush of mixed emotions. Exuberant that Dwilight felt ready to go back, but gloomy he would not be around anymore. "I'm—I'm going to miss you."

"Aye, lass. And I you. My home is still here, and you will always be welcome at my doorstep in Oxford."

"Thank you," she answered her throat tightening.

Quincy stood up when she heard a knock at the door. Eleanor Morrow opened it and looked frazzled at Quincy's presence.

"I didn't mean to intrude," Eleanor said.

"You're not," Dwilight replied, his eyes staring longingly at her. "We're playing chess. Though you would be a much better teacher."

"I need to finish packing anyway," Quincy smiled awkwardly. "I'm glad you're feeling better. I hope I'll see you soon."

She passed Eleanor to walk outside, but the Third grasped her elbow.

"Thank you," she whispered and released her.

Quincy nodded and quickly left the two alone.

***

Goodbyes were hard. Kalleigh hugged everyone and promised she would send the floor letters of her adventures. She had decided to take a year off and travel the world before deciding what she wanted to do with her Talent.

Next year would be even worse. Mon-Aye, Lindy, Alba, and Mikaela would all be leaving at the end of the next school year. And with Genevieve's expulsion for her physical altercation, it meant the opening and the promise of new Floor Three girls. Genevieve's expulsion left her feeling an odd mix of relief and sadness. She hated she was the reason.

"And now, Quincy and I will be the upperclasswomen guiding the impressionable new girls around Oakley," squealed Eloise, skipping around the room.

Colin met her at the door of the family room.

"Want help with your trunk?" he asked, shifting his weight clearly uncomfortable.

"Yes, please."

He helped dragged the trunk down the stairs.

"Thanks," she grinned when they got to the bottom.

"Are we okay?" he asked. His cheeks turning light pink.

She smiled and nodded. His shoulders straightened and he grinned. "Will you write to me this summer?" he requested.

She nodded and gave him a hug. When she released, his cheeks were now flushed red. The potential betrayal of a friend stayed in the back of her mind. But she couldn't live her life not trusting anyone.

What kind of life would that be? "I'll try," she replied. "But I can't guarantee they'll make it out of Miss Heatherwoods."

Colin grimaced. "Do you have to go back?"

Quincy nodded. "Court appointed. Besides, my mom is there. I don't think I could leave her behind."

"Makes sense. You're lucky you love your mum so much."

His statement took her by surprise. "And you're lucky your mom is alive," she gently rebutted.

"True enough." He smiled, but it didn't reach his eyes. They walked down the hallway toward their group of friends. "Would you fill out a request to spend Christmas holiday with me?"

Quincy grinned. "I'd finally get to see the horse you've been gushing about all year."

Colin laughed. "Exactly."

Eloise waved and they joined in the conversation. Quincy looked over at Monty who smiled. He looked exhausted. As they all walked outside towards the carriages and the eagles, she squeezed his elbow.

"Yes," he answered her. "I will make sure to rest this summer."

She rolled her eyes at him and laughed. "Good."

"If there's a problem," he whispered. "There's always a place at the house."

"Thank you."

Quincy mounted the eagle and looked out the window, watching Oakley disappear into the horizon. Back to Miss Heatherwoods.

Ready or not. She looked at the ceiling, wondering when she would see the raven again.

***

"How does a key disappear?" Wilbright pondered, digging through a clipping of an ancient newspaper written in German. "Translation?" he requested, handing the paper to Prieler.

"It's of no consequence." Prieler replied. "It doesn't tell you anything you didn't already know. A break-in at the supposedly impregnable bank. Of course, the box's location was in the VIP vault, so no one knew what it held. Local folklore claimed one of the old boxes in the vault held a magical key..."

"By then, the box's owner had passed, hadn't she?"

"Long deceased."

Wilbright closed his eyes, plans beginning to form. But none of them feasible. He didn't have enough information to begin with. He clenched his fists. It looked like his best choice was to visit the scene of the theft. First in the present to glean as much information as he could, then eventually travel back to the actual event itself.

The hawk in the corner of the room squawked and Prieler walked over to the bird. Prieler nodded to it, not saying anything. Without turning around, he addressed Wilbright. "It's best if we find this key, sooner rather than later."

"We must if we are to have any leverage," Wilbright added. "One is not enough."

A Future?

Prieler slowly nodded. "True, but it does stop her from opening the door without us. And there's still a piece in play."

Wilbright frowned at this new information. "Why was I not informed of this?" he demanded.

Prieler shrugged noncommittally. "We didn't trust this information wouldn't make its way to your uncle."

The hawk hissed, and Wilbright's face heated up. "You doubt me? Don't I want this door open as much as you!" his voice rose.

Prieler didn't flinch from the sound of Wilbright's voice, much to Wilbright's frustration. Instead, Prieler shrugged again. "I don't doubt it. However, your relationship with your uncle is a different story."

Wilbright remembered the dark look in his uncle's face the last time he saw him and he wrapped his arm over the other. Who was his uncle? Somehow Dwi had known. Why had his uncle kept this from him and not his little brother?

"You have nothing to fear," Wilbright coldly replied.

"We shall see."

Wilbright angrily left the room, slamming the door shut behind him.

"Temper, temper," Iblis laughed. Prieler looked at him, blankly. Iblis rolled his eyes. "You've become so boring."

"Why? Was your comment supposed to be amusing?"

"Spoilsport," Iblis crossed his arms.

"You're surprisingly pleased for having one key and them three."

The fire in Iblis' eyes grew. "How I truly feel would be of no use to us. Burning down this damp estate wouldn't be in your best interest." Iblis rubbed his fingers together and small sparks resulted from the friction. "Besides, we knew we would never get Chenoweth's key from him directly."

"But now the question is, have we planned everything correctly," wondered Prieler.

"We did," Iblis smugly said. "Otherwise we would have been outed already."

"We still may yet. The more pieces we move, the easier it will be for the raven to see us."

Iblis hissed. "My day of reckoning is still to come. Talin's weakness is thinking I no longer have any tricks up my sleeves." He smiled, a demented, cold look. It made him feel better imagining all the things he would do to that little girl and the anguish it would cause her guardian. He needed her to open the door. Then, he could finally have the delicious revenge he had been dreaming about for centuries.

"The little Scottish lord must hurry," Iblis said. "For we are all running out of time."

ACKNOWLEDGEMENTS

Without a substantial list of people this book would have never made it to your hands/screen.

Firstly, a massive thank-you to my parents. I'm seriously lucky. I can't thank you enough for reading multiple drafts because every time "it's finally done." Thank you both so much. And to my Granny Betty. I love you very much.

Also, to my long-suffering friends and idea bouncer-offers. Mikaela, I'm not entirely convinced that you aren't a Time Lord. Cassie, you give the best hugs and encouragement. Kaley, I always feel better after talking to you. Allie, you've seen me at my best/worst and we're still besties. Monika, most of my best adventures are with you and a cup of deliciousness. Kate Y, your optimism and strength are a constant encouragement to me. Kate K. for not teasing me with my silly drama and instead offering me tea. And to Jordan, Quincy Harris' Fairy Godmother.

To Sarah Gill: Life-long friend and ridiculously talented web designer. Please visit her at http://www.whatifcreative.org

To the Jetter family: Helen for hating Miss Heatherwood almost as much as I do and for the countless hours discussing this story and bringing it to life. Alex for your mad-Talent skills helping put this book together. Ian, Cedric, and Lyra, thank you for letting me borrow your parents.

To Daniel Burgess: There aren't any right words in existence to thank you for your Talent and time. Your art brings the story to life. Thank you for the lovely evenings spent at your home with your amazing family. Thank you. Eulalia!

To my editors: Rochelle Deans from Rochelle Deans Editing for making sense of the chaos that was Book 2. I'm so sorry it was so much work! Thank you for your help with the back of the book! And to Danielle Poiesz from Double Vision Editorial for all your help from the first book that bled into the second.

To my test readers: Orion, I'm so delighted you loved it. I had you and your family in mind when I created the series. Geoffroy, thank you for catching that moment that would have certainly come back to haunt me at some point. Janine, your early notes helped me make Quincy a better person and a more sympathetic character.

To coworkers, Facebook/Twitter friends, and anyone who have had to hear about keys, ravens, and time travel. I'm sorry, not really sorry.

And finally, for Joshua. Thank you listening to random sentences and, most of the time, completely out of context. Most of all, thank you for doing life with me.